TOMORROW WILL BE BETTER

Lying next to Frankie later that night, Margy was
overwhelmed with tenderness for him. She felt that
she really loved him and wondered how she had
ever let the first edge of doubt come into her mind
about it. She wanted to make him happy but she
had to acknowledge that the best way to make him
happy was to withdraw emotionally from him. But
she had to say something first.

"I'm proud of you, Frankie," she said. "I'm glad I
married you." His body grew a degree more rigid
under her arm. "And if it makes you happier not to
have me hold you, I'll take my arm away." But she
continued to hold him tightly, hoping against hope
that he'd say, I like it; leave it there. But he only
stirred impatiently.

"All right," she murmured. "There!" She was
rewarded by his sigh of relief as he relaxed. She
turned her back and whispered into her pillow.
"Why are you always so afraid that I'd hurt you,
Frankie?"

There would have been no answer, even if he had
heard what she said.

Other books by Betty Smith in this series

A TREE GROWS IN BROOKLYN
JOY IN THE MORNING
MAGGIE-NOW

TOMORROW WILL BE BETTER

Betty Smith

A TANDEM BOOK

published by

WYNDHAM PUBLICATIONS

A Tandem Book
published in 1976 by
Wyndham Publications Ltd
A Howard & Wyndham Company
123 King Street, London W6 9JG

Originally published in the United States by
Harper & Brothers, 1948
First published in Great Britain by
William Heinemann Ltd, 1949
Reprinted 1949
New edition 1974

Made and printed in Great Britain by
Hazell Watson & Viney Ltd, Aylesbury, Bucks

ISBN 0 426 17873 4

Chapter 1

There couldn't be a colder—a lonelier place in the whole world, thought Margy Shannon, than a deserted Brooklyn street on a Saturday night. She pulled her firmly held coat more tightly about her as she turned a corner. She was out walking the cold wintry streets because she was seventeen and had a job. She was independent now. She didn't have to be in the house by nine o'clock. She felt she had to use her hard-bought freedom even if it froze her to death. How easy to give up; go home and sit in the warm kitchen! But she had to hold out; get her mother used to the fact that there was a wider world outside the walls of the grudging home. So she walked the streets alone on a cold January night.

Margy had left school at sixteen after finishing two years at Eastern District High. She had looked forward to leaving school, getting a job, being independent, and having a little money of her own. She had been anxious to start leading a life of her own. She had found a job—an interesting job. She was mail reader in the Thomson-Jonson Mail Order House which had its offices and warehouses down near the Brooklyn docks; an hour's trolley ride from her home.

But the expected independence had turned out to be merely technical. Her mother kept the silver cord taut and vibrant with possessiveness, and Margy, like many Brooklyn girls who came of poor families, had to turn in all of her salary at home.

She earned twelve dollars a week. Like her father, she placed her sealed pay envelope on her mother's outstretched palm each Saturday afternoon. That was the tradition; a decent husband or a good child brought home the pay envelope unopened.

Flo gave Margy two dollars out of her envelope. Out of this Margy paid carfare to and from work and bought the daily bologna sandwich and cup of coffee which was the routine lunch of most of her co-workers. That left fifty cents a week for everything else; the hot dog she and a girl friend indulged in when they took a Sunday trolley ride to Canarsie in the summertime or the cup of hot chocolate with fake whipped cream on top and two crackers on the saucer which was the traditional treat at the end of a Sunday stroll in Brooklyn. An occasional dime-store lipstick had to come out of this fund, too.

Margy never had enough money for all the things a young girl wants so desperately. For instance she'd like to have one of the new-style wind-blown bobs, like her office friend, Reenie, had. But such a haircut meant frequent trips to the barber (with a nickel tip involved), to keep the hair in intricate trim. Since she couldn't afford that, she had to be content with her shingle bob with thin, fishhook curls pasted to each cheek.

Sometimes she dreamed a little dream. Suppose she were to get a raise! Would she tell her mother? She could take the extra dollar or two out of the envelope and reseal it before bringing it home. And what Margy could do with that extra money! Still and all, she thought, that would be cheating. She remembered what a grade-school teacher had said that time she had caught Margy sliding her eyes over to a seatmate's paper during a test.

"That's how a criminal begins," said the teacher. "He cheats in a test and gets away with it. Then he cheats in bigger and bigger things. Finally he ends up in Sing Sing."

Margy had no intentions of becoming a criminal. Yet . . . ? Who'd ever find out? It was like the old childhood dilemma: If you'd press a button and a Chinaman died in China, leaving you a million dollars, would you press that button? Sometimes Margy had decided that she'd press it very firmly; other times she had decided that a million dollars would never compensate for causing a death—not even a Chinaman's on the other side of the world. Well, she had never had a chance at the button and there was no immediate hope of getting a raise. So there was nothing to decide.

4

Margy planned to pass Frankie's house once more before she went home. She was not in love with Frankie but he was one of the few boys she knew. She had first become interested in him when he went up for his diploma the time both of them graduated from P.S. 18. She had known him only as "Frankie," an obscure, dark, Irish boy. But at graduation they called out his full name; Francis Xavier Malone. The name sounded important—like a mystery revealed. And Frankie, himself, had seemed important from that time on.

She had passed Frankie's house twice before in her walks around the block. This time she was rewarded. He clattered down the steps. She pretended to come out of a deep study with a slight start when he spoke to her.

"What do you say, Marge?"

"It's awfully cold, isn't it?" she replied in a tone that she tried to make lilting and provocative.

"You said it!"

He was off in the opposite direction, toward the corner candy store for a pack of cigarettes or to see if the morning paper had arrived. Margy cursed the luck that had made her walk around the block clockwise. If she had been walking the other way, he would have fallen in step with her and they would have walked as far as the corner together. Frankie wasn't much, she knew, but he was better than nobody. He would have served until a real boy friend came along.

Although it was only a little after nine when she got in, Flo questioned her suspiciously.

"Where you been?" she asked.

"Nowhere."

"Nobody goes nowheres on a winter night."

"I was just walking around."

"Nobody just walks around in the cold. You was somewheres and you're afraid to tell your mother."

"Oh, *Mama!*" cried Margy.

"I'm only telling you for your own good. If you run around and some man gets you in trouble, don't come crying home to me."

"I don't know any men. And even if I did, there's no place to go to get into trouble."

"There's places, and ways, too, if you're looking for

them," pronounced Flo darkly. "Tell me where you been."

"I was only walking around the block. And that's the God's honest truth. Let me alone, Mama. Please!"

"You and your father! Get up on your high horse the minute I ask a plain question."

"Where is Papa?" asked Margy, glad to change the subject.

"God only knows. And it's getting to be all hours. Night after night he leaves me sitting home alone, and . . ."

Flo talked on, off on a familiar subject.

It took Margy quite a while to get warm in bed. She finally accomplished it by pulling the covers over her head and breathing hard in the closed space. She relaxed in drowsiness, listening to the winter wind blowing against the window. How lucky I am, she thought, to have a home and to be warm. It must be terrible to have no place to go on a cold night—just to keep on walking the streets until you die from the cold. And if I get a raise, I'll be glad to give it to Mama. It's a wonderful thing to have a home and a family.

The dream started before she was sound asleep. It was an old recurrent dream: a reliving of the time when as a small child, she had been lost on the streets of Brooklyn. She knew the dream was coming and she knew the terror it held. Drowsily, she toyed with the idea of rousing herself before she drifted too far into sleep. But she could not fight off the delicious, relaxing weakness. She let herself sink into sleep.

It was summer in the dream; a hot summer morning. The dream started with the feeling of warm wind on her legs. She looked down. Yes, she was wearing socks and the new brown barefoot sandals that her mother had bought for her at Batterman's for forty-nine cents. She had been so proud of those new sandals. The happiness about them had been one of her first memories. And in the dream she was proud of the sandals all over again.

She was a child of five in the dream and her mother was a beautiful woman of twenty-five—at least she seemed beautiful to the little girl. In some inexplicable way, the mother disappeared and the child was lost. Lost on the streets of Brooklyn. She wandered from one street to another, panic growing in her. Then she turned a corner onto a familiar street and was happy because she knew her home was around the next corner. But there was a pair of huge iron gates at the end of the street, closing it off. She hurried toward the gates. She saw Frankie standing behind the gates. It was Frankie, the youth, not Frankie the boy of P.S. 18. The child was relieved. Frankie would open the heavy iron gates for her. But as she approached the gates, she saw Frankie grin and heard a click. He had locked the gates and she couldn't get past them. She sobbed.

A sound in the room awakened her. She sat up and listened tensely a moment before she realized that the sound came from her. She had sobbed aloud in her dream. What a dope, she admonished herself, crying in my sleep! And how come Frankie was in the dream? She put out her hand and felt the wall. She looked through her bedroom door into the parlor and saw the long narrow windows luminous from the street lights beyond them. I'm home, she assured herself. I'm safe in my bed. But if I go to sleep again the dream will continue. I'll count a hundred slowly.

But she was asleep before she reached sixty. This time she slept deep and dreamlessly—the way the young have a right to sleep.

Chapter 2

A woman hurried through the poor streets of Williamsburg accompanied by a little child who tried to keep up with her by trotting doggedly, stopping to pant, and then trotting faster to try to make up the time lost by the pause.

"This is the last time I take you along," scolded the woman absently. "Next time I'll leave you home alone."

The threat meant nothing to the little girl. Her mother's voice, forever lifted in monotonous complaint, was the rhythm of life itself to the child. If the voice had turned tender, the little one would have been confused. She'd have been rocketed out of the only world she knew into something terrifyingly alien.

"Every time the same," Flo fretted. "Every time you whine and whine, 'Take me! Take me along! I'll be good,'" squeaked Flo in a reedy falsetto.

The panting child looked up at her mother, wondering whom she was mimicking: Margy didn't know anyone who talked like that. The mother answered the child's thoughts.

"Yes, you! I mean you! And don't make out like you don't know what I'm saying, either." Her tone was aggrieved and the child felt guilty misery. "You're just like your father," the woman went on with vague indignation. "You never know what you want, and when you get what you think you want are you ever satisfied? No!" And so she kept on nagging.

Flo did not dislike the child. If the vein of essential truth in her could have been blasted free from its flinty layers of worry, bitterness and inarticulateness, her love for the child would have been revealed. She nagged and fretted at her because the child was her only emotional outlet; was someone to receive her voice; a symbol at which to direct thoughts spoken aloud. There was no one who listened so obligingly, who tried so hard to understand. Had she been challenged by God, Himself, for her ceaseless pecking at the little one, she would have said in defense:

"It means nothing. She doesn't understand what I talk about anyway." Then she would have added with her strange feminine refutation, "Besides, the quicker she learns that the world ain't all hearts and flowers, the better off she'll be."

They came to a crossing. Flo groped for the girl's hand. Margy, fearing that her mother wished to hurry her steps, put her hand behind her back and shook her head negatively.

"All right! Don't take my hand then. Get lost! See if I care."

They stood at the curb while Flo looked down the street that nobody liked. It was a one-block street, dead-ending at the twelve-foot-high iron gates of a grim, gray, charity hospital. The gates made a long narrow cage of the street. There was a feeling that if you turned into that street, the opening would close behind you and the locked gates ahead would hold you prisoner in that city block forever.

The street made Flo uneasy. Yet it fascinated her, too. Purgatory, she thought. Yes, it looks like Purgatory where lost souls walk up and down and nobody cares. It looks like nothing could live on that street; no trees, no chippy birds, no rubber plants, no geraniums.

I wonder if it's true what people say about this street? That murdered man they say, was found buried in a block of cement in someone's cellar. A prostitute in every second house. I wonder if *he* ever . . .

Quickly she dismissed the thought of her husband's possible unfaithfulness. Where would he get the two dollars? she reasoned. He gives me all his pay. My mother, God rest her soul, was right. Make him give you his pay envelope still pasted, she said. Make him promise the first night you're married. A man will promise anything, then, she said. I'm glad I made him promise six years ago. Because now he wouldn't promise me nothing. She spoke out of her thoughts to the child.

"Your granma was a good woman and don't you ever forget it."

Margy was puzzled. She couldn't figure out how Granma came in. She whimpered. Flo sighed in annoyance.

"*Now* what?" she asked.

"The street," whimpered the child.

"What's a matter with the street?"

"I don't like the way it looks at me."

Flo addressed the empty street. "This little girl don't like the way you look at her. So stop it now. Hear? If you don't, I'll give it to you, Street." Margy stared down the block with interest, actually expecting a miracle.

"It ain't stopping," she said. "It keeps on looking at me."

"Oh, you!" said the exasperated parent. "The street's got no eyes. It can't look at you. Besides, if the street is looking at you," she said with one of those changes so bewildering to Margy, "you don't have to stand there and look back at it. Let's cross over and don't let me hear no more silly talk out of you."

The child was afraid to cross the dreaded street. She reached for her mother's hand. The woman took revenge by duplicating the child's former gesture of independence. She put her hand behind her back and shook her head negatively. Tears came and stood in the child's eyes.

"See? How do you like it?" asked Flo. And the child had no answer.

She crossed the street hurriedly. The girl's thin legs worked like pistons trying to keep up. The woman walked faster when she reached the other side and the child began to lag behind. Flo was confident that the child would catch up.

That's how you got to learn children, she thought. Make fun of them when they're scared. Anyhow that's how I had to learn things.

A thought faintly tried to form in the back of her mind. And just what did you learn, anyway? asked this faint thought. Why . . . why . . . I learned how to get along in the world. Yeah? jeered the thought. Yeah! she answered. But the answer was without much conviction.

Flo had gotten so far ahead that Margy gave up trying to catch her. She turned around and went back to the street. She wanted to find out if it would still look at her in that funny way. She turned down into the street and slowly walked toward the gates, staring at each house, expecting something to happen. She came near the iron gates. To her surprise, they did not lock up the street. They were across the gutter on another street that went the other way. Her tiredness left her and she skipped across the street, forgetting to look both ways as her mother had taught her. She grasped the iron bars of the gate, pushed her little body close against it, closed her eyes tightly for an instant so she'd be more surprised at what she saw, then opened them wide to look through.

Her disappointed eyes saw nothing at first but gaunt gray buildings and gaunt gray walls. But as she looked, a gray boxlike truck drove up to the building. Two white-dressed men took a bed out of the back. But what a funny bed! No head, foot or legs. She knew it must be a bed because a man was sleeping on it. She thought it was funny that a man slept in the daytime. Her father slept in the nighttime. Another funny thing was that the man was sleeping with his clothes on. She saw his shoes sticking out from the bottom of the gray blanket. And Margy guessed that he was going someplace the very minute he woke up because his hat was lying ready on his chest.

A door opened and a lady dressed in white came out. The men smiled at her and the tall man said something. The white lady smiled back and took the sleeping man's hat and put it sideways on her own head. The tall man let go of the bed with one hand and tried to put his arm around her. All three laughed when the bed tipped a little.

. Just then a Sister came out and stood in the doorway and made a muff out of her wide sleeves. The three people didn't see the Sister and Margy whispered "Chickee!" trying to warn them. Somehow she knew that they weren't supposed to be having fun while that dressed-up man slept so tight on that funny bed.

Suddenly the white lady turned and saw the Sister. She pulled off the hat, put it back on the man's chest and ran into the building. The two men took a better hold on the bed and carried it in, with the Sister marching like a soldier behind them. The little girl waited but nothing more happened. The summer sun shone on gray emptiness.

Margy tried to puzzle out why the man slept in the daytime and out on the street, too, almost; why the men carried his bed as if they didn't care if he fell off and hurt himself; why the tall man wanted to kiss the white lady when she put the man's hat on and why they were so scared when they saw the Sister. The Sister hadn't scolded. She had just stood there. But they had acted as if she were hollering at them.

Margy walked down the cross street and came to where some little girls were playing a game called "Statchers." The leader took a girl's hand and spun her around and let go. The spun one froze in whatever position the release had left her. There were three statchers made and two to go. Shyly, Margy sidled up to the leader and held out her hand. The leader ignored it, whereupon Margy spun around by herself, staggered with pretended dizziness and came to rest on one wobbling leg, lifted her hand like the Statue of Liberty and stuck her tongue out as an added touch. All of a sudden the other statchers came to life and shrilly attacked the outsider.

"She don't live on this block," said one.

"Go 'way, you!" screamed another.

"Ger-rout-a-here!" commanded the leader.

"Git offa our block and play on your own dirty ol' block," warned the biggest girl.

As if on signal, the girls began swatting at her with their hands. They didn't hit her but swatted so close to her face that they made a breeze that moved her bangs. Margy cowered for a second with both hands over her face. Then she ran away down the street.

She turned a corner and sat down on the curb to get her breath back. She tried to figure the whole thing out and decided that the little girls had not wanted her on their block. She decided she'd do the same thing if any strange girl ever came to play on *her* block. That's the way to do, she thought. Everybody must play on their own block. And I must chase all the strange girls that come to play on my block.

A great noise rose from the cobblestones under her feet. A big brewery truck with stacked kegs of beer was coming down the street. It was pulled along by four giant Percherons. Seen from the level of the child's eyes, the sixteen hoofs rising and falling in labored rhythm seemed to fill the whole world. She forced her eyes upward, away from the fearful fascination of the flaying hoofs. The leather-aproned driver, his hands full of leather ribbons, was half sitting, half standing with his feet braced against the dashboard. He was pulling the reins back so hard that it made the horses hold their heads in a high curve. The big yellow teeth of one of the front horses were exposed and Margy was sure he was getting ready to bite her. A hoof striking a spark from the cobblestones drew her eyes down again. She thought fire was coming from the horses—fire that would burn her up if she kept sitting there. But she was too frightened to move. The horses' legs loomed up larger, seeming to come right at her. She shut her eyes tightly. As the horses stormed by, she opened one eye a little. It focused on a horse's leg and she saw something she had never seen before—a tuft of coarse hair attached to the leg. The tortured breeze made by the motion of the horses caused the tuft to blow. She opened both eyes wide and saw that all the horses had these bangs on their legs. As the truck went past, she stared at the wheels, fascinated by the way they turned, delighted with the shiny black of the axle grease in the hubs.

Well, the heavy truck went by without coming too close to her. The big kegs jigged up and down in an angry grumbling way but they did not fall off and roll over her as she had feared they might.

She sat there for a while waiting for more big horses with bangs on their legs to pound by. But only one other horse came along—a dark brown, skinny one who walked slowly with his head down. He wore a straw hat with holes for his ears to stick out, and pulled a little painted wagon that was piled up with fruit and vegetables. There was a big yellow and red umbrella over the driver's seat with the word BLOOMINGDALE's printed on it. A dark, skinny man walked alongside the wagon. He put his hand to the side of his mouth and sang a strange song.

"Straw-bebbs! Lawn-I'll-dadoes! Spinch! Tur-rmps! Green led-duz!"

He sang "led-duz" the way the priest sang "Amen" at High Mass. Women came out of houses, bargained briefly but passionately with the wandering greengrocer and retired indoors victoriously with tops of bunched beets or carrots waving like triumphant green flags.

The vegetables reminded Margy of dinnertime and in

her brief life she had learned one thing well: You had to be home at dinnertime. She started back in the direction from which she had come. Then, remembering the mean little girls, she turned and took another street. She turned the corner expecting to find the street with the gates. But it was a strange street without gates. Beginning to feel the oppressiveness of her naughtiness in leaving her mother, she tried to be a good girl by looking carefully both ways before she crossed the street. She turned another corner. No gates! She wondered where they were—began to fear that there never had been gates—that she had made them up. Maybe she had no Mama either. Or maybe she did and Mama didn't like her any more and let her get lost on purpose. Hadn't Mama said that the next time she was bad she was going to give her away to the ragman?

At that moment, a man came out of a house. After sleeping the night and half the day away in a windowless room, the first impact of fresh air almost killed him. He lurched as he drew a deep breath. Margy thought he was the ragman come to get her. She opened her mouth and bawled. The man staggered past without looking at her. He had a houseful of bawling kids. A strange kid bawling on the street didn't interest him.

Even after the man had lunged away out of sight, she continued howling. Eventually the howling settled down into a senseless gulping sobbing. A woman came by and stopped.

"What's a matter, little girl?" she asked.

"I'm losted."

"Lost?"

A fat woman came down a stoop and hurried over. "What's a matter?" she asked the first woman.

"Lost kid."

A woman with scant gray hair skinned back in brown kidskin crimpers showed herself at an open window. "What's a matter down there?" she called.

"Little girl lost!" announced the fat woman importantly.

"Yeah?" The crimped one's face lifted with interest as she folded her arms on the sill and adjusted her heavy breasts to rest on them. At last, she thought, something was happening down on the street—something to while away a little of dragging time.

More women came to opened windows—more appeared on the street. Each new window leaner asked, "What's a matter?" and the gathering women gave answer like a Greek chorus: "Little girl lost!" At dramatically paused intervals, Margy lifted her trembling voice and wailed, "I'm losted!"

"She must be lost," decided a newcomer.

"Yeah," agreed the others.

The fat woman tried consolation. "Don't cry, girlie. I was lost once when I was a little girl and my mama found me after a while."

Margy, after a dubious look at her, decided that a woman so big and fat could never have been a little girl. "No!" stated Margy flatly and ambiguously.

"Just tell me your name, girlie," wheedled the woman, "and I'll go find your mama for you."

Girlie stopped sobbing and closed her lips firmly. She had a notion that harm would come to her if she gave away her name. The fat one tried a more clever approach.

"Say! I bet-cher you don't even know how old you are!" Margy's vanity was challenged.

"I'm four-gawn-on-five," she announced.

The women smiled knowingly at each other, their exchanged glances saying, *Now,* we're getting somewhere.

"And now, Four-gawn-on-Five, what did you say your name was, again?" asked the fat one too sweetly. Margy drew her lips in tightly and stood mute. The woman tried another trick. She ignored the child and spoke confidentially to the crowd of women. "You know what? This little girl ain't got no name a-tall."

That didn't work. Wheedling, bribery, threats—nothing broke the child's silence. The fat woman gave up and reported her verdict to the crowd.

"She's stubborn. I only wish to Gawd that she was mine for five minutes."

The woman's tone was so threatening that Margy started to wail again. Someone suggested that a policeman be called. Women asked each other, "Who has a phone?" No one had a phone and the nearest candy store with a pay station was two blocks away. No one volunteered to go to the candy store; one woman refused to make the call because she didn't want to be questioned by the police. Another woman asked her what she had to hide and she answered, mind your own business and go yourself. An informal committee proposed that the fat woman accompany the child to the candy store, put in the call and leave the child there for the police to pick up.

"What? And me get arrested for kidnaping?" asked the fat woman. "Not on your tintype."

In the midst of the arguments, a stranger pushed through the crowd. The neighborhood women gave way grudgingly, looking her over with hostile eyes. She was too dressed up for that time of day. Good women were still in wrappers doing, or thinking about doing, their housework. They didn't like the tight way the strange woman's clothes fitted her or the strong *Djer Kiss* sachet powder she scented herself with. They kept their eyes on her while they whispered to each other out of the corner of the mouth.

"I got her number," said one.

"She's fly," said another.

The newcomer smiled and bent over the child. "What's your name, sister?" At the sound of the soft voice, the youngster stopped crying. The woman knelt and put her arms around her waist. The child gained confidence because the lady now looked no bigger than a child. "Come on. Tell me your name."

"If she wouldn't tell us, she certainly won't tell you," sneered the fat woman.

"I will so!" said the youngster suddenly and defiantly. "My name's Margy Shannon."

"Margy Shannon!" the women told each other. One of them called up to the window leaners. "Her name's Margy Shannon."

"Margy Shannon! Margy Shannon!" The name was passed from woman to woman, window to window. The sound filled the street and made Margy feel very important.

"Now tell me the name and number of your street."

"I'll tell you in your ear," said Margy.

The woman put her ear to the child's lips. Margy was delighted with the sweet, pink-candy smell of her. She put her thin arms around her neck, and while her eyes roved defiantly around the circle of women, she whispered the address which her mother had taught her after endless parrot-like repetitions. "But don't tell *them*," said Margy aloud.

Not a peep out of her, mused Flo Shannon, believing that her only child was trotting dutifully behind her. Pay no attention to them. That's how you learn them to depend on theirselves. That's the way I learned and so long as I turned out all right . . . Why do I keep thinking the same old things over and over again? Trouble is, I ought to go out more. More besides the store and to Mass. I ought to see different things. I always wanted to travel when I was a girl. But I got married.

I shoulda done better than Henny and a cold-water flat on Maujer Street. Being as I always had big ideas when I was a girl. You won't ketch me in no flat like yours, I told my poor mother, God rest her soul. If I can't marry somebody who'll give me a better home than Papa gave you, I'll die an old maid. And all my mother said was, I had big ideas, too, when I was your age and now look. My own daughter ashamed of me. And she cried.

But I wasn't ashamed of her. Only I thought I should do better—the big ideas I had. Then I had to go and meet Henny at that dollar racket. The way I used to love to dance!

Henny was different—at least while we was keeping company. The way he worked hard all day and went to night school studying civil service so's he could get on the cops. He musta had big ideas, too. But he changed when he married me. And now he turns out to be a shop worker —liable to get sacked any time—no pension for me when he dies. I'd be left to support the kid. . . .

Margy! She turned around, sure that the child was there. She was annoyed rather than alarmed when she found her missing. She figured that she was hiding in a doorway. Flo looked up at a street sign and realized that she was in a strange neighborhood. What am I doing over on Morgan Avenue? she asked herself. First thing I know, I'll land in Ridgewood. I was getting too deep in my thoughts. I shouldn't do that. I forget. . . .

"Margy!" she called out sharply. "You stop hiding on me now. Hear?" She waited. "I know where you are and when I get you, I'm going to give it to you. You see if I don't." Again she waited. She was aware of a hushed silence. The street seemed to be holding its breath and waiting.

Flo retraced her way, looking into hallways and behind doors and keeping up a one-sided conversation with an invisible child. The tirade of nagging changed into a game of fear.

"Now, Margy, Mama didn't mean it. Stop hiding and come out and Mama won't spank you. Mama will even buy you an ice-cream toot." She waited.

"Let's play hide'n-go-see," she suggested craftily. "I'll shut my eyes and count ten, you come out, and then it's my turn to hide. Ready?" she lilted.

A street echo answered, "Ready!" and it seemed the child was there hiding somewhere and willing to play.

The woman closed her eyes and counted an honest ten before she opened them. She lifted her voice in an almost forgotten childhood chant: "Come out, come out, wherever you are!"

No child appeared. But as if conjured up by the chant, a little old man materialized. He shook his finger at her and said, "It's dumb to play games with little children that ain't there." Before he had finished the sentence he put his hand behind his ear and waited tensely for her reply.

"I'm not playing. I lost my little girl."

"How's that again?"

"My little girl is lost."

"Find a cop. Tell him to take you home. He has to. We pay taxes. Maybe you think you don't pay taxes. But you pay rent, don't you? And when you pay rent you pay taxes. So you pay the cops. So go find a cop and say you're lost and don't bother me."

"I'm not lost," she shouted. "I'm not bothering you neither. My little girl is lost."

"That's different. Go back where you lost her and she'll be still standing there."

"She's not a one to stand," she screamed.

"She'll be walking around the block, then. Lost people keep going around in circles. Did you know that?"

"Never mind." Flo was anxious to get away from the garrulous old fellow. "I'll find her."

"I read that in a book once. I was quite a reader in my

day." Flo moved away. He spoke louder, trying like the Ancient Mariner to hold her with his voice. "I could tell you what I read in my time and you'd be surprised. To look at me, you wouldn't know I had it in me—the things I found out from reading." But she was getting farther away.

"Tell me some other time," she called back to him.

"When?" he shouted eagerly. But she was gone beyond the sound of his voice. He spoke sadly and quietly to himself. "I'm a poor, lonely, old man. People ought to talk to me more. A pity. I got things I could tell people. . . ."

Flo came to the gates of the hospital and saw a nun walking with bowed head in the yard. "Sister, did you see a little girl pass by?" she called. The nun shook her head gently and smiled sadly.

The little girls were still playing statchers.

"Was there a strange little girl here?" Flo asked them.

"Yes!" shouted one girl. "No!" shouted the others.

"Which way did she go?"

Two children pointed right, one pointed left and the leader said she didn't know.

Flo went from street to street, frantic, fearing that she, too, was becoming lost. She asked everyone she met had they seen a little girl and each one said, no, and looked at her strangely. She groped in her pocketbook and found her ebony rosary beads. She fingered them as she walked the streets and droned out Hail Mary's and Our Father's in a hot whisper. When the beads had been told, she spoke directly to God and promised she'd never be mean to the child again if only He'd let her be found.

Her mind, always eager for an excuse to walk in the past, went back to the child's birth. She remembered the newborn child being placed at her side for nursing. She remembered lifting one of the tightly curled hands—how gently she had forced open the tiny perfect thing and exclaimed over the wonder of the well-made fingernails that looked like infinitesimal pearly shavings. How a great tenderness had come upon her when the tiny hand closed over her finger! How she had promised Holy Mary that nothing harsh would ever happen to the child that she, Florence Shannon, had brought into the world.

And now the child was gone. It was as though the child had hardly been.

As she walked and prayed, memories came and dissolved in other memories. She remembered the child of a year ago. Then she lost that memory. She found and clutched the memory of the little one learning to walk—the unsteady balance on feet set down wide apart on the oilcloth kitchen floor; the faltering first step; the swaying indecision; the hard sitting down on the floor; the breath-held second while the mother waited for the cry of pain—instead, the baby's face split by a wide grin of pride—the getting up, the step, the fall—repeated a dozen times until the baby mastered the important trick of putting one foot before the other and managing to stand upright while so doing.

The memories unreeled back to the birth agony. Flo paused in her rapid walking as a labor pain formed in her mind. The pain became an actuality. She felt a dull throb. It will rain before night, she thought. The stitches hurt whenever it's going to rain.

Now she was back in the pregnancy. Was it yesterday or the day before she had come upon that old dress? She had worn it last four—no—five years ago; had removed it to undress when the labor pains started. She had hung it on a nail in the closet. And it was only yesterday—no—the day before that she had taken it from the nail. It had not been pressed in all those years. The heavy material still held the curve where her swollen body had stretched the skirt until it strained at the seams. It was as though the child were as yet unborn and still within the sheltering curve of the skirt.

She walked faster to outdistance her thoughts. But the thoughts quickened and would not be outwalked. Only yesterday! Only yesterday, she thought, everything was. Today, nothing. The present was evil. Only the past was endurable, she decided. In the past there had been her sheltering mother; Flo's love for the boy she married; the baby. Now in the present there was nothing. Her mother was dead; her husband had become a surly stranger and the baby was gone.

Dead! Yes, she admitted it. Drowned in Newtown Creek, or buried under a sudden slide of coal piled high and conical in the yards on the bank of the creek. They wouldn't find the body until next winter when people needed coal.

She wept bitterly.

Then she turned her home corner and saw Margy sitting on the curb before their house licking on a Neapolitan ice-cream sandwich that the sweet-scented stranger had bought her.

Relief flooded through Flo and she felt as though her leg bones had melted and she would collapse where she stood. Then murderous rage pushed aside relief. Here she had been crying her heart out for a dead child and all the while the object of her grief had been safe and serene on the home block, enjoying ice cream. Flo swooped down on the child who had smilingly risen to meet her, holding out the ice-cream sandwich as an enticing overture.

"I'll learn you to scare the life out of me!" screamed Flo.

She slapped the ice cream out of the child's hand. It fell into the gutter. She slapped Margy first on one cheek and as the child swayed, on the other cheek to counteract the sway. She kept slapping back and forth and the child rocked from side to side like a last-standing bowling pin that is reluctant to fall.

The child was small. Her eyes were near to the ground. She saw low things enlarged. Now as her mother tramped the ice cream, the white, brown and pink spots that jumped up to fasten themselves on her new sandals seemed enormous.

Flo was working herself up into a fearful fury. "I'll learn you to run away," she screamed. "I'll learn you to want your own way all the time. Wait till your father gets home. He'll give it to you."

The child stared down on the trampled ice cream. Flo yanked her arm to make her look up. "Why don't you cry?" she demanded in furious curiosity.

The child looked at her, confused. Often her mother slapped her because she *did* cry. And now she was angry because she *didn't* cry. The child was mixed up, but the same tenacity that made her withhold her name from the women made her withhold her tears.

"Stubborn!" pronounced Flo, even as the fat woman had pronounced it. "Stubborn like your father. But I'll knock that out of you even if it takes all my life." She slapped her again. The child's eyes grew hot with stinging pain.

But she did not cry.

The Graham Avenue trolley bucked limpingly across the intersection at Ten Eyck Street. Henny Shannon folded the Brooklyn *Eagle* at the page where he was reading and stuffed it in his hip pocket. He picked up a discarded *Journal*. He took it because of its comic strip that he could read to Margy after supper. He walked to the front of the car as a signal that he wanted to get off at Maujer Street, the next corner. The motorman, with a kind of futile apprehension, put on speed. Maujer was a block before Grand. Grand was the big intersection where half the passengers transferred. The car had to make a long stop there and the motorman hated to lose time by stopping a short block before to let out a lone passenger. What the hell, figured the motorman, it's only a short block to walk back.

Henny tapped the motorman on the shoulder and announced, "Maujer's my stop."

Defiantly and without looking around, the motorman said, "Keep your shirt on. I'm stopping, ain't I?" The car winced to a halt.

Henny paused before he swung off the steps. He had some information to give. He said, "I happen to be a workingman, Mac."

The statement was not a revelation. It was a reminder. What Henny meant by the words was: Look! All day I'm shoved around by the foreman, the superintendent and the big boss. I can't even sneak in the toilet for a smoke without the foreman coming after me. *You* get shoved around, too. Brother, do we have to shove each other around?

"I'm a workingman, myself, Mac," said the motorman. Those were his words. But his meaning was: I know all about it, friend. I go through the same thing myself. Every day.

The men parted in a glow. There had been brief communication and understanding between them.

Henny's steps dragged as he walked up Maujer Street toward home. It had been a tough day in the shop. Now, instead of coming home to a safe place, a loving wife and a happy carefree young one, he was returning to grim, silent antagonism or the worse alternative of monotonous, whining, nagging complaints about this, that and the other thing.

Some kids were playing shinniger in the gutter. Henny stood and watched. A boy teed up a blunt peg on a stone. He tapped the shinny sharply with a sawed-off length of broomstick. As the shinny leaped into the air, he whacked it smartly with the stick and the peg hurtled in an awkward arc toward a boy standing spreadlegged to receive it.

Henny remembered his own shinniger days. His hands closed on an imaginary stick. He was back twenty years— so real was the memory of the feeling of the stick in his hand; the ecstatic bump of his heart when the stick connected with the peg suspended in the air for the millionth part of a second. He was envious of the boys. They had what he could never have again in his life—moments of wild joy. He heard them call to each other, using nicknames.

He had had a nickname as a boy. "River" Shannon, they called him. Sometimes just "Riv." He had pretended to be angry when someone called him by the nickname. But how he had loved it! He thought briefly of the song from which his nickname had been derived.

> *Where the River Shannon's flowing.*
> *Where the three-leaf shamrock grows.*
> *Where my heart is I am going . . .*

He stepped closer to the boy with the stick. He wouldn't volunteer, of course. But just suppose the boy said: "*You* show us how to do it, Mister." Oh, he would give them some pointers all right! But the boy never so much as noticed him. Futility flooded Henny. Then there came upon him a great urgency to exert authority. He raised his voice and spoke to the boys.

"You boys don't want to go and play shinniger," he told them. "Dangerous game. Many a kid's had his eye knocked out by a shinny."

The boys stopped playing and stared at him. Then one by one, they told him off.

"Aw, go fly a kite, Mister."

"Go 'way back and si'down."

The smallest player held his nose and pulled an imaginary chain. The boy with the stick shoved his face close to Henny's.

"Mister," inquired the boy conversationally, "why don't you just go to hell?" Henny raised his hand to strike the boy. But the boy did not flinch. He pushed his face an inch closer and said, "Hit me! Go on and hit me!" His voice dropped to a low, hard, threatening tone. "Just go ahead and try socking me one." Henny saw the boy's knuckles whiten as he tightened his grip on the stick. And he wasn't more than twelve or thirteen years old!

Henny stepped back, frightened and ashamed. What's got into me, he thought, a guy of thirty picking on kids in the street. He turned and walked away. The boy called after him.

"It's just that we don't want to get shoved around, Mister."

It was an apology. The low, hard, threatening quality was gone from the boy's voice. It was only a youngster's voice now—a voice with tears behind it.

It's just that we don't want to get shoved around!

Shoved around! Henny made that remark every day. He heard others make it. People saying it and meaning it when they said it and yet getting shoved around just the same. A drunk in a saloon being ejected and clinging to a kind of pitiful dignity, stating that he would go, but don't shove. Don't *shove.*

Still and all, thought Henny, we shove each other around more than the cops or bosses do. You'd think we'd stick together against the big shovers instead of being little shovers ourselves. Ah, well, he decided, it's a cockeyed world.

Flo heard Henny's step on the stairs. She was startled. He was home, then, and no supper ready. Where had the day gone? And she had forgotten the meat she had been shopping for when Margy got lost.

. Nervously she slid a frying pan over the gas plate and lit the flame under it. She looked at Margy sitting in a corner, her small hands cupped over some small secret.

"It's all your fault," she told the child. Margy looked up, her eyes round with surprise. "And now your father's home and he'll give it to you." The child blinked her eyes in confusion. This angered Flo. "Don't look at me like that and make out like you don't know what you did today. You know all right."

When her mother's back was turned, the child opened her fist and looked at the bud she had surreptitiously picked from the geranium plant on the window sill. She wasn't supposed to pick the buds off. Mama said she'd whip her if . . .

That was it! That was what Mama was talking about. Mama mustn't see. She'd take it away from her. She kept her head low over her hands. She started to pull off each tightly wound petal. She wanted to know what was packed so carefully inside. Afraid that her mother would take the bud away from her before she came upon the mystery of its core, she tore the bud in half.

She found that there was nothing—nothing. The darkness of desolation came over her. The feeling of the morning came back. Again she heard the horses' storming hoofs; again she saw them bearing down on her.

"I was losted," she called out suddenly as her father entered the door.

"What?" he asked, looking to Flo for an explanation.

"Nothing," answered his wife.

Hurriedly she cubed cold boiled potatoes into the hot fat of the frying pan. She meant to tell Henny later about the episode; tell him in her own way; build up the story to put herself in an aggrieved light. She didn't want to tell the story with the child's bald statement as a beginning.

"Nothing," she repeated. "She's such a one for ideas."

As Henny hung his hat and coat on the nail behind the door, Margy ran to him and hugged his leg. "Losted all day," she whispered.

"Did she lose something?" he asked Flo.

"No." She broke two eggs into the frying pan.

"Horses are big," explained the child. "They'll walk on me." She hid her face against his leg and trembled.

"No, they won't," he assured her, patting her back awkwardly. "I won't let no horse come in here." He turned to his wife. "What does she mean?"

"I don't know." Flo laid raw onion rings in the bubbling fat.

Henny sat down to the table. Margy, with a child's sudden change of mood, climbed up on his lap. "Read me the funny sheet," she demanded.

He opened the *Journal* at the comic strip and explained the pictures to her. "Here is Buster Brown talking to his dog, Tige."

"Why is his name Buster Brown?"

"Because he wears a Buster Brown suit."

"Why is that a Buster Brown suit?"

"Because it's got a Buster Brown collar."

"Why is that a Buster Brown collar?"

"Because a boy whose name is Buster Brown wears it," explained her father.

It was like the geranium bud. At the beginning the explanation had promised much. But torn apart, there was nothing.

"Why? Why? Why?" burst out Flo, irritated by the repetition of the word. "Always asking *why*."

"That's how she learns," said Henny.

"Stop talking and eat your supper," said his wife, setting the plate before him.

Margy slid to the floor as he picked up his knife and fork. Henny stared at the plate. On it were two fried eggs, fried potatoes and fried onions. He opened his mouth to protest but closed it without saying a word. Through many evenings of the same routine, he knew how the conversation would go.

"Eggs?" he would inquire. "Again?"

"What's a matter with eggs?"

"Nothing. Only the same every night. . . ."

"Last night we had chopmeat."

"Is there nothing else besides eggs and chopmeat in the store?"

"Eggs and chopmeat is cheap. Maybe I could cook fancier if you'd give me more money."

"Give? You mean if I earned more."

"If you'd talk up to your foreman . . ."

"And get sacked?"

"Other men ask for a raise."

"Asking ain't getting."

"If you had more push . . ."

"Listen! I work hard all day. When I come home nights, I expect . . ."

"And what about what I expect? I slave in the house all day and when you come home all you do is let me sit and look at the four walls."

He sighed. No, he wouldn't say, "Eggs again," and start up the whole business.

He reached for the ketchup bottle and coated the food thoroughly with the thick, red, pungent stuff. Then he propped the folded *Eagle* on the sugar bowl before him.

"You eat yet?" he asked.

"Long ago," said Flo.

"You just couldn't wait," he stated quietly and bitterly. He began to eat and read simultaneously.

"Why should I wait? Eating with you is like eating with a statcher—a statcher that reads the paper."

Guiltily, he pushed the paper aside and concentrated on eating. That word, statcher, clicked open a door in Margy's memory.

"Look!" she called shrilly. "See me! See me now!" She spun until she was dizzy, then stood on one wobbling leg, lifted her hand in salute and stuck out her tongue—her pose of the morning.

"What's got into her?" asked Henny.

The mother spoke sharply to the child as she set a cup of bitter, black coffee before the man. "Stop acting so silly, now, or your father will give it to you." The child came out of the pose.

"I forgot something," said Henny. He got up, groped in his coat pocket and brought out a small slab of hard pink candy wrapped in tissue paper.

"What's that?" asked Flo.

"Only a penny," he apologized obliquely. "I got it off of a stand."

"You'll spoil her." Yet in a queer way, Flo was pleased that he had thought of the child.

So! Margy had it straight now. All day her mother had been telling her that she'd "get it" when her father came home. Margy had thought *it* meant a spanking. Instead it was candy all the time. She took the candy and tore off the paper.

"What do you say?" prodded Flo.

"Ta-ta," acknowledged Margy brightly.

As she removed the paper, the sweet smell of the candy reminded her of the lady who had brought her home when she was lost.

"Such a nice lady," said Margy to the candy.

"Candy," corrected Flo.

Margy held the candy to her cheek. "Nice lady," she crooned.

"What does she mean?" asked Henny.

"Nothing!" Flo gave orders to the child. "Stop playing with it and eat it."

"No!" said Margy automatically.

"Eat it!"

"No!"

"Do as I say!"

Margy became frightened. She didn't know what was happening but somehow the candy was getting her into trouble. She opened her hand and let the candy fall to the floor. It broke into three pieces. Margy looked down expecting colored drops would come from it like the ice cream.

"Pick that up!" commanded Flo. Margy folded her hands behind her back. "All right, then," said her mother reasonably. "I told you you were going to get it but you wouldn't listen." She turned to Henny. "Do you know what she did today?"

"What?" He sighed.

"Well, she ran away."

The child, now frightened, backed into a corner, her eyes on her father. Henny drank some coffee before he spoke.

"Why didn't you watch her better?"

"Watch her? I never took my eyes off of her."

"Then how could she run away?"

"She laid her chances and sneaked off and before I could turn around, she was lost."

"All kids get lost once in their life. All kids want to run away."

"I never did," said Flo. "I thought too much of my mother to cause her any trouble."

"Now don't start in about your mother," warned Henny.

"No? Well, let me tell you: If ever there was a saint in heaven, my mother was one."

"All right! All *right*," answered Henny.

He picked up the *Eagle*, turned it back to the front page and folded it carefully. Here it was—the nightly quarrel. Each night he hoped to avoid it. He tried to avoid saying anything that would get her started. But it was no use. No use! There was something in the woman that made

28

it necessary for her to prod and nag, refute and win. In his dim fumbling way, he had long ago decided that quarreling took the place of lovemaking as far as Flo was concerned. Well, he'd accommodate her.

"All right," he repeated. "Listen! The only decent thing your mother ever did was to lay down and die."

She gasped without screaming, as if a pail of icy water had been thrown in her face. She was hurt and took refuge in dignity.

"If it wasn't for my mother, I wouldn't be here today," she stated.

"And I'd be one happy man."

"Oh, yeah?" she sneered.

"Yeah! It stands to reason. Your father sleeps with your mother and I got to pay penance for it all my life."

"You filthy . . ." she was trembling. "My sainted mother never . . ."

"No. She found you in a head of cabbage."

"Little pitchers," warned Flo, indicating the child standing in the corner.

"She has to find out things some way," mumbled Henny. But he was ashamed of what he had said.

"She hears enough dirt on the streets. Does she have to hear it in her own home, too?"

"You call this a home?"

"Is it my fault? I try to make it a home. I work my fingers to the . . ."

". . . Bone," he broke in.

"And nights I have to sit and look . . ."

". . . at the four walls," he quoted wearily.

They spoke faster and more furiously, each jumping in to take the other's lines. It was like a stale play where each actor had his part letter-perfect and could play the other's part, too.

Soon their words meant nothing. The furious tones carried all the meaning. Margy trembled with fright in her corner. She wanted to hide but was afraid to call attention to herself by stepping out of the corner.

Finally the neighbors, who had first listened eagerly, then became bored at the trite dialogue, took a hand. The people upstairs stamped on the floor for quiet. The people downstairs banged on their ceiling with a broom handle. People on Grand Street shouted at them across two yards.

"Shut up!"

"Shut your windows or shut your traps!"

A boy flying pigeons on an adjoining roof threw himself flat on his stomach and leaned over the roof's edge. Inspired, doubtless, by his close association with birds, he shouted to the fighting Shannons to lay an egg.

Henny stuck his head out of the window and shouted at all of the hecklers: "Go to hell. Go to hell, all of youse!" But there were tears in his voice. He closed the window, shutting out the warm, murmurous, summer night.

There was silence in the kitchen of the flat. Flo sat with a spent look on her face. The room was growing dark but she did not think to light the gas.

After a while she got up and carried his supper dishes to the sink. Then the aftermath of the quarrel, with both ashamed, set in.

He spoke with quiet despair. "What's happened to us, Flo?"

It's not my fault, she started to say. Instead she pulled in her lower lip between her teeth. She would say nothing more. She was spent with quarreling and relieved that it was over. He went on as if explaining something to himself.

"I was a boy living in a rear house on Scholes Street. My folks," he went on, "were greenhorns from the old country. So they got shoved around. To get even, they shoved me around. I use' to hang out around the Jews' pushcarts on Moore Street closing time. Other kids swiped stuff off of them just because they was Jews. But me, I worked for them. I helped them carry their stuff in nights. They paid me off with fruit and vegetables that wouldn't hold overnight. My folks needed that food.

"My folks! My mother did the best she could. My father," his voice tightened with bitterness, "rest his soul, he didn't know no better and I won't hold nothing against a dead man.

"Yes, I was a boy living in a rear house on Scholes Street. Bigger kids beat me up. And when I came home crying, my old man walloped me for letting myself get beat up. That was to learn me to be tough, he said. But I didn't want to learn to be tough. I didn't have it in me.

"I had the ideas all boys has. I was dope enough to think I stood a chance a being president of the United

States. They fooled us in school. They learned us that every American boy stood a chance a being president. I believed that like I use' to believe in Sanny Claus. Well, I got over that when I got in long pants.

"Then I got this here idea that I could be a cop or a fireman or the guy what drives a railroad train. A free country. Anything could happen. Well, ideas was free anyways. It turned out I didn't have no chance to be nothing.

"I was pushed out when I was thirteen. Get a job, my old man said. Get any kind a job just so it brings in a few dollars a week. And I been working ever since—not what I want to work at but anything I can get.

"I'm stuck! And I'm stuck till I die.

"But I didn't start out stuck. No. When I started keeping company with you, Flo, I thought you was the prettiest girl in Williamsburg. We bought furniture on time from Fehmel's. You had that bedspread you crocheted when we was engaged. Everything in our house will be the best, you said. I said, a flat on Maujer Street's the best I can do right now. You said, it's only for now, Henny, we'll live in a better place someday. I'll help you. It takes time, you said. You got to crawl before you can walk, you said.

"Six years ago! Furniture ain't paid up yet. Bedspread's been in hock all these years. It's only for now, you said, then. It's only for now, we say when we're young. And one fine day we wake up and find out that what's only for now is the whole Goddamned thing!

"Still and all, I had my ideas. I use' to think you was the prettiest girl in Williamsburg."

They were silent for a long time. He sat with his thoughts. She sat within arm's reach of him and her hand quivered with the impulse to put it on his cheek in a gesture of love. She remembered the shy way he had said, "I'd like you to be my girl," the first time they had ever danced together. Remembering, some of the old tenderness came back to her. She had a flash of understanding him; the dreams he had had—his fundamental decency that made it so hard for him to cope with harsh living.

She knew she had it in her woman's power to give him hope and dreams again. All she'd have to say was: Never mind, Henny. I love you. We still have each other. And all this *is* temporary. Everything will be better someday. Wait and see.

She could say that. That's all he wanted to hear. He'd be happy all of a sudden. He'd put his arms around her. . . .

In a panic, she murdered her tender thoughts. She fought down the impulse to show him affection. She knew what any demonstrativeness would lead to. Another terrifying nine months—new stitches—another mouth to feed.

Her eyes sought her child in the darkened room. Margy was sitting under the washtubs playing with two shoe boxes and some clothespins. She put all the clothespins in one box, then took them out and put them in the other box.

She should have a doll, Flo thought. Every little girl should have a doll. I never had one. I use' to say that if ever I had a little girl I'd see to it that she had a doll. She ought to have a doll.

Her husband spoke, joining his voice to her thoughts. "We use' to say that if we had kids we wanted them to have it better than we had it. So what do we go and do? We shove our kid around the way we got shoved around. We don't learn nothing. That's the trouble. That's why we're stuck. We don't learn nothing from what we went through."

He got up and paced the small kitchen. "Did I ask to be born? Did I ask to be a millionaire? No. All I asked for was a fair chance. I tried to be a good boy; a halfway decent man. But do I stand a chance? Will our kid ever stand a chance?

"Questions. Always questions and no answers. Who's got them answers and where are they keeping them?"

He put his hat and coat on.

"And *now*, where are you going?" asked Flo.

"Down to the corner."

"You won't find no answers in a saloon."

"I know. But at leas' I'll find other guys there with the same questions."

He closed the door gently as he went out.

Flo sat in the dark and thought: I mustn't let him get talking that way again. It makes me remember the real truth about my mother and I don't want to remember the real truth. I want it to be the way I made it up—that she was a saint. If I had to keep remembering all the time how bad things was at home, I couldn't live. It's better to remember things the way they shoulda been insteada the way they was. I got so that I don't hardly remember the way they was and that's a very good thing.

She called her child by name and Margy turned her face toward her. The white face and fair hair made a pale blur in the shadows.

"Come over here, Margy." But the child turned her face away. "Aw, come, baby, and after a while I'll light the light and read you the funny sheets. Come to Mama."

The child came to her mother. Flo lifted her to her lap. "Listen, baby. Mama didn't mean to slap you so hard today when you got lost. The hitting didn't mean nothing. It's just a way some mamas has. Just remember that you are always your mama's little girl."

Somehow the child understood that she could cry now and her mother wouldn't punish her for doing so. The child broke then. She folded her arms tightly about her mother's neck and whispered, "I was losted all day."

The tears came.

The mother sat holding the child tightly. She pressed her face to the child's wet cheek. She cried, too.

And they were two children who cried because it was dark and they were lost.

Chapter 3

Margy grew up learning to accept things as they were. She learned to make the best of things. She was grateful for little concessions and considered herself lucky when things went her way. She had her few moments of bitterness and rebellion when she thought that things ought to be better; that her parents should have more understanding and proceed on the premise that she was not a bad girl when she misbehaved or was disobedient; but that she was merely thoughtless and stupid when she did things that angered her mother.

In thoughtful moments she grieved at the continuous antagonism between her father and mother. But most of the time she figured her parents' way of life was the way of all life; the way that folks lived along together.

She knew always the pinch of poverty but seldom the stranglehold of actual want. She endured the tight, nervous discipline of her home, knowing the compensating freedom of her school life. (At least school seemed free in comparison with home.)

So at seventeen, with two years of high school behind her, she felt ready to lick the world. She had the optimism of the young to whom all of life shines endlessly ahead; the young who are sure they can make their own proud destiny in spite of the tritely spoken wisdom of the older people who have had their chance at licking life and have come out of the unequal fight with bloody and bowed souls.

When Margy set out to find her first job, her father made a little speech. He spoke out of his own experience and told her that the two most heartbreaking chores of life were looking for a new flat and for a new job. He said that nothing beat you down like being dispossessed or having to give up living quarters because you couldn't pay an unexpected or arbitrary rent increase, and then going out to walk the streets to find another flat within your means. Maybe you found it, only to be turned down because the landlord didn't think your job was good enough to guarantee the rent. Or you were turned down because you had committed the economic crime of having children. Not, explained Henny in all fairness, that you could blame the landlord. Kids *did* wreck a place.

It was the same with looking for a job. If you had never worked before, you were tagged "inexperienced" and few bosses wanted to bother about breaking in a new hand. If you *had* worked before, the question hardest to answer was: Why had you left your last job? If you had been fired, you had no proper references, and bosses were leery of hiring you. If you had left of your own accord, you were considered a troublemaker or a sorehead; a dissatisfied worker. And what boss wanted such a man in his shop?

That's why, Henny explained, he had clung to the job he hated. He knew the odds were against his finding a better one. And that's why, he told Margy, she shouldn't get the idea that looking for a new job was all pie.

Margy listened but she didn't believe a word he said. She had finished her formal education the last Friday in June and was all for going out the next day and starting to work. Her parents urged her to wait a little while; she'd have to work long enough in her time; that the transition from schooldays to workdays should be made slowly. Margy gave in to them. She made the transition slowly. She didn't start looking for a job until the following Monday, three days later.

She set forth equipped with a neatly clipped HELP WANTED FEMALE column from the Sunday classified ad section of the newspaper, and two letters—one from her high-school principal saying she was intelligent and industrious and one from her parish priest saying she was intelligent and decent. The priest's letter was more important than the principal's. It proved definitely that she was a Gentile. It eliminated her having to clear the hurdle of intolerance.

She tried the Manhattan ads first because she wanted to work in New York. She thought of it as a glamorous place.

She dreamed of a new world; of the daily ride to and from Brooklyn over the Williamsburg Bridge which spanned the East River, the river she had read about in her history course in high school.

She had another foolish, sentimental dream. It was about getting paid on Saturday in New York, and buying a box of Loft's Special Candy out of her pay and bringing it home to her mother. She dramatized her mother's pleasure; how Flo would wait each Saturday for the weekly treat. And some weeks the treat would be "parleys" which were very wonderful, indeed.

These warm dreams got a thorough douche of icy water after she had replied to two ads. The two jobs she had tried first had been filled hours before she arrived. The man at the second place explained that thousands of boys and girls who had participated at hundreds of high-school graduation exercises over the last week end were loose in New York—avid for jobs; any kind of jobs. He went out of his way to tell her this because he had a daughter who had just graduated from Girls' High in Brooklyn and he knew how it was.

The third ad marked on her list said: *General Clerical Worker Wanted.* It was a small office consisting of one hard-looking woman, a desk, chair and typewriter. The woman asked Margy could she take dictation directly on a typewriter. Margy looked blank. Thereupon the woman said that she dictated very slowly and motioned Margy to sit down to the machine. Margy said she guessed she could type from dictation. Of course she didn't know how to type but it looked easy. You merely hit the letters to spell out words, she thought. The woman gave her a sheet of paper, then lit a cigarette while waiting for Margy to get set. Much to Margy's embarrassment, she couldn't put the paper in the typewriter. She tried and tried but the gadgets about the roller confused her. The woman watched her a moment half sneeringly, half pityingly. Then she spoke. She spoke in a tired, tough voice.

"You put up a good bluff, sister, and I love a gal what puts up a good bluff. But you couldn't follow through. You just couldn't follow through. I need somebody I can count on and you looked like that somebody—a little dumb but honest. But you don't make the grade. Let me give you a tip, sister. Forget about working for a living. Glaum on to some guy who'll marry you and support you. Have a couple of kids and forget the business world. And now," the woman said, bored and tired, "beat it!"

Margy backed out of the place. In a way she was glad she hadn't been hired. Yet she would have liked to work there a while just to see what the business was. There had been a half-written letter on the typewriter desk. The heading said: *Mail Service. Daily Tip.* Then the letter started out: *Why throw good money after bad? Widow of famous jockey, having important connections . . .* That's all she had been able to read.

Margy had a nickel left out of the half-dollar her mother had given her. It was three o'clock in the afternoon. No use answering any more ads. Everyone would know she was a failure—had spent the whole morning in a fruitless search for work. Else why would she still be looking in late afternoon?

When she got home and made her report, Flo was full of I-told-you-so's. "I told you not to go to New York," said Flo. "I told you you'd stand a better chance in Brooklyn. I told you it was silly to go so far away from home to work. I told you that there's everything in Brooklyn that you could ever find or see in New York. But did you listen? No! So now you found out your mother was right."

Flo was one of those loyal Brooklynites whose fighting loyalty to her birthplace had been inherited from her parents. They and their neighbors had seriously considered setting up cannon and ramparts to fight a civil war for Brooklyn's liberty back in the old days when Brooklyn, a great American city in its own right, was absorbed by census-hungry New York City and demoted to "borough."

Margy had no antagonism toward Manhattan. But like her mother, she considered it a separate city and she looked upon it as any outsider would: a distant, unknown, glamorous place. She sure would have liked to work there.

Well, she had tried to get a job there and failed. Now she thought of Brooklyn fondly. She worked up a feeling of honesty, uprightness and civic pride and decided that Brooklyn was the only place to work in. She left for her second day's hunt for a job with a clipping from the *Standard Union,* Brooklyn's own paper, in her purse. The ad stated that the mail-order firm of Thomson-Jonson wanted mail readers, no experience required, but willing to learn.

The Thomson-Jonson Mail Order House had its warehouses and offices in downtown Brooklyn. Margy was to learn later that it was a small concern catering to small farm owners in Long Island and New Jersey.

A trolley could take her to within a block of it. She got off at the wrong stop on purpose so that she could detour by way of Fulton Street and walk to the place where the wonderful big department stores were. She wanted to look at the windows of the stores. She walked as slowly as dared a job-hunting citizen, and thoroughly enjoyed the hats and dresses exhibited behind the big plate-glass windows. She stopped a long time before Abraham & Straus's window admiring an Empress Eugenia hat. Then she turned into a narrow side street on her way to Thomson-Jonson's.

She was about to pass a tiny flower shop with most of its stock exhibited on the narrow strip of sidewalk before the store when a sign in the window stopped her. GIRL WANTED, it said, and for the moment, Margy forgot about the mail-order house. Margy thought how wonderful it would be to work in a flower store; to handle beautiful flowers all day long; pick them out for customers—to receive the compliment: "I leave the order in your hands"; to arrange the order artistically and wrap the flowers up in that soft, shiny, green paper. And as she stood staring at the sign, she began to dream. Maybe on a Saturday the man would let her take home some roses almost full bloom, that wouldn't keep over Sunday. How wonderful to take home a bunch of flowers to her mother each Saturday! That would be almost as good as Loft's Special.

She entered the store. It was no larger than an ordinary bathroom. Cut flowers in green pails were set on the floor on either side of a narrow aisle leading to an icebox. A small table, on which were a cash register and a roll of thin, green, waxed paper, stood in front of the icebox. A dark, gaunt youngish-looking man stood at the table, working. Several dozen full-blown red roses were on the table. The man was pulling off the outside petals of a rose until nothing but the core remained. He put the core on its long stem into a pail from which dangled a sign: ROSEBUDS,

50¢ A DOZEN. He looked up as she came in, finished pluck-ing a rose and wiped his hands on his black apron.

He thought she was a customer. "What's yours?" he asked.

"I happened to be passing by," she began.

"I got some nice glads, guaranteed to open up. . . ."

"No. I don't want to buy anything. I happened to see the sign in the window, girl wanted, and since I'm looking for a job . . ."

He stared at her intently for a second, then he picked up a rose and depetaled it before he answered, "The job's filled."

He did need an assistant and Margy had been the first one to apply. In his brief second of scrutiny he had de-cided that she wouldn't do. She looked honest and intelli-gent but she wasn't the type he had in mind. You see, he had a wife home. The lady shared his board greedily but, for reasons best known to herself, sneeringly refused to share his bed. That made life lonesome and dreary for him. Now he didn't exactly expect to get a partner in adultery for ten dollars a week. But he did want a curvy, sweet-smelling girl; someone he could stand close to at the table while together they made new flowers out of old; someone he could accidentally brush against as they passed each other in the brief, narrow aisle. In short, he wanted a girl who would flood the small cubicle with a definite aura of tremulous yielding femininity—someone with a curl to her hair and bows on her dress and slow-swinging legs with high-heeled, rosetted slippers at the ends of them. Certainly this plainly dressed, neatly combed girl wasn't the type.

Margy couldn't let loose of her dream all in an instant. "But you still got the sign in the window," she argued.

"I didn't get around to taking it out yet," he lied.

"I see," she said inadequately. "But thank you just the same."

"That's all right," he answered graciously, glad to have the episode finished so quickly and amicably.

Margy walked out slowly, staring covetously at the pails of flowers. She walked around the block slowly and came back to the store. The sign was still in the window. An unexplained feeling of anger gave her the courage to enter the store again.

What's yours? he started to say when he looked up and recognized her. "I told you I don't need no girl."

"Then why do you fool people by keeping that sign in your window?"

"Just because I feel like it, maybe. Anyhow, it's none of your business."

"All right," acknowledged Margy in defeat. "But do me a favor."

"What?" he asked grudgingly.

"Tell me why you don't want me to work for you?" The question took him by surprise. "You see," she explained, "I have to get a job. And if there's something wrong with me, it would be a favor if you'd let me know so that I can fix it, and not have so much trouble getting a job."

"Well, for some jobs, you'd do fine," he said. "Like for instance in a office. But for a job like this, where you meet the public, you got to have class."

"How do you mean?"

"Well, you ain't classy enough. That's all."

"I see. Well, thank you."

"That's all right."

I haven't got class, she thought, walking over toward Thomson-Jonson. That means, I'm not smart looking; no style, no personality. And it's my clothes. If Mama would let me buy my own clothes, I'd have class, all right. I wouldn't buy this tacky blue suit and these shoes with sensible heels if I were picking out my own clothes. Well, when I get a job and bring home pay each week, Mama will have to let me go out and buy my own clothes.

She daydreamed, as lonely but hopeful young people will. She dreamed she was wearing one of those very low-waisted short dresses. It would be old-rose Georgette crepe with an accordion-pleated skirt whose hem would dip in under her knees as she walked. There'd be a big bunch of purple artificial violets on the shoulder; black net stockings with high-heeled, patent-leather opera pumps—more classy to have them plain, no bows on the toes. The hat would be a purple cloche to match the color of the violets and a black patent-leather handbag to match the shoes. And *Quelques Fleurs* perfume.

She saw herself walking into the little flower store and saying casually, "I understand you need a girl. Will I do?"

"Yes, yes," the man would answer eagerly. "You're exactly the type I'm looking for."

"All right. Take the sign out of the window."

"You bet!" He'd take it out.

"Now tear it up, please." He'd tear it in two. After the sign was torn up, she'd tap her foot, look around and say coldly, "I've changed my mind. I don't think I'd care to work here."

"Do me a favor and tell me why?" he'd ask humbly.

"Well, if you want to know, this store hasn't any class. I'd like to work in a more classy place, if you know what I mean."

"I see," he'd answer, a broken man. "Thanks for telling me."

"That's all right," she'd say, and maybe she'd add a debonair, "Any time." Then she'd swing out of the store on her patent-leather, high-heeled pumps, leaving behind a memory of *Quelques Fleurs* perfume to haunt him until such a time as it was absorbed among the scents of the roses, lilies and carnations or whatever seasonable blooms were in stock at the time.

It said on the door: LEGAL DEPARTMENT. Under that it said: MANAGER OF CORRESPONDENCE DEPARTMENT. The third line was EMPLOYMENT DEPARTMENT. Way off down in the corner of the glass door was the aloof name of WAYNE PRENTISS. It was a small mail-order house and Mr. Prentiss was three departments by himself.

Margy's first impression of Mr. Prentiss was that he was polite and nice looking but rather old. Why he must be all of thirty, she guessed.

After a few routine questions, he gave Margy a blank to fill out. She stared down at the sheet wondering what to do. She didn't have a fountain pen! He saw her dilemma and took his own fountain pen from his pocket, uncapped it and handed it to her point end toward him. That's what gave Margy the impression that he was polite.

Margy wrote backhand instinctively. But they had taught her the Spencerian method in school. She held the pen in the approved fashion, wrist on paper and made the prescribed warming-up circles. She touched the pen to the paper and instead of an M the pen gave birth to a huge sprawling blot. She dropped the pen in a panic and made the blot worse when she pressed the fresh, white, oblong bit of blotter on it that Mr. Prentiss handed her. When she picked up the pen again, her hand was trembling so much that she couldn't rest her wrist on the paper. Mr. Prentiss got up and went over and stood in the niche formed by the open office door and the wall.

"Come here," he ordered.

Margy stopped trembling and turned ice cold. It was going to happen! Her mother had warned her! A man will try to take advantage of a girl looking for a job, Flo had said. Then her mother had given her instructions. In being interviewed, advised Flo, always stand between the doorway and the man so that you can turn around and run out at the first sign of the man trying to make love to you. And never, warned Flo, set foot inside an office in which there is a couch. Say, politely, that you changed your mind, or that you'll come back tomorrow: any kind of excuse. Then get out of the building as fast as you can.

Margy wondered desperately if there was a couch that she had overlooked in the room. Without moving her head, she rolled her eyes in all directions looking for the couch. She decided it was behind the door. She was trapped!

"Come here, please," repeated Mr. Prentiss.

And Margy went to him. Her mother had taught her to be wary of men, but she had trained her also to obey orders instantly and without question. So obedience triumphed over fear.

There was no couch behind the door and Mr. Prentiss looked anything but lecherous, bending over the water cooler which was the only piece of furniture behind the door. He was filling a paper cup with ice water.

"Drink this slowly," he advised. She obeyed. He took the emptied cup from her and said, "Now stand up straight and take three deep breaths." She breathed quiveringly. He wasn't satisfied. "Breathe from the diaphragm. Like me." He gave a demonstration. She breathed according to his theory.

As they walked back to his desk, he said, "Now don't be nervous. Remember this: You have your services to sell and we are in the market to buy service."

He put a fresh application blank before her and placed

the pen by its side. She stared down at the blank. Instead of putting her at her ease, his kindness confused her, made her uneasy. She couldn't understand why any boss needed to be considerate when there were so many people looking for work. She suspected an ulterior motive in his kindness.

He felt her confusion and being a kindly person he tried to help her out. "Everyone has to get his first job," he explained. "Everyone has to start somewhere. Even I had to go out with my law diploma under my arm—figuratively speaking, of course—and walk the streets hunting for my first job." He smiled at her and she tried to smile back.

As she filled out the blank, he thought of his own experiences getting a job. He was the son of a widow. His father, who had been manager of a small department store, left his widow a small trust fund and a mortgage-free house in Bay Ridge, Brooklyn. The boy, Wayne, had finished two years of college and was working as apprentice bookkeeper in a mercantile house when he was drafted in the First World War. After getting out of the army, he had used the little money he had saved to go to a New York law school at night. Often he and his mother discussed how fortunate he was to be able to finish his education, in spite of the war.

A few years ago, he, too, had answered a Thomson-Jonson ad for a young man with some knowledge of law. He had started at twenty-five dollars a week, and by dint of industry, as the success stories have it, he had made himself indispensable in various departmental ways and now was earning thirty-five dollars a week. Mr. Prentiss considered that he had had a very lucky break; getting a good law education and a nice interesting job immediately on passing the bar exam. He felt that he had to pay for this lucky break in some way. He was considerate of other job hunters who came under his power.

Margy filled out the blank but left the top line empty. She looked up at him hesitantly.

"Stuck?" he asked.

"It's about my name. I don't know . . ."

"Last name first . . ."

"I mean I was christened Margaret but everyone calls me Margy."

"Why?"

"I don't know. Maybe because Margy's easier to say

43

than Margaret. No matter what name you have," she explained, "in Brooklyn, they change it to end with y or ie."

"In some parts of Brooklyn," he amended.

"Yes," she agreed, worried that she had said too much.

"Well, what's in a name," he quoted. "Shakespeare said that," he explained.

Margy hunted around for a tactful reply. If she said, yes, he might think she was smart-alecky. If she said, did he? Mr. Prentiss might be flattered that he knew so much. On the other hand, he might consider her stupid. She straddled the issue.

"Shakespeare said a lot of smart things," she said.

"He hit the nail on the head every time. Every single time." Thus Mr. Prentiss evaluated the great playwright.

The application blank was filled out at last. Margy, more at ease now, was sorry that the episode was finished. She had begun to like Mr. Prentiss very much. She thought he was learned and kind.

He signed his name on the blank, clipped her two letters to it, put it in his desk drawer and stood up.

"Twelve dollars a week to start," he said. "Hours, eight-thirty to five." Since it was an old-fashioned office without pushbuttons, he raised his voice and called out, "Miss Barnick?"

A plain, lean, dark-faced woman of forty or fifty walked into the office on silent rubber-heeled shoes.

"This is Miss Shannon," he said. "We're trying her out as reader." To Margy, he explained, "Miss Barnick will be your supervisor."

"Follow me," ordered Miss Barnick.

"No use starting her in today," said Mr. Prentiss.

"I thought I'd show her around so she won't waste time in the morning."

"A good idea, Miss Barnick," approved Mr. Prentiss. "Report at eight-thirty tomorrow morning, Miss Shannon."

"Thank you," said Margy. "Thank you very much."

"Good luck," he called after her.

It was a big office with broad, flat-topped desks end to end. "This will be your desk," explained Miss Barnick.

Margy fell in love with the desk. It was so big and shiny and neat. There were half a dozen wire baskets in a neat row at the far end and a glass bowl filled with strong pins. In front of each basket were placed pads with paper of various bright colors: White slips with ROUTINE printed on them; yellow, INQUIRIES; pink, COMPLAINTS; and the dark blue bore the startling word, THREAT! There was also a pad of gummed mailing stickers.

"Ruthie, here, who sits next to you, will break you in," said Miss Barnick. Ruthie and Margy smiled at each other. Miss Barnick sailed across the room followed by Margy. "This is the washroom," she said. "I'll leave you now."

"Eight-thirty tomorrow," checked Margy.

"It would be better if you got here ten minutes before. The person that gets ahead in business," pronounced Miss Barnick somberly, "is the one who comes to work ten minutes ahead of time and leaves ten minutes after closing time. I might as well tell you that we don't like clock watchers here."

"Yes, ma'am," said Margy respectfully.

Miss Barnick went away. Margy, because she thought it was expected of her, went into the washroom. She pulled off her hat and ran her comb through her hair. There was another girl in the washroom. Margy deduced that she had just been hired, too, because the girl wore a hat. She was powdering her nose. The two girls sized up each other in the mirror.

The other girl had a nice hair style, Margy thought. It was shingled boyishly in the back and the sides frizzed out from under her hat in a permanent wave.

The girl submitted to the scrutiny for a while, then turned to smile at Margy. A gold-capped front tooth winked wetly.

"Didn't you ever see a doll before?" the other girl challenged good-naturedly.

"I was just admiring the way you got your hair done," explained Margy.

The girl pulled off her hat. Her ash-blond hair was smooth and shiny in the back where it was unwaved, and cloudily dull and confused at the sides where it stood out in two bushes.

"It's lovely," breathed Margy.

"Thanks," said the other girl. "You just been hired?"

"Yes."

"Me, too. I was walking out of what's-his-name's office when you came in."

"I didn't notice you," said Margy.

"You looked too scared to notice anything."

"I think this is going to be a nice place to work," said Margy.

"A job's a job." The girl shrugged.

"I had a little trouble with my name," said Margy, awkwardly getting around to making a friend. "I finally put down Margy Shannon."

"What *is* your name?"

"Margy Shannon."

"You can't have trouble with that unless they don't like the Irish here." The girls laughed. "My name's Irene. You know, Reenie for short. Reenie O'Farron. Irish Protestant," she added.

"I'm Irish Catholic," revealed Margy.

Both girls had a pang of disappointment because they were not of the same faith.

"I go out with a Catholic feller," said Reenie, meaning to show that she was liberal.

"So do I," said Margy. She didn't, of course, but she felt that she had to exchange confidence for confidence. "Not steady," she added.

"What are you doing this afternoon?" asked Reenie.

"I thought I'd go home."

"You can always go home when there's no place else to go."

"That's true."

"Let's take in a show," suggested Reenie.

Margy did some quick mental arithmetic. She had forty-five cents in her purse. A nickel would have to be saved for carfare home. A sandwich might cost a dime. Her mother might ask what she did with the money. She could say that she had to go to a lot of places before she found the job. . . .

"Let's!" agreed Margy recklessly.

Margy was very happy. It had been a wonderful day. She knew she was going to like the job. She thought Mr. Prentiss was wonderful and Reenie was going to be a very exciting friend. She shuddered at the idea that the florist might have hired her and that she might never have set foot in Thomson-Jonson and might have missed out on everything. In a way, she thought, I'm glad I'm not classy.

Chapter 4

Margy liked her job and was extremely conscientious about her work, especially the first few weeks. She read all the letters through from beginning to end. Miss Barnick explained that this wasn't necessary; in most cases a letter could be classified by its opening sentence. Margy tried to do it that way but invariably became interested in the contents and read the letters through. Ruthie told her not to worry—that after she had read ten thousand or so she'd be tired of letters.

Margy waited eagerly for Threat! letters to turn up. These letters threatened lawsuits because the writer alleged the goods received were misrepresented in the catalogue, or that the price was more than quoted or that money had not been refunded for returned merchandise. Margy had been instructed to deliver such letters immediately to Mr. Prentiss after first pinning the classifying Threat! slip to them. Sometimes she delivered as many as four such letters to him a day. Sometimes days went by without a single Threat letter in her pile. Whenever she went into Mr. Prentiss' office he gave no indication that he was aware of her presence. He never looked up or said thank you. He was quite the busy executive with no time for polite amenities. She began to think that she was mistaken in her first idea that Mr. Prentiss was a kind, friendly human being.

Then she got into trouble.

It grew out of her habit of reading all the letters through and getting too interested in the writers. She answered one of the letters! Many a time, a crank letter came in or a foolish letter and the girls showed these to each other just for a laugh. One such foolish letter came to Margy's desk.

A farmer near Trenton, New Jersey, evidently believing

that anything could be had by mail, wrote in asking Thomson-Jonson to get him a wife. His only specifications were that she be young and a hard worker. His wife had just died and he needed a woman to help handle the chores around the farm.

Margy answered his letter during a lunch hour. Romantically she advised him to wait until true love came his way; not to marry merely to get someone to work for him. Then she had filed the farmer's letter in the "No Answer Required" basket and that was the end of the episode (or so she thought) except she'd have a feeling of half-shame from time to time when the idea occurred to her that she had done a silly thing.

But the farmer wrote to Margy asking *her* to marry him! The letter, addressed to Miss Margy Shannon in care of Thomson-Jonson, went to the desk of a reader newer than Margy. The girl read it, studied it, classified it as Threat! and carried it in to Mr. Prentiss. He sent for Margy.

"Miss Shannon," he said, "you understand that employees are not permitted to receive personal mail here."

"Yes, sir," she said. "I know. I never let anyone write to me here."

"Are you sure?"

"Yes, sir."

"Nevertheless, you've received an extremely personal letter at this address."

Margy became frightened. Who could have written to her? Was it someone to whom her family owed money and who meant to embarrass her so that the debt would be paid quickly? She recalled how once her father had bought a dime ticket for a church raffle from a man in the shop; how he had won a turkey and how they had delivered it to him at the shop; how the foreman had told him he'd be fired if he didn't keep his personal life the hell away from his work.

I'm going to get fired, thought Margy, and they don't give you references if you get fired. And how can I get another job without references? And I'm supposed to get a two-dollar raise at the end of the year.

"I don't see how that could be, Mr. Prentiss," she said fumblingly. "I don't know anyone who would send me a letter—not even to my home."

"I won't make a mountain out of a molehill," said Mr. Prentiss. "The letter happened to come to my department. I won't report this to your supervisor. It might lead to your dismissal, you know."

She mumbled, thank you, and waited. He said nothing more. She turned to go.

"Just a moment. You might want to read the letter," he said. "Technically, it's your mail." He permitted himself to smile briefly.

She stood in front of his desk and read it. Her face got hot and red with embarrassment. He took off his glasses and watched her as she read. When she finished, she looked at him. She noticed how young—almost boyish—he looked without his glasses. She handed the letter back to him.

"Don't you want to keep it?" he asked. "After all, a girl doesn't get a marriage proposal every day."

"No, sir, I don't want to keep it." Her eyes were hot with unshed, shamed tears.

He tore the letter in two and threw it into his wastebasket. "We'll consider the incident closed," he said. "But don't let it happen again."

"No, sir," she promised.

She waited. He waited. She thought: There're a lot of things I could talk to him about if we were in the same class. He thought: I'd like to find out all about her; where she lives, what kind of parents she has—her hopes for the future—what her thoughts are. It would be easy to fall in step with her some night when she's leaving and just walk along with her and talk. But she'd misunderstand. There'd be talk. The bosses wouldn't like it. Not good policy to mingle with the help, Mr. Thomson had advised him that time when it got around that he liked that red-headed Marie a little. And his mother! The thought of disloyalty to his mother (disloyalty according to his mother's definition) made the whole small episode with Margy a little distasteful to him.

"That's all," he said curtly.

He watched her walk out of the office. It was quite a while before he put his glasses back on and started work on the accumulated Threat! letters on his desk.

Margy thought only of Mr. Prentiss the rest of the day.

She became very sad thinking about him. The refrain of a poem she had been made to memorize in grade school came back to her.

For of all sad words of tongue or pen,
The saddest are these: It might have been.

Yes, it was all like Maud Muller on a summer's day, the judge coming by while she raked the hay. Ships that pass in the night, thought Margy. That's Mr. Prentiss and me. If only it had been that I went to college like he did—or that I was a supervisor here. Then maybe he'd give me a second thought. But in the first place, he's too old. No, that doesn't matter. It's better that the husband be older than the wife.

She dreamed a while in the slow period of the afternoon. She ended up her dream by deciding that it couldn't be. A girl marrying the boss was more romantic than practical. Of course, she had read a lot of stories about secretaries marrying their bosses. But it always turned out that the secretary was a society girl who was working under an assumed name in her father's organization just to prove to her father that she could earn her own living without his help. And when the boss married that girl it was all right because the boss was a rising young executive and the old man had had his eye on him for some time. So he made him vice-president the day he married the daughter. Sometimes the stories had it that the boss's son was working incognito in the firm and he fell in love with the secretary who had no idea at all about his real identity. In this case, the secretary was always breathtakingly beautiful with a bouncing pert personality.

With sighs of regret, Margy set aside the dream of marrying the boss. By closing time she had rationalized away her shame at receiving the letter and being called into Mr. Prentiss' office about it.

"After all," she explained to Reenie as they left the office together, "it's not really my fault. I didn't ask that farmer to write to me."

"Look at it this way," consoled Reenie. "Fifty years from now it will all be forgotten. If you do happen to remember it, you'll brag to the other old ladies in the poorhouse how you had a chance to marry a guy once and you turned him down."

"I really didn't have a chance to . . ."

"A proposal's a proposal," said Reenie firmly, "no matter which way it's dragged out of a man. And you've got refusal number one out of the way."

"Do you think somebody will really propose to me someday?"

"Of course. And you mustn't say yes right away. You must say no three times before you say yes."

"Would you?" asked Margy.

"I always do," said Reenie.

"What?" asked Margy, a little shocked as she got Reenie's meaning. "You couldn't have said yes, because you're not married."

"I wasn't talking about marriage in my case. I was talking about holding out a little, you know, before you give in."

"Oh, Reenie!"

Suddenly Reenie laughed and then said, "Shame on you for thinking bad thoughts about a friend."

Margy was relieved. "You were only fooling, then." She gave Reenie an affectionate shove. "Oh, you! Always full of jokes."

"That's me," admitted Reenie. "The girl who'll do anything for a laugh. And do I feel sorry for you!"

"Why?"

"Because next Saturday when you go to your confession you'll have to tell the priest you thought evil thoughts of a friend."

"I never did!"

"And you'll have to tell him you lied to a friend."

"When did I ever lie to you?" asked Margy.

"Just now when you said you never did."

"Let's talk about something different," said Margy.

Reenie looked at her friend's face and saw it was grave and downcast. She put an arm around her and hugged her close for a moment. "Oh, Margy," she said, "don't take things so serious. Learn to make and take a joke, 'cause if you don't, it's going to be an awful dreary life for you."

A week or so later as Margy, Reenie and Ruthie were leaving the office, they saw a sprightly, coquettish, little old lady talking cutely to the private detective who stood in the doorway at closing time to watch that the girls didn't carry merchandise out of the place. The lady was in gray: gray dress and toque with a bunch of artificial purple violets at the side; gray suede pumps and gloves and purse; sheer gray silk stockings. There was a sharp, spicy scent about her; carnation perfume.

"I'm waiting for my best beau," she told the detective as the girls passed. "He always takes me to the theater and supper on my birthday."

The three girls stared at her with frank curiosity and lingered near the doorway because they wanted to see the "best beau." Each made a guess as to his identity. Margy decided he was Mr. Betz, the old but dapper accountant who wore a white carnation in his buttonhole each day and who wore fawn-colored spats when cool weather started up.

She was astonished when Mr. Prentiss stepped out of the elevator and the old lady claimed him by slipping her arm through his. Best beau, thought Margy, feeling something like distaste. Hm!

Mr. Prentiss tipped his hat to the girls as he and his mother were about to pass them. Mrs. Prentiss stayed her son by a slight pressure on his arm. She smiled at the three girls, each in turn, and looked straight and a little appealingly into each face as she did so, as if saying, Please, you who are so young and have so much before you, don't take from me this son who is all I have.

She turned her head to smile at a fourth girl who stood with one elbow resting on a radiator, staring insolently at mother and son. When Mrs. Prentiss saw the girl's red hair, she knew instantly that she was the Marie her son used to talk about so much. The little old lady's sweet smile twisted into a sneer of hate. She pressed closer to her son's side and drew him out of the building.

The three girls walked down the street a little behind the mother and son.

"The girl what marries him will be lucky," said Ruthie. "He's such a good son."

"Who wants to marry a good son?" asked Reenie. "I'd rather marry a good *man*. Any day!"

"Well, I think it's cute," said Ruthie, "the way they're more like sweethearts than mother and son."

"And I think it stinks," said Reenie.

"Reenie!" said both girls simultaneously and disapprovingly.

"Just for the sake of argument," said Reenie, "Ruthie, would you marry a man like that—so hotsy-totsy with his mother?"

"Yes, I would!" said Ruthie courageously.

"Would you, Margy?" asked Reenie.

"I'll let you know," said Margy. "That is, if he ever happens to ask me."

Chapter 5

Mrs. Prentiss sat upright in her chair, her little feet straining down to touch the floor with the tips of her toes. The well-trained Gage and Tollner waiter hovered over her, reverently presenting his tray of pastries as though he were offering gifts of diamonds and rubies to a queen.

"Let me see now." She tilted her head to one side and put her forefinger in the deep furrow of her right cheek. "They're all so lovely. I can't decide between the apricot tart and that baby mocha éclair."

"Take both," suggested her son.

"Oh, I wouldn't think of being *such* a greedy."

The waiter shifted his weight from one foot to the other. It took the place of a sigh. She looked up at him and smiled, her cheek furrowing where once it had dimpled. The familiar contraction of the muscles that once controlled a deep flashing dimple gave her the same feeling of captivating feminine power that had been hers when she was twenty.

"Poor waiter," she murmured understandingly. "How you must detest weak women who can't make up their minds."

"Oh, no, ma'am," he demurred. He smiled gallantly at her in penance for the sighing shift of weight. "Take your time. That's what I'm here for."

"Why he's nice!" Mrs. Prentiss cried out at her son.

The waiter looked pleased and embarrassed. Her son wished to hell she'd choose *something* and get it over with.

"Well, I'm not going to keep this nice man waiting a second longer." She shut her eyes hard the way a child does and described a slow circle with her forefinger, chanting slowly, "I'm going to take THIS one!" As she exploded the word *this*, her forefinger stiffened and she opened her eyes. She was pointing at a Neapolitan.

"But I don't want that one," she wailed.

This time the waiter sighed audibly as he reshifted his weight.

"Give her those first two," ordered Wayne. With skilled alacrity, the grateful waiter slid the tart and the éclair onto her plate.

"No, no, no," she squealed, stretching out the palms of her hands with a pushing-away gesture. A couple at the next table stopped eating, looked up and stared at the little drama.

"Oh, Mother!" said Wayne impatiently. "That's all," he said to the waiter. The waiter was glad to get away.

Mrs. Prentiss removed the last remaining roll from a plate and pulled the plate toward her. She picked up her knife. "You've simply got to help me eat these." She began to cut the éclair in half. The beige cream oozed out.

"Mother, please stop. Either eat them or leave them."

Sudden tears flooded her eyes. "But I was brought up not to be selfish," she explained. She transferred a gooey half of each pastry to the plate and extended it to him. "Please? Pretty please?"

"I don't want it," he said. The interested couple gave him a dirty look. "I hate sweet things." She set the plate down. Her hand trembled and a tear rolled down her cheek. He was in a panic. He had to say something and say it quickly. "I hate sweet things," he repeated, swallowed hard, and added, "Except you."

Without warning, a gush of evil-tasting liquid filled his mouth, like the time when as a boy, he had become seasick on a ferryboat. He gulped down a glass of ice water.

Her cheek furrow deepened as she smiled at him through her tears. Suddenly she felt safe, happy and beloved. The interested couple at the next table smiled tenderly at the little old lady and went back to their dinner.

Mrs. Prentiss ate her pastry, handling her fork with graceful movements, her eyes roving to neighboring tables as she chewed daintily.

He looked at her and tried to see her as a young girl. His father had worshiped her—or so she always told her son. She had been too delicate to have a baby. She told him that, too, a lot of times. But she had had him. Why? he wondered. Because she couldn't help it or because she wanted to give his father tangible proof of her love? Was it because she had been conscientious and wanted to make return payment for room, board and the protective status of wife? (She had been poor and pretty. The man she married had been fairly well off.)

He wished he knew how it had been with her.

"Mother," he asked, "why didn't I ever have a brother or sister?"

"Lonesome?" she returned brightly.

"No."

"I tried to be a playmate to you—when I was young, I mean younger. Besides it's nice, just the two of us. We're not only mother and son. We're two good friends, aren't we, dear?"

"Yes, Mother." He fought back a sigh.

"But could I have been sure that the others would have turned out like you, I would have had more." She waited, looking at him a little tensely.

"Thank you, dear," he said gallantly.

He stood in their Bay Ridge basement kitchen and watched an extra drop of water from the closed tap trickle down the copper bowl of the sink. He pulled out his handkerchief and wiped off the drop. He did it from force of habit. Ever since the age of six, his weekly chore had been to polish that copper sink. Twenty-five years of polishing each Sunday morning! Except when he was in the army, of course.

He turned off the gas. The milk was heated exactly the way she liked it, a skim beginning to form on the surface. He poured it into a tall thin glass and set it on the tray next to the flowered plate holding two Nabisco's. With the tray in one hand and the other hand on the light switch, he looked around the kitchen, the way a housewife does before she closes the door of one of her rooms behind her. The saucepan! He set the tray down and rinsed out the saucepan, dried it and hung it on the end hook. He watched for a moment until it stopped swinging.

She wore a dainty, much-tucked, long-sleeved, batiste nightgown. Her hair was in two braids, tied with narrow lavender ribbons. The rose silk, shirred lampshade attached to the bed above her head was kind to her.

"It's nice," she said, smiling down at her tray, "that we can give each other these little comforts and luxuries. Sunday, you're going to stay in bed until noon and I'll bring you a breakfast tray. I'll get up early and cook everything you like."

"Oh, no, Mother! I couldn't let you."

"But you will let me. It's my privilege and my pleasure. And it's only fair. You wait on me and I wait on you."

He yielded. It was easier to yield than to argue with her. After a while he asked her if she was comfortable.

"Like a kitten," she said.

"Is there anything else you want?"

"No. But don't run away. Sit and visit with me a while."

He sat on the slipper chair by her bed. The seat was so low that his knees stuck up and almost touched his chin. His pants got pulled up too tightly around his seat. He fidgeted, trying to relieve the strain on the seams without actually pulling at his pants.

"How did things go at the office today, dear?" she asked. She put her hand on his knee.

"So-so. Routine. Nothing interesting."

"Nothing?"

"Except I found a pretty lady waiting for me in the hall." He pressed her hand. He was rewarded by the look of radiant pleasure in her face.

"Tell me: That girl, Marthy, who asked the farmer to marry her. Whatever became of that?"

"Oh, Margy! *He* asked *her*."

"Poor thing! I suppose she had dreams of marrying a rich farmer and not having to work any more."

"Oh, no. Nothing like that. She just felt she had to give him some advice and he misunderstood. You know how young girls are."

"I should. I was a young girl once, believe it or not."

"I believe it."

"And that other one. Has she been transferred yet?"

"Who?"

"You know the one I mean——the impudent-looking one with the dyed red hair."

"Marie?"

"You know all their names, don't you?"

"Well, they work for me. No, she hasn't been transferred. I really need her in my department. And her hair isn't dyed. That's the natural color."

She wagged her finger at him. "Ah, we women may fool you men, but we never fool each other."

He stretched out his legs under the bed and put his hands in his pockets. He felt more comfortable.

"I hope you'll marry someday, son," she said. "But to someone who's worthy of you. I'd like to hold a grandchild in my arms before I . . . before I . . . well, before I cross over."

"I'll have to make it snappy." He smiled. "I'll be forty any year now."

"You have so much time. Your father waited until he was forty to marry. Then he didn't do so badly." She bobbed her head in a sassy little coquettish way. "Even if I say it who oughtn't."

"I'll wait, then. Because . . ." he half spoke, half sang, "I want a girl just like the girl who married dear old Dad."

"Never mind," she scolded prettily. "There's a lot of truth in those old sayings and those old songs. Otherwise they wouldn't have *lived*. So don't make fun."

"I wasn't." He took the empty tray from her. "Happy birthday," he said. "And many more." He leaned over to kiss her cheek.

Her arms went around him. She held him close. "You're a good boy, Wayne, a *good* boy. I don't know what I'd do without you."

He had what he considered a disloyal thought. He wondered how it would sound if a young girl told him she wouldn't know what she'd do without him. He knew he was held. He couldn't marry while his mother lived. He didn't want her to die. Yet, he wanted a wife—children. He wanted to love a woman and be loved by her. There had been times—a few (he didn't like to remember them) —he called those times "bought love." Buying had seemed a desperate expedient at the time. But the aftertime had brought no surcease—no contentment. He sighed out of his thoughts.

"What, dear?" asked his mother.

"Nothing. Only it's the other way round. I don't know what I'd do without *you*."

Chapter 6

Margy waited until the supervisor's back was turned before she looked at the clock. Twenty minutes to quitting time. All day she had waited for the hour but now that it was near, she hated the day to end. The office was her neat and orderly world—more home to her than her parents' flat. She slowed down. Her work was about up but she didn't want to finish before Reenie. It didn't seem a friendly thing to do.

The supervisor was at the other end of the room. Margy took a chance and spoke to her friend. "I like your new dress, Reenie."

"I got it over on Pitkin Avenue."

"It's a sample, I bet."

Reenie was flattered at the implication. "Sure. They wanted twelve ninety-eight but I beat them down to nine fifty. That's what it cost wholesale, the man said—they always say that. Anyhow I got it for nine fifty only I should come back and bring my friends."

Margy examined the dress covetously, wishing she could take advantage of friendship, go to the same store with Reenie and bargain for a similar dress. There was something familiar about the dress. It was old-rose Georgette, one of the new long-waisted styles with the belt halfway between the waist and knees. The accordion-pleated skirt was short enough to reveal Reenie's kneecaps. There was an artificial blue rose fastened to the shoulder. Margy thought violets would be better. That was it! It was exactly the kind of dress Margy had dreamed of wearing when she went back to tell the florist his store wasn't classy enough for her. *Her* dress had violets.

"Only," complained Reenie, smoothing down her boyish chest, "I got to wear such a tight brassière with it.

The skirt's so short it hikes up in front if my chest sticks out."

"Did you get a hat to match?"

"I couldn't find one. So I had to get a black."

"Oh, well, black goes with everything."

"Wait'll you see it! It's one of these here new cloche shapes." (She pronounced it clock.) "First I thought I'd get me a finalé hopper style."

"But all the cake eaters wear those."

"They're classy just the same. Anyhow, being's I had to wear it for work, I thought this here cloche would be better."

Margy looked down at her own navy-blue serge skirt in distaste. Her entire wardrobe consisted of a blue serge suit, a lightweight coat, a few blouses and some slips and pants. In spring and fall she wore the suit. In winter, she added the lightweight coat and in summer she wore the skirt and a blouse without the jacket.

She had started off the outfit with a white Georgette blouse which she had to launder each night. When it turned yellow, she dipped it in pink Rit and all the girls assured her that they honestly thought it was a new blouse. Well, it had been dipped many times, each time a different color. Now it was navy blue. She dyed a slip navy blue and the blouse, skirt and slip looked almost like a dress.

Winter was coming on. Margy wanted a new winter coat and a dress like Reenie's to go under it. She was sick and tired of her navy-blue ensemble.

"I'm thinking of getting a new coat, myself," she confided to Reenie.

"Don't think," advised her friend, "just go out and get it."

"But you don't know . . ." Margy bit off the rest of the words. She couldn't tell Reenie how her mother was about money. But Reenie guessed.

"Talk up," she said. "Tell your mother you can't hold your job unless you have some new clothes. That always works."

"I couldn't."

"Why? You're over age, aren't you?"

"I was eighteen last June."

"The day I was eighteen, I went to my mother and said: 'Look, Mom, I'm my own boss now and I don't have to give in all my pay. From now on, I'm paying board.' "

Ruthie, who sat on the other side of Margy, broke into the conversation. "That's exactly what I told my mother, the day Ed gave me the ring."

Reenie glared at her for presuming to join in a conversation she had no right to listen to in the first place.

"I was just saying," apologized Ruthie.

"So," concluded Reenie, lowering her voice and pointedly ignoring Ruthie, "I handed her five dollars and kept the rest and to this day I'm paying board."

"But your mother has a job of her own."

"So's your father," countered Reenie. "If I were you, Margy, I wouldn't hand in all my money. I'd start right now paying board."

"I might as well wait a little longer," temporized Margy.

"Wait for what? When again will you want nice clothes so bad? How often in life are you young? Soon enough you'll get married—settle down—kids. Soon enough you won't care about nothing no more."

They saw Miss Barnick bearing down on them with a black cloud settling on her face. Intimidated, they stopped talking, looked up and smiled ingratiatingly. The supervisor felt a pang of compassion. They were good girls and worked hard and it was only in the last few minutes of the day that they wasted time. Once Miss Barnick had been young and she had known the delicious happiness of girlish confidences. Her face started to break up because she wanted to smile at them, but didn't quite dare. She was afraid that if she showed understanding the girls would take advantage of her and where would her job be if she couldn't maintain discipline? The breaking up resolved into a frown but she went past without reprimanding them and to Reenie and Margy it was like a reprieve before execution.

Margy's fingers flew. The shining pins flashed through the yellow, red, blue, green and white slips. She was up on her mail ten minutes before closing time. According to an unwritten office law, she was allowed to go to the washroom now. She gathered her toilet articles from her desk drawer—a powder-saturated puff wrapped in a clean handkerchief and a wafer of Cashmere Bouquet soap wrapped in a bit of torn towel. She tucked her crackled patent-leather purse under her arm.

"Wait for me!" pleaded Reenie, standing up as she pinned a red slip on her last letter. With a deft movement she got her things out of her drawer.

As they opened the door of the washroom, a wave of high-pitched conversation hit them. The girls were gossiping about Mr. Prentiss. One said he never would marry because his mother wouldn't stand for it. Someone else said he'd never marry because he was madly in love with Marie and she just couldn't "see" him. An older girl suggested mildly that in all probability Mr. Prentiss was still single because he didn't care to marry.

"But he must care," wailed a girl.

"Why?"

"Because we have to have *something* to talk about."

Just then, Reenie, standing in the open doorway, said sweetly, "Come right in, Mr. Prentiss." The girls stood petrified but relaxed when only Margy walked in and shut the door behind her. The girls didn't think Reenie's joke was funny. It happened almost every day. No matter whom they were talking about when Reenie entered, she always said, "Come right in," using the name of the person being discussed. It was always Margy playing straight to Reenie's clowning who came in. And the girls were always annoyed because even though familiar with the gag, they were taken in by it every single time.

The small washroom was crowded with girls making ready to go home. They stood before the mirrors, powdering, outlining their lips in moist, gleaming reds, and running ten-cent combs through their hair. Their eyes never left their reflections in the mirrors. They watched the flash of their teeth when they smiled; rolled their eyes so's not to lose sight of themselves as they turned their heads sideways while they made the slow rhythmic motion of pulling the comb through their hair. They talked to each other, their eyes meeting in the mirror.

The boxlike room was warm with mixed smells: the sweetness of face powder, the fainter exotic smell of lipstick and the warm female odor of hair. The pungent smell of wet soap cut through the more cloying odors.

Most of the girls had brought their pocketbooks. "Hold my bag for a minute, will you?" they asked each other. A girl who was washed, combed and made up, stood to one side holding four handbags. Margy and Reenie, first extracting lipstick and comb, added theirs to her load.

"What was the name of your last servant girl?" she asked in pretended protest. They smiled thanks at her as they crowded in before a washbasin.

Margy looked down the line. Three tiny-stoned rings, belonging to the engaged girls, gleamed on the porcelain. Days when Margy got to the washroom earlier, she heard them say to each other as they stripped off their pledges lovingly, "Don't let me forget my ring, now. Hear?"

Margy and Reenie washed their hands quickly, anxious to get at the more important business of makeup. Margy looked up as she dried her hands and her eyes met Reenie's in the mirror. They smiled at each other like friends meeting after a long parting.

"Know what?" asked Reenie, idly.

"No. What?" Margy replied. A girl giggled.

"When I was a kid, my mother used to give me a slap when she caught me looking in the glass. 'There's a devil behind every looking glass,' she used to say."

There was a small pause while the lined-up girls froze in their actions. Eyes traveled along the mirrors to Reenie. They were one—held tenuously by an old folk saying most of them had heard at home. Then the thread snapped and there was chatter and head tossing and little scented clouds as puffs were banged against noses and made to give up the last fractional gram of powder.

The old girls (some as old as thirty) stood aside, yielding the mirrors to the younger ones. They had passed the years when the innocent ritual of self-adoration was so important. Their toilettes were brusque and practical: a vigorous washing of the hands, a wet edge of a towel rubbed angrily behind the ears, and they stepped aside without a sigh to make way for those who carried the banners of first youth. It was as though they had put beautiful young foolishness behind them forever and now were concerned only with cleanliness—as though they had traded hopeful, tremulous youth for antiseptic womanhood. They listened to the chattering of the youngsters and their older eyes met in the mirrors over the heads of the young girls and they exchanged looks of superior wisdom. As they listened, they pushed back the cuticle of their fingernails with a towel or dug underneath the nail with a short file.

Margy, passing her cool dampish puff over the planes of her face, and half lost in dreaming delight in the sensuous feeling the smoothing made, had a sudden queer feeling. She felt that the moments of this time would be marked in her memory for always; that in years to come, an instant picture, complete in all details, would come to her at unexpected times. And she'd see the washroom again and hear the girls talking—talking about men and clothes. Funny, she thought, when girls talked about clothes, they thought of men, and when they talked about men, they thought of clothes.

There was a sudden hush in the room and Margy came out of her musing. Reenie was talking and the girls always listened when Reenie had something to say. Margy caught the end of what her friend was saying.

". . . last night. And my mother wasn't home."

"Session?" asked two of the girls simultaneously and hopefully.

Reenie was insulted. "Certainly not!"

Just then Miss Barnick opened the door. "Oh! Excuse me, girls." She started to back out.

"Come in, Miss Barnick," chorused the girls. "It's all right. Come on!" They shoved each other aside to make space. "Come on! There's room."

"No. Thanks, girls. I'll come back later." The supervisor withdrew.

Miss Barnick had some understanding. She knew the girls were under her thumb all day and she thought it unfair to intrude in the last moments of the working day. Let them blow off steam by themselves, she thought.

"Barnick's a good sport," said Ruthie.

"But an awful sourpuss on the job," Reenie reminded her.

"I guess she's got to be strict," said Margy. "The way we carry on and all. If she didn't jump on us once in a while, there'd never be any work done."

The girls more or less agreed with Margy. Then Ruthie said, "Go on, Reenie."

"Go on where, Ruthie?"

"You know."

"I don't know what you're talking about."

"*Reen-*ie!" chorused the girls, protestingly.

"Oh, yeah. About last night. Well," said Reenie, "first I

showed him the snapshots from my vacation last year in Bear Mountain. He made out like he was jealous of the fellers in the pictures with me. Then he played the piano. He just finished this here course—*you* know; learn to play in ten easy lessons without notes? And then . . ." she stopped, tantalizingly.

"Then what?" chorused the girls eagerly.

"Well, by that time it was pretty dark in the parlor and I asked him to turn on the light."

"Were you paralyzed or something?" asked Ruthie.

"Oh, you!" said Reenie in mock exasperation. "Anyways, he made believe he couldn't find the light. So he said, 'Let's dance.' We put a record on the victrola, *you* know, 'I'll be Loving You, Always'?" A girl started humming the song and continued humming under Reenie's talking. "So we danced a while in the dark. Then we sat on the davenport." Reenie paused for a long time.

"*Then* what happened?" Several combs paused in mid-air.

"We talked. That's all."

There were oh's of disappointment and frank statements of disbelief. Reenie said nothing more. She turned her eyes downward with an indrawn dreamy look on her face and rather shyly became absorbed in twisting the bottom of her lipstick and making the bit of scarlet come and go at the top of the gilded container.

The girls put the finishing touches on their faces and some of them joined in humming the song. Reenie sang a line.

Days may not be fair, always,

she sang in a low whisper that sounded sad and wistful to Margy.

The dismissal bell shrilled shatteringly. There was a petrified pause, then the girls' voices, released from the spell of the low-talking workday, rose high in a paean of freedom. The girls had themselves back for a while. Their time no longer belonged to the House—not until the next morning anyhow. They exchanged their self-conscious giggles for uninhibited laughter; their subdued confidences for conversation screamed across the room.

Reenie dipped her fingers in water and sprinkled Ruthie

while she was putting her engagement ring back on. "I christen thee, Dumb-Ox!" she intoned. Ruthie scooped up a handful of water to throw at Reenie. She missed and the water spattered the pocketbooks held by the obliging girl. The young girls laughed screamingly; the old ones smiled indulgently. The young ones all tried to get out of the washroom at once. They jammed the doorway and good-naturedly shoved each other out.

After they had left, the older girls conscientiously turned off running faucets, released stoppers, collected forgotten combs and powder puffs and tidied up in general. And their faces had the preoccupied look of patient mothers picking up after little ones.

Margy and Reenie were in the first elevator going down. The elevator boy who ran errands for them and had to take a lot of kidding from them during working hours now had the girls at his mercy. Although the car was packed and everyone impatient to get away, he made them wait for the beautiful Marie who was floating sinuously and leisurely down the long corridor to the elevator.

"You babes take a look at what's coming," suggested the elevator boy, "and learn something."

"Already you taught us all you know," quipped Reenie, "and still we don't know anything."

"Oh, yeah?" retaliated the boy futilely.

As the beauty approached the elevator, the boy said, unctuously, "Step up, please."

"Next stop, Waldorf-Ritzstoria," sneered Reenie.

Marie paused before she obeyed the boy's polite request. Her heavy white eyelids lifted and two black-rimmed ovals of jade made brief contact with the boy's pale brown eyes. Margy saw his knees tremble as he slid the door shut. She was sorry for him because he yearned for something he could never have. Yet, he was lucky in a way, she thought. All his life he'd carry the memory of those early evening moments when he had held the elevator for her hoping to get that green-eyed glance in reward.

The copper-haired beauty stood among them and the other girls turned drab in contrast. She flooded the tiny closed space with her *Djer Kiss* perfume and she seemed indifferent to the sensation she caused.

Margy stared at her frankly. This was the girl whom, according to office rumors, Mr. Prentiss was in love with;

the girl his mother wouldn't let him marry. If I only had her looks, thought Margy, the whole world would be mine. Reenie had a similar thought, for as the elevator grumbled to a stop, she whispered to Margy:

"If I had her looks I'd be in the Follies instead of slaving away in this dump. Her looks and my brains."

"You said it!" hissed a girl jammed up against Reenie.

Friends lingered on the corner for the last of the day's exchange of confidences. "Look," said Reenie, taking pains not to meet Margy's eyes, "if I were you, I'd pay board from now on. Then you can get a warm winter coat." She looked up at the darkening November sky and shivered. "Winter will be here before you know it."

"I don't know whether I want a new coat or not," lied Margy out of a kind of loyalty to her mother. Reenie slipped her arm through Margy's.

"Don't get mad. I mean it in the right way."

"I'm not mad. I'll get a new coat when I feel like it." However, she decided to speak to her mother about it that very night. She had to do something if the girls were beginning to notice she had no decent clothes.

Reenie tried to apologize. "I guess I opened my mouth and put my foot in it."

"No, you didn't Reenie," said Margy thoughtfully. There was an embarrassed pause.

A lumbering trolley came down the street. Reenie spoke with clumsy cheer. "Anyway, here comes my covered wagon."

"You going to see Sal tonight?" asked Margy. Sal was short for Salvatore, an Italian boy with whom Reenie was in love. He was the one Reenie had talked about in the washroom.

"No. I saw him last night."

The trolley stopped at Reenie's signal. As she boarded it, she called out in usual farewell, "See you in the morning, Margy."

Margy made the usual answer: "Not if I see you first."

Margy went around the corner to catch a Graham Avenue trolley.

Chapter 7

Reenie stopped at the fish store on her block and bought a filet of flounder for fifteen cents. For an additional nickel the man fried it in a black cauldron of much-used cottonseed oil. For another dime she went the limit and ordered a portion of French fries. He threw a handful of wedge-shaped cuts from partially boiled potatoes into the oil. It was a meal for two and it cost thirty cents and a word of thanks.

Reenie's mother was sitting in the rocking chair near the window, her shoes off and her puffed feet resting on a chair. She wore her uniform. She worked part time in a lunch wagon. Her hours were from ten to four for which she received half-pay, ten dollars a week.

She had gotten the job by answering an ad for part-time work. The ad claimed the work would not interfere with household duties. Maizie stood on her feet six hours a day. The work wouldn't have been too hard except that she had a kidney disorder which kept her feet and ankles swollen. She accepted this as part of life, It had never occurred to her that her life could be easy or pleasant.

"Mama!" Reenie called out when she came in. "What did you take your shoes off for? Now you won't be able to get back in them in case we want to go to a show or something."

"I don't want to go out," she said. "All I want is to get off my feet." She sighed and brought her feet down from the chair.

"Stay sitting, Mama," said Reenie.

"I got a fix supper. I thought we'd have something plain. After looking at food all day, I don't feel much like cooking."

"I brought supper home with me," said Reenie. "All we need is bread and coffee." She was rewarded by the look of pleasure and relief on her mother's face. "I'll make the coffee. You stay sitting and I'll push the table over by you."

"You shouldn't a done that, Doll," said Maizie. (She called her Doll when she was pleased with her.) "Take the money out a my pocka-book."

"No. This is on me," said Reenie.

"You pay board, Doll. You're not supposed to buy food out a your own money."

"Eat and forget it," ordered Reenie.

After the meal, Maizie from force of habit ran her greasy hands down the side of her uniform where during the working day a towel was folded over her belt for that purpose. The towel was gone and two grease stains appeared on the livid green of the harsh cloth uniform. Reenie looked at them with distaste.

"Why don't you put something else on, Mama?" she asked.

"I've got nothing else to wear."

"Wait a minute." Reenie went to the closet and brought out a dress on a wire hanger. "What about this dress? I bought it for you Christmas. I wanted you to have something classy. So what happens? It hangs in the closet."

"It's too good to wear around the house, Doll. I'm saving it."

"Saving it for what? To be buried in?"

"No. For when I go out someplace."

"But you never go out."

"I went out last night to the Woman's Aid meeting, even though my feet was killing me. Just so's you could have the house for yourself," she said accusingly. "And I didn't ask no questions when I came home either," she added pointedly. Reenie flushed but refused to take the hint to tell what had transpired the evening before.

"Well, why didn't you wear your new dress to church instead of that old uniform?"

"I kept my coat on. Nobody saw."

Reenie got a box out of her mother's bureau drawer and put it in Maizie's lap after first taking off the cover. Reenie took out a handful of photographs and sat on the arm of her mother's rocker so they could look at the pictures together. The first picture was that of a tall, rather handsome, well-dressed woman.

"Look, Mama, that's you, twenty years ago."

"I know." Maizie sighed.

"You were a classy dresser in your day. I mean classy, considering the dumb styles they had then."

"I know." Maizie sighed again. She took out a set of hair puffs from the bottom of the box. The hair smelled of camphor. The puffs were a lovely chestnut color. "I had these puffs made up out of my own combings, twenty years ago."

"I wish my hair was a pretty color like that," said Reenie.

"I use' to pin them on top a my head. Like this." Her rough hands held the cake of bright chestnut hair on top of her iron-gray, overcrimped hair.

Reenie closed her eyes and moaned, "Don't, Mama!"

"Why, what's a matter?" asked Maizie.

"Nothing. Let me put the box away now."

When Reenie came back out of the bedroom her mother said, "I tell you what, Doll. I'm going to try to fix up more. I'll find a cheap dentist and get my teeth fixed. And I'll get some nice clothes. I use' to be so crazy about clothes when I was young—like you're crazy about them now. And maybe I'll even get my hair touched up. Lots of women do, you know."

"Sure. Why not? I'll go with you when you have it done. Maybe I'll even pay for it."

Out of what, her mother wanted to ask. After you pay in board home you need every penny for clothes. You got to dress classy because you're in love with a shoeshine boy. He'd lose interest in you in a hurry if you didn't keep dressed up. He's no good and I know it but I got a keep still and say nothing.

"Forty-three ain't so old," said Maizie. "If I get myself fixed up I might meet some nice man and get married again. Then I wouldn't be a drag on you in my old age."

"You'll never be a drag on me. Besides that's not the question. The question is when are you going to start all this fixing up?"

"Soon's my feet stop swelling up so much."

Nothing more was said for a long time. Reenie in defensive detachment and in the hard, truthful way of the young knew that her mother's trouble would not disappear because Maizie hoped it would. Reenie had great hopes for herself and great assurance that nothing could ever happen to her, that is, nothing that had happened to her mother could possibly happen to her. There was a pang of pity and a twinge of irritation because her mother wouldn't face the truth. The swelling had started five years ago and had not lessened with the years. Five years ago there had been merely a streak of gray in the chestnut hair. Now it was all gray. How could anything ever be better for her mother?

But Maizie, like so many people born to nothing, had her hopes to sustain her. She had been young with all the hopes and dreams of the young. The hopes and dreams had never materialized. Maizie had never come into wise or disillusioned maturity because she still had that young hope that things would be better.

Like Margy's father, she was a decent person; hard-working. She had had to make compromises all along the way. She made them cheerfully, always believing they were a temporary expediency; that tomorrow, next year some miracle would come to pass and the good life she dreamed of would fall into place.

Of course it hadn't happened—never would. Her husband had died when he was twenty-nine. The only legacy he left his wife was a pretty six-year-old daughter. Maizie had been optimistic in her grief. It was like the phrase of hope in Chopin's "Funeral March."

I'm young yet, only twenty-seven, she had assured herself. I'm not afraid of hard work. I'm not bad looking and I have a wonderful child. So many women have nothing. I have Irene. I'm so lucky. I'll work hard and give her everything a girl should have. If my life ever seems hard to me I'll know it's because I'm making life easier for her.

Well, what happened? The child was pretty; worshiped by her mother. She grew up a little spoiled; always wanting to know why she couldn't have what other girls had —pretty clothes, a home she needn't be ashamed to bring her friends to. And always Maizie promised that things would be better "after."

She remembered Reenie's first dance in her second year of high school, held at the Hotel St. George in downtown

Brooklyn. Reenie was invited and needed an evening dress. Maizie said she'd see what she could do. The days went past and there was nothing that Maizie could do about getting an evening dress. There just wasn't any money.

Reenie had an idea. She asked her mother for two dollars. For what, Maizie automatically wanted to know? Well, it seemed there was a nightgown in a store on Grand Street. It had a full skirt and a square neck trimmed with lace. Reenie said it would look like an evening gown if it had a long slip under it.

They bought the nightgown. Reenie had a pink slip; Maizie had a pink slip. Maizie cut the bottom off her slip and sewed it onto Reenie's slip. The girl tried on the combination and thought it was beautiful. Reenie was young, pretty and thin. Anything looked beautiful on her. But Maizie knew that the other girls would laugh at her. They wouldn't be fooled into believing a nightgown was an evening gown.

The day of the dance, Reenie stayed after school for some last-minute committee work in connection with the dance. Maizie waited until five minutes past three, then she went to her grocer's.

"Look," she said. "I just got word my sister's husband died." (She had no sister.) "I want to send flowers but the bank closed at three and I can't draw money no more today. I was wondering could you lend me ten dollars till tomorrow and put it on my bill?"

"Ten dollars is a lot of money for flowers for the dead," commented the man.

"I know. But it's my only sister and I want to do the right thing."

"I don't even know if I got that much." He rang up No Sale and counted the money in the cash register. There was twenty-eight dollars and some change. "Eight dollars is all I got," he said.

"That will do," she said eagerly. "I know of a cut-rate flower store."

He stared at his little hoard. He knew she didn't intend to buy funeral flowers. He had so little money himself, just enough to feed and clothe his four children. But he got his living from the neighborhood. He depended on each and every customer. He didn't want to offend one of them by refusing a favor. He was not without insight. He knew she wouldn't have had the nerve to come borrowing from him unless it was some kind of crisis. Though he had little money himself, he certainly had more than the families whose needs supported his family. He had this understanding, too. He gave her eight dollars.

"Thanks, thanks," she said fervently. "I'll pay it back soon's the bank opens in the morning."

She knew she had no money in the bank and so did he. But both knew it would be paid back, a quarter or a half a dollar a week.

"Only one thing," he said. "If my wife happens to wait on you, don't say nothing. You see, she don't understand about business and how sometimes you like to oblige a steady customer."

"I won't say nothing to nobody," she promised. "And I'll always deal here as long as I live in the neighborhood."

"That's all I ask," he said. "Good steady customers what pay their bills every Saturday night. You see," he said, "I like to be softhearted but I got to live, too."

She rushed over to Pitkin Avenue and found a dress for six ninety-eight. It was heavy glistening white rayon satin with cherry velvet bows on either side of the modestly low square neck. As she handled the material of the skirt, she shuddered unaccountably. The thought came to her that it seemed to be the same heavy white stuff that lined caskets. She shook off the thought, reasoning that it had come to her simply because she had told the grocer she wanted the money for the dead. She decided it was a wonderful dress for the money. She bought a Juliet cap made of gold-color cords with a large green stone in the center, for forty-nine cents.

She got home half an hour before Reenie, pressed the dress and spread it out on the girl's bed. Reenie came home excited. It was nearly six. She didn't want to eat, she said, because there wasn't enough time. Maizie stood listening while Reenie went into the bedroom, expecting to find the nightgown and slip laid out. She heard a little squeal of pure happiness. Reenie came out holding the dress to her. Her eyes were wide and dark with excitement and her cheeks were flushed with happiness.

"Mama! Oh, Mama," she moaned. "You're the best . . . the most wonderful mother . . ."

"Just so it fits," said Maizie, embarrassed at the demonstrativeness she had never had before from her daughter. "Don't cut off the tags till you see."

It fit. The child looked wonderful. She sat waiting for her escort, her knees crossed and swinging her foot because she enjoyed seeing the play of light on the material.

When the bell rang, Maizie took off her apron and smoothed her hair. Reenie jumped up and grabbed her coat. "I won't ask him to come up," she said a little too quickly. "We're late as it is."

Maizie understood that Reenie was ashamed of the flat and she didn't blame her at all. She looked out the window and saw Reenie and a boy get into a taxi. They had to walk between staring kids lined up on either side. The boy wore white flannels and a blue serge coat. He handed Reenie a small white florist's box. That's all Maizie saw before the cab drew away.

Maizie sat and dreamed. Her little girl would amount to something. At sixteen, she had made a good start: a dance at a swell hotel, an evening dress, an escort in a cab and a corsage. Maizie dreamed of greater triumphs, greater glories for her daughter.

But the dress was never worn again. Reenie left high school the end of that year and got a job. The dress lay in its box on the top shelf of the closet. Two years after the dance, Reenie happened to be cleaning out her closet and she brought out the dress.

"Look what's here, Mama. Isn't it the tackiest thing? But the night I wore it I thought it was the most beautiful dress in the world. Gee, I must have been a dumb bunny."

There was a knock on the door. Apprehension quickened in Maizie. It was a little boy come to tell Reenie that she was wanted on the phone in the corner candy and stationery store. Maizie saw the girl's eyes widen and darken and the crimson wash of happiness come to her cheeks and she looked again like the girl of sixteen who had come running out of the bedroom holding the dress.

"Going out tonight?" asked Maizie.

"I don't know yet," said Reenie, breathlessly, as she grabbed her coat and flung herself out of the room.

She came back in a little while. All the joy and happiness was gone from her face. "I'm *not* going out tonight." She took her coat off slowly. Maizie cleared her throat.

"I don't like to say nothing," she said, "only he's not good enough for you."

"Why isn't he?" she flashed back at her mother.

"Well, he's Eye-talian."

"So what? Everybody's *something*. We're half German and Margy's Irish."

"But your parents was born here, so was Margy's. His come from Italy."

"He's as much American as I am."

"Besides he's Catholic and you're a Pratt-a-sent."

"What's religion got to do with it? He can go to his church and I can go to mine."

"It don't work out that way. If there's children, there's fights. If they go to your church, his family and him will always be mad. If they go to his church, they'll get weaned away from you."

"I could turn Catholic."

"I'll tell you the truth. I'd rather see you laying in your coffin than married to him."

"Mama!"

"I didn't mean that." She knocked wood. "I brought this home to show you." She took a copy of the *Menace* out of her uniform pocket. "A customer gave it to me. Read it. You'll find out about the Catholics."

"I don't want to read it. I bet you carried that around all day waiting for a chance to shove it at me. I'm surprised at you, Mama. I bet you really believe that every time a Catholic boy is born they bury a gun under the church."

"Such talk wouldn't get around," said Maizie slowly, "if there wasn't some truth in it."

"Well, don't worry," said Reenie bitterly. "Sal wouldn't marry me if I was the last girl on earth."

"What's a matter," asked her mother indignantly, "don't he think you're good enough for him?"

"That's right. I'm not good enough for him." Reenie put her coat on again.

"I thought you said you wasn't going out," reproached her mother.

"I'm just going down to the store to phone Margy. I want to ask her something." When she got to the door, her mother said:

"Doll?"

"What, Mama?"

"It was thoughtful of you to bring home the fried fish and potatoes. Don't think I don't appreciate it."

"I told you to forget it. And don't forget, Mama, you're going to start fixing yourself up."

"As soon as . . ."

"No! You start tomorrow."

"All right, Doll."

They smiled affectionately at each other.

Chapter 8

Usually Margy read coming home in the trolley. But tonight her library book lay unopened in her lap. She was thinking out some way in which she could ask her mother to let her keep enough of her pay to buy a new winter coat. She couldn't figure out any way except to ask outright. She cringed from that. In order to forget the matter for the time being, she concentrated on examining her fellow-passengers, a favorite game with her.

Most of them were working people. The young girls like Margy read library books or magazines and the older women did endless tortuous tatting or intricate cotton crochet work—small needlework that fitted into a purse. The young men, newspapers folded expertly into a narrow oblong, read with intense interest the dope on the Brooklyn ball team's chance for next season.

The older men, wearing work pants so stiff and shiny at the knees that they looked oiled, sat dumbly relaxed with gnarled hands resting bluntly on knees. It was as though the hands refused to give up the curve used in the manual work they had done that day; were enchanted; had frozen in the essential curve to fit their work and would stay that way in readiness for the next day's handling of tools or levers or heavy crates. They sat there, their eyes dull and filmed with weariness. They were worn out, beaten down. They had to conserve themselves each nonworking moment in order to replenish their strength for the next day's work. And their killing work brought them nothing except enough rest and food to enable them to work. Time did not march on with them; it went around in a circle. They lived on memories of the hopes they had had as young men and on some lucky break in the future that would release them from a hard life. For the moment, nothing mattered to them except the throbbing feeling of rest.

As the car bumped through Williamsburg toward Greenpoint, workers got off at various corners. A new kind of passenger replaced them—middle-aged housewives who had been visiting friends or married daughters in other neighborhoods, and who now were belatedly getting home to prepare supper.

They stood on corners, blocks ahead of the coming car, and as it drew near stepped out to the curb and signaled worriedly as though afraid the car would not stop for them; afraid it would pass them by and they'd be left stranded in an alien neighborhood with night coming on.

They mounted the car steps with grateful eagerness and teetered unsteadily to a seat. Then while they fumbled in their broken-strapped purses for a nickel for fare, they looked up to smile ingratiatingly at the conductor as if apologizing for making him wait.

They wore black—bunchy dress and sagging coat; a slightly mashed, too youthful hat, probably a daughter's discard, set straight on their heads. They sat spread out and breathing heavily, looking like pumpkins squatting on the ground in late fall ready to squash apart if a wintry wind went among them.

Yet each had been a tremulous young girl once, full of dreams and natural vanities. But they had had to fight poverty and they were licked from the start. The lost fight had taken full payment from them.

Watching them, Margy thought: I'll never get like that. I'll be more like Mama. She's nearly forty and slender as any girl. But I guess she's so thin because she always looks at the sad side of life. But I won't be sad and I won't be fat either. I'll stay just the way I am. I won't let myself go to pieces no matter what kind of a life I have. Thus Margy.

She stopped in at Alexander's before she went home. She ordered a two-cent soda. The man poured an inch of chocolate syrup into a glass, filled it with seltzer water to the top and gave it three professional digs with a long spoon to mix it. He replaced the spoon in its long glass of water. He watched her drink it, knuckles resting on white-aproned hips, waiting for her verdict.

"Good!" she approved. He nodded, satisfied. He relaxed. She bought three penny chocolate twists, the kind with hard crackling marshmallow inside.

"You'll spoil your supper, Margy," he warned.

"I'm buying these for after," she explained.

Then it happened—the hoped-for event that made her stop by the store each night. Frankie Malone came in. She turned her back and pretended to be absorbed in the magazines on the rack.

"Let's have a pack of Fatimas," he ordered. She heard a coin ring on the glass showcase. She turned around in simulated surprise.

"I *thought* it was you," she said.

"What do you know? Well, what do you say, Marge?"

"I'm spoiling my supper with soda and candy." As she said it, she realized how banal it sounded and was filled with despair. Always she planned to say something bright and interesting when she met him, and always she said something inane.

"That's a lot of hoo-ey. Nothing can spoil a meal if you're hungry."

"That's right."

They stood and talked. They said nothing of importance, nothing of interest. They were held at the soda fountain by an unexpressed but common bond. Both dreaded the plunge into turbulent family life after an orderly day at the office; each tried to delay the inevitable homecoming by conversation. But they ran out of talk soon enough. Frankie, feeling obligated to round out the meeting correctly, mentioned that the Neighborhood Center House was starting up its monthly dances that night.

"Would you like to go . . ."

"Yes!" she jumped in too eagerly.

". . . to the one next month?" Her yes had come so quickly that he had had no time to rearrange the last words of his sentence. He felt like a heel. "I'd take you tonight, only . . ."

"I know," she said, anxious to make amends for her eagerness. "A previous engagement . . ."

"Nothing important." He didn't know why he had to say that except it seemed the correct ritual when talking to a girl about another date. "Only I made the date some time ago and I like to keep promises. I'm funny that way."

"That's a good way to be," she said.

"A month from tonight, then?"

"Thanks. I'd love to."

"It's a date?" he verified.

"A date," she agreed.

Walking away from the store he thought: Why did I have to go and stick my neck out? I don't want to take her. She's not much fun. I'll have to get out of it some way.

She ran up the steps in a glow. Her first date! But it was twenty-eight days off. She wondered how she could wait that long. She prayed that he wouldn't change his mind. She was jealous of the girl he was taking that night. Already the unknown girl was a serious rival. She decided that her mother would just have to buy her a new coat— at least a new dress. She'd just *have* to.

Just before she opened the door, she smelled onions frying and heard fat sizzling in the pan. Same old supper. She sighed, glad that she had had the soda to take the edge off her appetite.

"Hello, Mom." Flo's return greeting was a sharp sigh. As her mother set a plate on the table, Margy asked with her father's inflection, "You eat yet?"

"Long ago," said Flo.

"Keep mine hot, then, till Papa comes home. I don't like to eat alone."

"God knows when your father will be home. It might be all hours," predicted Flo mournfully. "That's why I never wait for him."

Henny always got home between six and six-thirty but his wife had this fixed idea that he was an unpunctual man.

"Still and all, I guess I'll wait," said Margy. "I don't care much for fried eggs, anyhow." It was a most unfortunate remark.

"Considering," said Flo bridling, "the little money that comes in this house . . ." Margy couldn't bear to have the inevitable nightly argument about food and money.

"What I started to say," Margy amended hastily, "is that I don't care much for fried eggs without onions. Are there onions?" she asked.

"Of course," reproached her mother, "I might not have much money to cook with, but . . ."

"I changed my mind," broke in Margy. "I won't wait for Papa. I'm too hungry."

On the way to the sink to wash her hands, Margy flung her arm about her mother's waist and hugged her briefly. Through the tilted mirror over the sink, she saw her mother's mouth go crooked in a tremulous smile.

Poor Mama, she thought. *Poor* Mama. What goes wrong with people that they feel they have to put on a mean act all the time like Mama does?

Margy answered her own question. I guess she must have had a hard life. And still has.

Chapter 9

The violent impact of family
life hit Frankie Malone like a blow in the face when he
opened the door. They were all in the kitchen, his mother,
father and his three sisters. There was the smell of corned
beef, cabbage and potatoes all cooked together in one pot.
There was the smell of wet wash and the fainter, more
acrid smell of beer.

As he closed the door behind him, he saw his mother
swish the beer around in the can to make foam come up.
"I got out a big wash today," she explained. "And washing
always makes me drink like a fish." In a very unfishlike
way, she took a big draught from the can.

Although it was prohibition, the Malones had no trouble
getting their beer. Patrick Malone was a cop. He was a
fairly honest one. He exacted no protection money from
the speakeasy on the corner. He knew he wouldn't get it
anyhow. The place was not on Malone's beat and the
speakeasy proprietor had to pay the regular cop enough
as it was. The regular cop wouldn't have stood for Malone
muscling in anyhow. So the only tribute Malone exacted
was this nightly free bucket of beer.

Patrick Malone sat by the window in his short-sleeved,
button-down-the-front undershirt. He was a big man and
the buttons pulled at the buttonholes making little dia-
mond-shaped spaces through which bits of his red-haired
chest could be seen. The pants legs of his cop's uniform
were rolled up to the knee, and his feet, sore and tired
from walking a hard-pavement beat all day, were immersed
in a dishpan of warm water in which Epsom salts had
been dissolved. He added to the smell of the room by
smoking a pipeful of cheap, strong tobacco. He took the

pipe out of his mouth as he greeted his first-born, his only son.

"Well, how's the big financier tonight?" he inquired.

"Don't always keep picking on the boy, Patsy," came Mrs. Malone's automatic, pleasantly spoken warning.

"What you trying to do? Make a mully-cuddle out of him?" asked Patsy.

"Just leave him alone. That's all I ask," said his wife.

But Malone was not to be denied his regular evening diversion. He took the pipe out of his mouth and leaned confidentially toward his son.

"Tell me, Malone," he said, "how's Soup-Meat Consolidated doing? Is Cabbage still keeping a head?" Suddenly he roared with laughter. "That's good, eh? Cabbage. Head. Get it?"

"We get it, Pop," said Cathleen, the oldest girl, eighteen, who was sitting at the table with a small mirror propped up against the mustard jar, and plucking out hairs from her already hair-thin eyebrows. "We get it," she said, "and you're the only one thinks it's funny."

Before Malone could think up a reply to that one, the sound of sudden fiddle music filled the air. Noreen, the middle daughter, a girl of twelve, had brought out her fiddle and began knocking off the stipulated half-hour of practice she had ducked that afternoon in order to play on the street. She played "Humoresque" harshly and badly. She never got past the first line because the note beginning the second line always went wrong and she started over again. With each new start, she played the line faster, hoping like a hurdler to get a good running start to get over the barrier. But she never made it.

Malone, knowing when he was licked, subsided. He couldn't hope to put his jokes over with that competition.

The motivation for his pleasantries was that his son Frankie was learning the brokerage business from the ground up. At least that's how the small Wall Street firm for which Frankie worked as messenger explained away the meagerness of the salary. So far all he had learned about the brokerage business in two years was that it was quicker and cheaper to hire a young man to go around delivering envelopes than to stamp and mail them. Frankie was ambitious and hopeful. He really believed that he'd be vice-president of the firm someday if he was willing and honest and economical. He had no trouble with the first two traits. Willingness was thrust upon him. He knew that if he didn't do his work efficiently and cheerfully he'd be fired. That made him willing. He had no opportunity to be dishonest even if he were inclined that way. He was entrusted with little more than orders to buy and sell. He had no opportunity to handle or misuse money. Economy was the hardest of the three virtues he had chosen. He earned eighteen a week and gave half of it to his mother. The rest went for his needs and an occasional date. The first week he went to work, he made a resolve to bank one dollar a week out of his pay come hell or high water. He stuck to that resolve and now he had a little over a hundred dollars in the Bushwick Savings Bank.

His father had taken it for granted Frankie would go into civil service when he grew up; be a policeman, fireman or even a letter carrier. But Frankie chose otherwise and Mr. Malone never got over resenting it. That's why he ragged his son about being a big financier.

His mother set a plate of corned beef, cabbage and potatoes, the usual washday dinner, before him. She snatched the mustard jar from behind Cathleen's mirror. The girl let out a squawk. Noreen hit a false note for the sixth time. Old man Malone took his red hairy legs out of the dishpan and dried his feet. All of a sudden, Frankie didn't want to eat. He pushed his plate away. Quick as a flash, Mrs. Malone pushed it back with the stern injunction:

"Eat!"

"I guess I'll wash my hands first," he said. His mother put his plate in the oven.

When he came back, he had changed his four-in-hand for a bow tie. His mother knew by that sign he had a date for the evening. With a flash of jealousy, she wondered who the girl was.

The kitchen had more or less calmed down when he returned. He settled down to trying to eat. Noreen had gotten past the hurdle of the sour note and was sawing away doggedly on the fiddle. Cathleen was finishing her eyebrows. Doreen, the six-year-old sister, was coloring pictures in the newspaper with crayons. Malone was bent over the bottom drawer of the cupboard getting out his books and pamphlets.

Although Patsy Malone was forty-five, he still had hopes of becoming a rich man before he died. To that end, he was taking a mail-order course in embalming. When he signed up for the course, he told his family that he had made the decision because he'd be out on pension in two years; set for the rest of his life as far as salary was concerned. Yet he'd be young enough to start up a business of his own. The Malones had a couple of hundred dollars saved up and Patsy was going into the undertaking business in partnership with his sergeant, who was also going out on pension in two years. When the family demurred at the nature of the business, Patsy settled all arguments once and for all by saying he didn't care how they felt; as far as he was concerned, there was lots of money in the dead.

Now he pushed back some soiled dishes and set up his book and pamphlet on the table. He settled down to study. He had one firm habit which invariably emptied the kitchen in two minutes. He studied his lessons aloud. The family never got over a feeling of queasiness at listening to the macabre details of preparing a body for the grave.

Now as he read, everyone hurried what he was doing. Frankie ate faster and faster in order to finish his supper before his father read something really gruesome from the book. Hastily, Mrs. Malone drained the last of the beer from the can. Cathleen speeded up her plucking. Doreen picked up her crayons and newspaper. Noreen fiddled harder and louder, coming into the homestretch.

Then Malone started reading aloud about exchanging embalming fluid for blood. Cathleen shuddered and pulled out the one hair in her left eyebrow that kept the brow a continuing arch. Now she had a broken arch.

"Look what you went and made me do with your old reading," she sobbed as she ran out of the room.

Noreen slammed her fiddle and bow into their wooden box and yelled: "I'm done. I did it. Give me a nickel for the show now."

Mrs. Malone gave her a dime and told her she had to take Doreen. Noreen howled but her mother was adamant. Noreen left, dragging the willing Doreen with her.

Frankie pushed his plate away with a definite motion and got up from the kitchen table. His mother asked him a question that was being asked in a thousand homes in Brooklyn that evening:

"You gawn out tonight?"

"Can you blame me?" he answered bitterly. He left.

Mrs. Malone was glad to get rid of the chattering girls. They'd be home in a couple of hours or so; you just couldn't get rid of them. But Frankie was different. He stayed out late when he went and his mother never had any idea where he was.

Malone stared at each one as they left. "What's a matter with them all?" he asked.

"You're the one that's drivin' the children out of the only home they got," she said.

"What did I do now?" he asked.

"You shouldn't go and tease Frankie about his job. It's not becoming of you. And you shouldn't be reading about letting out blood when he's eating."

"If you had your way, you'd make a regular milk-soup out of the boy."

"I happen to understand him. He's different than you. *He's* sensitive."

"I happen to be a sensitive man myself but I don't go around blathering about it all the time. And now if you're done with criticizing an ambitious man, I'll be getting on with my studies." He resumed reading aloud.

"And I'll be letting the dishes go till after, and sit in the front room so's I won't be interfering with your great studies." She went into the parlor.

Now that Malone was alone in the kitchen, he felt no need to read aloud. He read to himself, barely moving his lips as he did so. But it was no fun that way. He was a gregarious man and couldn't bear to be left alone for a moment. He took up his stuff and followed his wife into the parlor.

"Listen to this, Mama," he said. Mama groaned. He read aloud with relish.

In five minutes she was sound asleep.

Frankie was taking a girl named Irma to the dance. For a wild moment, he considered marrying her just to escape from his family. But he changed his mind after a moment's sober reflection. Irma wore her skirts too short and too tight. In fact everything about her was too much. Her shingled hair was much too short and her chest too fashion-ably flat. Her rouge was too raspberry and her lipstick too wet. Her long black earrings were too jetty.

He looked at her with critical eyes and wondered what was the matter with him. He had first been attracted to Irma because she was flashy. He decided it was the con-trast with Margy. If he just hadn't happened to run into Margy Shannon that night, Irma would have seemed okay. Margy made Irma seem boisterous and rowdy. It should have been the other way. Irma should have made Margy seem quiet and plain. Was there no in-between girl? he wondered—someone with the bang of Irma and the reti-cence of Margy.

He wondered why the hell he bothered to think about girls, anyhow. He could get along without them in every way except dancing. He loved to dance and was consid-ered a good dancer in the neighborhood.

Chapter 10

Henny came in as Margy started to eat. Again there was the hurried lighting of the gas flame, the thump of the lump of lard, the cubes of cold boiled potato splashing into the melting grease, the prickling smell of the browning onion rings and the crisp crack of eggs broken against the pan's rim. These were the symphony of home—family sounds carried over from Margy's babyhood.

"You're late," announced Flo briefly and bitterly.

Margy felt she'd scream if he'd tell about the motorman's not stopping and if he didn't tell about it, she'd scream too because it would be like the end of his life had come.

"Had a little argument with the motorman," explained Henny. "He didn't feel like stopping at Maujer Street to let me out. So I looked him up and down and said in a polite, quiet way, 'Listen, Mac!'"

He went on relating the incident as though it had happened for the first time that evening. As he sat down and reached for the ketchup bottle, he asked his wife the old familiar question. Margy forestalled Flo's bitter answer.

"Sure, Pop. Mama ate. But don't you think it's cute to eat with me?" she asked with aching archness.

She put her hand on his left wrist. His right hand with its stiff workman's curve closed laboriously over her hand for an instant and then he withdrew it in embarrassment.

"Remember," Henny reminisced, as he started to eat, "how you used to sit by the washtubs and play with clothespins and make out like they was dolls?"

"Yes," sighed Margy. "I sure was a dumb kid."

"Dumb!" exclaimed Flo indignantly—Flo to whom the past was perfect. "You was the smartest child on the

88

block. Yes, you was. And good, too. I never had to raise my hand to you."

"Except in self-defense," said Margy, meaning to get a smile out of her mother.

"What? How?" Flo didn't get the joke. "No. I never hit you."

Vividly, as though it had been yesterday, Margy remembered her mother slapping the ice-cream sandwich out of her hand into the gutter. "Remember the time I got lost?" she asked.

"You never got lost." Flo refused to remember that time.

"All children get lost," stated Henny.

"Not her. I guess I'd remember if she ever got lost," said Flo.

"Well, maybe I just strayed a little," said Margy. She smiled at her father. He smiled back. She directed her smile at her mother. The woman resisted but Margy held the smile. At last Flo's face broke up like a jigsaw puzzle that would have to be reworked. She smiled.

There was a kind of peace and good will in the little flat for a while. But it couldn't last of course. Margy hoped her father would stay home that evening. She was tired of the nightly quarrel that began when he made the first move to go out. He got up from the table and went over to the door to get his coat.

"Going out?" asked Flo.

"Yeah."

"Again?" No answer. She took his silence for hostility. "You couldn't stay home even one night?" she asked with what seemed like sweet reasonableness. He seemed to consider the question.

"No," he decided.

"Why?"

He knew why, but he didn't have the right words to explain so she'd understand. He found some lame words.

"Because there's nothing here, home. And after a man works hard all day . . ."

"And after a woman works hard all day," countered Flo, "she don't want to be cooped up nights, neither. At least you see other people in the shop all day. I don't see nobody. All day I look at the four walls . . ."

On the pretext of washing her hands, Margy let the water run noisily into the sink. As she turned her soaped hands one over the other in slow, tight, agonized movements, she listened to the water and tried to make it shut out the well-worn and familiar-since-childhood words of accusation and bitterness. But the voices rose higher and cut through the sound of the running water.

"I might as well be married to that door," said Flo.

"Well, do you want to go out with me?" invited Henny drearily.

"Out where?"

"Just out."

"To one of your beer parlors?"

"No. Just out," he persisted vaguely.

"There's no place to go and you know it," she stated flatly.

"There's places."

"Where? Just tell me where. Tell me one place."

"I don't know," he conceded futilely.

"If my mother, God rest her soul, was living, I'd have a place to go. I can tell you that."

But on the cue, "mother," he had the door open and was on his way downstairs.

Margy dried her hands slowly. "I suppose you're going out, too," said Flo.

"No, Mama." Margy had been planning to go to the library to exchange her book. But she said, "No, Mama."

"I'm surprised. I guess you're staying home because you got no place to go."

Margy began moaning inwardly. "I could find some place to go, I guess," she said.

"Hah!" called out Flo triumphantly. "Then you're only staying home because you feel sorry for me; because your father leaves me sit every night."

Margy knew that her mother wanted them to stay home to prove that they loved her and wanted to be near her. Flo wanted this, but she didn't know how to deserve it.

"I'm staying home because I have a lot to do."

"What?"

"I got to rinse out my slip for one thing. I should wash my hair but I guess I'll only put it up. Oh, I have a lot of things to do." She sighed convincingly.

As she hung up the towel, she looked in the mirror and saw her mother's unguarded face. Flo looked almost happy. Margy knew that she, Margy, had lost out again. She felt she had a right to go out after working all day. Then she thought of how little her mother had out of life. She reasoned that if staying home made her mother happy, it was the least she could do. After all, thought Margy, she has nothing and I have my whole life before me.

That was Margy's whole philosophy, her golden hope—that she had all of life before her.

She undressed and got into her bathrobe, made of an imitation Navaho blanket. She washed her slip, stockings, brassière and step-ins. She wound dampened ends of her hair up on aluminum curlers. She filed her nails and though the polish was unchipped, she removed it and put on fresh lacquer. Then she ironed her damp flimsy lingerie into dryness. She took as long as she could with everything, but at eight-thirty she was finished. She wasn't sleepy enough for bed. Besides the day seemed incomplete, as though there was something more that had to happen.

She went into the parlor and switched on the light. The room was both familiar and strange—familiar because it had always been there and strange because it was used so little. Like the other rooms of the flat, it was barrenly clean. The lace curtains were coldly starched and the familiar shiny-leaved rubber plant stood on a taboret between the two front windows. The dull, brown velours, overstuffed davenport with two matching armchairs stood at familiar angles, and the looming, dully polished victrola stood catty-cornered in its familiar place.

That victrola! It had been the only luxury of their lives; bought on time, a dollar a week, twelve records free. Margy remembered the happiness of getting it all paid up and really *owning* it. But the handle had snapped in two one night. Henny had taken it to be repaired but had waited too long to call for it. The repairman couldn't find it; denied it had ever been brought to his basement shop. His denials had been so passionate that he almost got Henny to believing there never had been a handle in the first place. To replace that handle was just something that the Shannons couldn't accomplish.

The machine had stood silent for years, a symbol of the futility of their days. The lost handle was proof to Henny of his constant contention that he was always being pushed around and it was another strike against him as far as his wife was concerned. She had gloated over his negligence the way a philatelist gloats over a rare, newly acquired stamp. It had been another link in the chain of recriminations that she was everlastingly forging against her husband. A queer thing that a lost handle could become so much a part of the stuff that formed a family's life.

Margy put the "Missouri Waltz" on the turntable. She knew it couldn't play without being wound yet she had an unreasonable hope that some miracle would make the music come. In a small frenzy of desperation she stuck her little finger in the handle hole and tried to turn over the machinery with her fingernail. Then she began turning the record with her hand. A phrase of music came grudgingly. She twirled the record faster. The music came limpingly and incomplete. She hummed along with it, trying to make it a whole thing. Suddenly she stopped. She had not heard her mother come in but she knew Flo was standing behind her. She waited for the first words.

"You'd think we was made out of money," began Flo.

"I've only had the light on for a minute."

"Light in the kitchen! Light in the front room! House lit up like a Christmas tree!" Margy turned off the light. Her mother's voice continued from the darkness. "It's not that I'm stingy but we have to watch every penny."

"I know."

"If I had my way I'd have a light in every room. But how would we make ends meet then? I'd just like to show you last month's electric bill."

"You don't have to, Mama. I know."

Back in the kitchen, Margy tried to get absorbed in her book but Flo couldn't bear to be shut out. She kept still as long as she could, then spoke out.

"Do you think *I* like it?" Margy looked up, confused, trying to make the transition from Iris March of *The Green Hat* to the Maujer Street flat. "No, I don't like it," continued Flo. "Scrounging, living this way." She sighed. "What big ideas I used to have! I pictured myself dressed to kill—my daughter in fine clothes."

"Mama, I need a new winter coat," said Margy, suddenly.

"Can't afford it," came the automatic answer. "Your old coat over the suit will do another winter."

"I'm past eighteen now and . . ."

"Eighteen? Why it was only yesterday you was a baby."
Then a look of naked fright came on the woman's face.
She wondered what Margy was leading up to. Was there
a man? Was she planning marriage? "Why did you just
say you was eighteen?"

"Because I *am* eighteen."

"Everybody's eighteen sometime in their life."

"Well, Reenie's been paying board since the day she
was eighteen."

"That girl's a bad influence—the way she dresses. The
less you got to do with her, the better off you'll be."

"Reenie gives her mother five dollars a week. But I'd
give you seven."

"What are you talking about?"

Margy blurted it out. "I want to pay board home instead of giving in all my pay. That way I could get a new
coat and a new dress once in a while."

"What for?"

"Well, I'm invited to a dance and I'd like a new dress.
That's why I thought . . ."

Flo seemed to consider her daughter's request. "All
right," she said finally. She spoke quietly and reasonably.
"Pay board, then. Yes, pay board. Deal out seven one-
dollar bills on the table every Saturday. But if you lose
your job, your board stops and you can go find a free
boarding house. If you get sick while you're boarding here,
nursing is extra."

"Don't start carrying on, Mama. All I'm asking is a few
dollars a week out of my pay."

"Yes, pay board," droned on Flo unheedingly. Suddenly
her tears came. "When my own mother, God rest her soul,
was living, I was so happy to help her. I gave her all my
pay and wished I could give her more. I used to carry her
around in my hands. I just couldn't do enough for her."
She began to sob.

Margy was sorry, sorry, sorry that she had started anything. She should have known she couldn't win. Now she
had the added trouble of trying to undo the whole thing.

"All right, Mama, I won't pay board then. I thought
there was no harm in asking. I'll keep on bringing home
all my money. Only don't cry."

After Flo had permitted herself to be persuaded to dry
her tears, she felt that she had to explain her attitude.

"It's not that I'm mean," she said. "There's not a kinder person in the whole world than me. If I had plenty the best would be none too good for you. But you got no idea how hard it is to keep a home together on so little."

"I said all right, Mama."

"You got your whole life before you. You'll have many a good day yet. My good days are all behind me. When a woman gets my age, what has she got to look forward to? Nothing. Only her children. And it's a sad thing when children turn on a mother."

"I'm not turning on you."

"It's a wonder," continued Flo, "that I do so good considering the little money comes in this house. And do I get credit? No! Do I get a salary for my work like you and your father? No!" She addressed an imaginary companion. "My daughter thinks she gives me too much. My daughter thinks I spend all the money on myself."

Margy took off her bathrobe. "Mama, if you don't stop, I'm going out."

"A dance!" said Flo quickly. "You said you wanted a dress for a dance. What dance? Who you going with?"

"Nobody. Nothing," said Margy. "I was just talking."

Just then a boy came to the door with a message that she was wanted on Alexander's phone. Glad of an excuse to get out of the house for a few minutes, Margy threw on her dress and coat and followed the boy.

"Hello?"

"This you, Margy?"

"Who else?"

"Well, you sound funny over the phone."

"You always say that, Reenie. Well, what's up?"

"Listen! I thought I'd ask you. I'm thinking of changing."

"On account of Sal?"

"Yeah. It would be hard on the children—if we got married, I mean." Reenie thought of what her mother had said. "There'd be hard feelings on his side if they went to my church and I'd get mad if they went to his."

"Well, if you love him, you might as well take his religion."

"You're not saying that just because you're Catholic yourself?"

"I don't know. You asked me and I told you."

"There's only one thing bothers me: The idea of going to confession and telling all the bad things you thought and did out loud to a stranger."

"Oh, I guess a priest who has to hear a couple of hundred confessions a week won't be knocked off his feet by your sins."

"I don't like to be bawled out."

"They don't . . . I mean, I don't know how it is in other Catholic churches, but in my church, he just listens, and when you're through, he tells you to say so and so many Hail Mary's and Our Father's for penance."

"So you just don't sit in a box with him and talk it out and listen to a lot of advice?"

"Not in the church I go to."

"Well," concluded Reenie, "I'll think it over some more."

"Listen, Reenie, I'm going to a dance."

"Swell! Who's the guy?"

"Oh, just some fellow I've known for quite some time."

"You never *told* me."

"There's nothing to tell. He's just a fellow."

"But I tell you *everything*."

"I'll tell you all about the dance afterwards."

"Do that."

They waited, the wires hummed. There seemed to be nothing more to say.

"Well," said both simultaneously and laughed.

"Will I see you at the office tomorrow?" asked Margy with sudden unexplained anxiety.

"Why not?"

"Well, I just thought . . . Okay. See you tomorrow, then."

The boy was waiting outside the telephone booth. "Pick out what you want," Margy told him. He chose a strip of licorice. Margy paid Alexander the penny. That was the kid's reward for fetching her. He hung around the store all evening, calling people to the phone at a penny a call.

"Who phoned?" asked Flo.

"A girl from the office. She won't be in tomorrow and she asked me to tell the supervisor."

Margy told the lie simply because if she had said Reenie

95

phoned, she'd have to listen to a diatribe against her friend for the rest of the evening.

It was ten o'clock and quiet in the house. Flo was making regular trips to the parlor to peer out the window to see if Henny was coming home. Margy found she was hungry. She got out one of the penny bars of candy and started nibbling on it while she read.

"Don't spoil your stomach with that trash," said Flo, "I'll make you a nice sandwich." Obediently, Margy set the candy aside.

Flo took special pains with the sandwich. When it was finished she put a paper doily on the plate under it. Wordlessly and rather shyly, she pushed the plate along the table to Margy.

The girl looked at it and her eyes blurred with tears. Flo had extravagantly trimmed off the crusts because Margy liked sandwiches that way. And the extra touch of the lace paper doily! She looked up and smiled. Flo turned her face away from the eyes that looked so bright with tears.

"Would you like a cup of coffee, too?" Flo asked humbly.

"No, Mama. The sandwich is wonderful. The best fried-egg sandwich I ever had. Thank you. Thank you a whole lot, Mama."

Flo's heart turned over. She thought: She asks for a new winter coat and all she gets is a sandwich and she says thanks—for that. She gives in too easy. She ought to have more fight in her. It's all right for her to give in to me. But suppose some man gets hold of her and she gives in so easy? Or she might marry somebody just because she feels sorry for him and she'll never complain if he's mean to her. I'm so scared that she'll always get the dirty end of the stick. She's too much like her father—don't know how to stand up for her own rights.

Margy's thoughts ran along the same line. I wish I was more like Mama so I could get my own way in some things. Nothing big—just things like getting a new winter coat or a new dress. But I can't fight. I get sick when I argue. Oh, well, this is only temporary. Everything will be better someday. I'll *make* it better. After all, I'm young yet.

Her mother spoke aloud. "You're young yet, Margy. After all, you have your whole life before you."

"Yes," Margy said. "Yes."

Each went back to her thoughts. Flo thought: I must do better by her otherwise I'll lose her because she'll marry the first man that comes along. And she's such a *good* girl.

Margy thought: I understand sometimes why she's the way she is. I wish she'd try to understand me. I try my best to see how it is with her—and with other people, too. All I wish is that someday someone will come along and try to see how it is with me.

Chapter 11

Frankie and Irma stood in the vestibule of Irma's house saying good-night.

"It was swell. Thanks for taking me," she said.

"Aw, it was nothing."

"They had some swell records tonight. I could have danced forever."

"Me, too," he said politely.

It had to be you, it had to be you,

she hummed brightly. "And I *do* mean you, Frankie."

"Do you? Well . . ." He shifted uncomfortably.

"Listen. I don't have to go up yet."

"Your mother might worry."

"Horse feathers!" She put her arms around his neck. "Let's be frank and earnest," she said. "You be Frank and I'll be Irmest." She giggled. "Listen! We been dancing together the whole evening. You know the way I feel because you must feel the same way, too. So . . ." She rubbed her nose against his. Suddenly her arms tightened about him and she pressed her body against his. He was terribly embarrassed.

"No. But thanks just the same," he said. "I mean I've got to get up early to go to the office."

She was incredulous. "You mean you don't *want* to?"

He said the first thing that came into his head. "I'm just not excited."

"That's the first time I ever knew you were a . . . a sissy," she sneered.

"And that's the first time I ever knew you were a . . ." He stopped. He was too polite to say, whore.

98

It took Frankie a long time to get to sleep. He worried that he'd be tired on the job next day. He worried whether Irma thought he was a fairy. He wondered whether there was any girl in Williamsburg who could enjoy dancing without wanting to be made love to at the end of the evening. Again he thought of Margy. She seemed decent and sensible. He had heard talk in the neighborhood that her mother was very strict with her. Maybe he could have a pleasant evening with her without all that embarrassing stuff afterward. The question was: Could she dance? Well, he'd have to find out. He decided not to get out of the date with Margy. He'd take her to the next dance. Relieved at making the decision, he soon fell asleep with his mind at ease.

Margy, sleeping the deep sleep of the young in her narrow, white, iron bed, had no way of knowing that Frankie's disappointing evening with Irma would change the course of her life.

Chapter 12

Reenie's mother slept restlessly. After her quarrel with her daughter, tears had made her face swell up almost as much as her ankles. Reenie was in the kitchen. She set out two cups and saucers and measured water into the coffee pot for the morning. She put out two spoons and took two oranges from the bottom shelf of the icebox and placed them on the cake of ice on top. She knew that her mother, working in the lunchroom, hated to handle food at home.

She looked around and wished there was something more to do. She had made a decision and needed to write a letter to Sal. The letter would change things with them and although she had come to the decision she wanted to put off the announcement of it. She wanted to be a little longer, the way she was now. Finally, she wrote the letter:

Dear Sal:

I spoke to my mother about changing. She cried and went to bed sick. So I can't do it just yet. No use asking you to change Protestant. I know you won't. Well, Sal, we tried our best to do the right thing—get married. Everything seems to be against it. But I love you and I'll never love anybody else. I believe now, what you so often told me, that we have a right to belong to each other. It would be better if we were married. Then there wouldn't have to be all this sneaking around. So I am writing to tell you that it is okay with me. I would not say it was okay except I know we'll get married sooner or later. Next Wednesday night, when my mother goes to her church meeting, we can be

alone in the house a couple of hours. I would not
want you to think I ever did this with any other
man. It is only because I love you so . . .

Just then, her mother moaned in her sleep. Reenie
jumped and made a big blot on the sheet. She got another piece of paper and copied the letter all over again.
She didn't want Salvatore to think she was a sloppy girl.

Chapter 13

Miss Drusill and Miss Lange, the permanent residence workers at Neighborhood Center House, decided to wait five minutes more before they turned on the lights in the recreation hall. Already the boys and girls were gathering on the street before the House. They'd swarm in the moment the lights went on, eager to start dancing. The Misses Drusill and Lange didn't want to let them in before Miss Grayce arrived because Miss Grayce liked to stand in the doorway and greet each arrival personally. Miss Grayce was a volunteer worker who came all the way from Central Park West, New York, to Williamsburg, Brooklyn, once a month, to teach the young people dancing and social usage. Being greeted at the door by the hostess was part of the course. But Miss Grayce was late again and certainly, decided the ladies, you couldn't keep the young people waiting on the street much longer. They agreed to wait another five minutes.

Miss Drusill and Miss Lange were plain-looking, conscientious, middle-aged spinsters. They had never had children but they knew how to love and care for the children of others. They had never had lovers but they had understanding and wise advice when young girls came to them with love problems. They had never known ambition —except as dedicating their lives to the poor could be called ambition—yet they knew how it was with boys who were anxious to get ahead. They had never known personal criminal tendencies, yet they appeared frequently before the police, convincing the officer in charge that such and such a boy was not a criminal, merely an exceptionally bright boy who had chosen a wrong outlet for his capabilities.

They were well loved in the neighborhood. The people depended on them for so much. Yet, they were but two women and there were thousands of children and young people who needed their help. They couldn't have kept the House going if it weren't for the volunteer social workers. These men and women, all of good family and many with wealth, gave freely of their money and, what was more important, of their valuable time. Miss Drusill and Miss Lange frequently assured each other they couldn't do without the volunteer workers. They were grateful.

Miss Grayce was different. The resident workers felt that she had no true vocation for the work; that she used it to escape boredom—or as a stopgap between betrothal and marriage. Miss Grayce always brought some of her friends with her. The friends were inclined to find the young people "amusing." The resident workers worried about the friends. They did not like their young people to be patronized. However, they always ended their discussion of Miss Grayce by agreeing that she was popular with the young people and after all it *was* nice of her to give her time.

They turned on the lights and opened the doors. The boys and girls rushed in. Just as the last of them were going in, the car drew up to the door. Miss Grayce had finally arrived. This time she brought her fiancé and his friend along with her.

"Oh, dear, oh, dear!" said Miss Drusill.

"If we had only waited five minutes longer," sighed Miss Lange.

Margy and Frankie saw the three New Yorkers arrive, the fiancé carrying a batch of new dance records. To Margy, they seemed like people from another world; a smoother, more polished world—a world she knew of only by reading about it.

Margy and Frankie were off in the first dance. Any fears he had had about her dancing were dispelled. She was what was known in the neighborhood as a nifty spieler. Like all Brooklyn girls she had a sure instinct for rhythm. She had learned to dance on the sidewalks of Williamsburg to the music of wandering German bands. Reenie and the other girls showed her new dance steps and she practiced with the girls whenever a rainy day cut short their after-lunch walk around the block. Her step suited Frankie's and she followed nimbly where he led.

"You dance nicely," she told him shyly.

He returned the compliment. "You're not so bad yourself."

Miss Grayce came along and introduced Margy to another boy. Miss Grayce liked the young people to change partners. Her premise was that no good came from the same couple dancing too much together. Besides, introductions and meeting of new people was part of the social function of the dancing class.

"Miss Shannon, may I present Mr. Ricci?" suggested Miss Grayce with bright correctness. Although Margy had known who Carmine Ricci was since grade-school days, she was considerate of Miss Grayce and played along.

"Pleased to meet you, Mr. Ricci," she said.

"Likewise," he responded.

Miss Grayce got a new girl for Frankie and fluttered off to unscramble the other couples. Then she announced a morris dance.

"Let's sit this one out, Margy," said Mr. Ricci. "I wouldn't be caught dead in a hick dance. Morris dance, my eye! I know a square dance when I see one."

"Okay, Carmy," agreed Margy.

They found seats near the victrola. Margy looked over the warm happy scene and thought how nice it was to have a place to come to; where you were welcome; where you fitted in.

Miss Grayce had put her fiancé in charge of the victrola. He stood there, changing records and talking to his friend. Margy listened idly, enjoying the rise and fall of the well-modulated voices. Then a sentence came out of the context of their conversation which made Margy sit up straighter. The friend of the fiancé said it.

"What an outsider needs over here is an interpreter."

At that moment, the figure of the dance brought Frankie Malone and his partner near the victrola. Frankie heard the last remark and jerked his head to stare at the New Yorkers. The fiancé smiled and saluted Frankie with a careless flick of his fingers. Frankie ignored smile and salute and followed the dance figure until he came to where Margy and Carmy were sitting. He pulled his partner out of the dance which was ending anyhow. They stood behind Margy and her partner. The men continued their conversation.

"Take Grayce. She understands them fine. It's merely a question of getting the accent and she has it down pat. You should have been at the apartment the other night when she did an imitation of the fellow who complained about his partner."

"Sorry I missed it."

The morris dance ended. One of the gentlemen obligingly put a tango on. As the dreamy notes of "On the Alamo" came up, Carmy jumped to his feet.

"A dance with dips! Just my dish! Let's go, Marge."

"I don't feel like a tango," refused Margy. Carmy turned to Frankie.

"Mind if I muscle in?" he asked.

"Go ahead," consented Frankie. Carmy asked Frankie's partner for the dance.

"I'll try anything once," she said.

Frankie sat down beside Margy. They didn't speak to each other. They listened to the two gentlemen at the victrola who had resumed their conversation. One was telling the other about Miss Grayce's take-off on one of the kids.

"Well, it seems that this girl, or should I say, 'goil' "— the fiancé waited for his friend to smile—"wore a tight skirt . . ."

"Skoit," corrected the friend.

"That's right. Of course I'm not good at imitations— not as good as Grayce anyhow. According to her it went something like this:

" 'I'm dant-zin wid a goil, see? An' her skoit's so tight, we ain't makin' der dips all the way, see? So I tells her in a nice way . . .' "

As Margy listened, the world that she was used to swung into a different focus. Occasionally there is a moment in a person's life when he takes a great stride forward in wisdom, humility or disillusionment. For a split second he comes into a kind of cosmic understanding. For a trembling breath of time he knows all there is to know. He is loaned the gift the poet yearned for—seeing himself as others see him.

Margy, listening to the gentlemen, saw her kind of people as others saw them. She'd given little thought to any world outside her own. She had been born in a certain environment—had taken it for granted. Her kind of people were different from each other in small things but alike in the fundamentals. Some were kinder than others; some meaner. A lot were poorer than most; a few better off than their fellows. Some were ambitious and a lot didn't care about anything except living from day to day. She knew some who seemed happy and she knew too many who complained all the time. But all were confined in the same rigid frame that boxed in her life. The only difference among the people she knew was that some squirmed more than others in the box.

She was not entirely ignorant of people in other environments. She read the novels of her day. *Black Oxen, This Side of Paradise*—books like that. Certainly the characters in those books were different from the people she knew. She had supposed those fictional characters were as unusual, as unreal as characters in fairy tales or mystery stories. Now she had to wonder whether these fiction people weren't the real people and her kind the unreal ones; the ones unknown to the world at large, whose lives were just as fantastic as those of people in books.

She tried to figure out why Miss Grayce would give of her time to the Williamsburg young people just to get a laugh out of them. That seemed mean. Yet she knew that Miss Grayce was not a mean person or she wouldn't be there in the first place. Margy decided that Miss Grayce was a "pleaser." She liked to please the poor but she liked to please her friends, too. If she could please them by making fun of some Brooklyn boy, all right; she felt that that made her a good hostess. But it still made Margy feel uncomfortable.

The tango ended and the fiancé put on "Beautiful Ohio."

"You wouldn't want to dance?" suggested Frankie half-heartedly.

"No," said Margy.

"Let's get out of here."

She hesitated at the door. "Maybe we ought to say good-by to Miss Grayce, and thanks."

"Nuts!" said Frankie.

"Still and all . . . to be polite . . ."

106

"Okay. Make out that you didn't hear what those two guys said; make out that you still believe that Miss Grayce puts herself out to come over to Brooklyn to bring sunshine to a bunch of poor slobs. Go ahead! Tell her you had a *gorgeous* time." His lips twisted sneeringly over the feminine adjective. "Do that and stay a sucker all the rest of your life."

So she left without saying good-by and thanks. She had had such a nice little speech prepared, too. She had planned to speak very carefully and bring in words like "skirt" and "girl" and pronounce them right, and maybe when next Miss Grayce was asked to do her imitations, she'd back out, saying: "But I was wrong. Really, they don't talk like that. I was speaking to a little Brooklyn girl and honestly her diction was as good as ours." Well, it had been a moment's rosy dream—Margy setting the world right.

Frankie and Margy walked through the streets toward her home. For a long time he said nothing, then, with his face straight ahead, he said:

"Her skirt *was* too tight. Miss Grayce noticed that I had trouble dancing with Irma and Miss Grayce took me aside and told me to tell her exactly what was bothering me. So I told her. And Miss Grayce said what a shame but Irma felt that she was dressed right for the dance and I must be a gentleman and put up with it. So I did. And while we're dancing, Miss Grayce keeps smiling at me and I think everything's on the up and up. And all the while she's figuring out how to do an imitation of me to give her friends a laugh.

"I *don't* talk the way she says. And even if I do, I'm not ashamed of it." He leaned against a lamppost, his eyes searching for something on the ground. "What the hell!" He kicked viciously at a burned-out matchstick. "Must I say gur-r-rl because she says it that way? Sounds dumb to call a bird a burd. I guess I'm the one who should be doing impersonations." He straightened up. "Ladies and gents! I will now give you a few impressions of uptown New York Miss Grayce!" He put one hand on his hip and fluttered the other one. "My dear, there was this here dee-lish-us gurl wearing a green blues and a pink skurt . . ."

Suddenly the spirit went out of him and he abandoned

the impersonation. To Margy's helpless horror, he began to sob. He wept standing there under the lamppost. He talked between sobs.

"I'll go away from here and make a lot of money. I'll come back someday with my pockets full of ten-dollar bills. And every kid on the street who talks the way I do will get a ten-dollar bill off of me," he boasted boyishly. "And I'll send all the poor kids to camp every summer just because I always wanted to go and never had the chance."

Margy tried to find the words to tell the boy not to grieve because Miss Grayce had betrayed him; that it didn't matter—it didn't matter at all because she, Margy, believed in him and was sure he'd amount to something someday. He'd be an important man.

In fact, she told him, he was important already because he had become important to her. And as they walked and talked, he found it easier to believe Margy's words than Miss Grayce's cruelty. He began getting the feeling that he was somebody after all; that this quiet girl knew of all the potentialities within him. And so the twenty-year-old boy thought that he had fallen in love with her.

And because Margy was all ready to fall in love with someone—anyone, and because she was sorry for him and had a woman-need to save someone from hurt, and because at the moment of his tiny crucifixion she had been able to stand at his side and lessen a bit the ugly impact of man's thoughtless inhumanity to man, she felt a warm, protective glow toward the boy.

And, as women are so prone to do, she mistook this protective glow for love.

Chapter 14

Spring was all right that year. Margy had a boy friend; someone to go places with and someone to talk to. Frankie took her to the movies Wednesday nights. Saturdays they went to a dance and had a chop-suey supper afterward. Sunday afternoons they took trolley rides to Prospect Park or Coney Island and on the Fourth of July they went to the Statue of Liberty—both for the first time. On paydays he presented her with a box of Huyler's candy. In short, they were "going steady."

Flo suspected something of the sort and gave Margy reproachful looks while she waited for the confidences her daughter withheld.

"I used to tell my mother, rest her soul, *everything*," hinted Flo.

"Did you, Mama?"

"Yes. There was this here feller wanted to keep company with me but I asked my mother first. She didn't like him so I told him I could never get serious with him."

"You don't tell me!"

"But you're different. You keep things from your mother."

"No, I don't."

"Maybe there's something you ought to tell me?"

"What makes you think so, Mama?"

"Well, you're different—different than you was last year."

"I'm a year older, that's all."

"No, you changed in other ways. You don't talk much to me no more."

"Oh, Mama, talking always leads to an argument."

"When do I argue with you?"

"Well, you don't then. You just talk me out of things."

"Like what?"

"Like when I wanted a new coat last fall."

"So you're still brooding over that coat! Let me tell you," said Margy's mother, "that you have mighty little character if you feel that way about a coat. What's a new coat? You'll have many a new coat after I'm dead and gone. Many's the time you'll say, 'Why did I torment my poor mother so just because she couldn't buy me a coat?'

"Such ideas over such a little thing like a coat when you have your whole life before you! If I was only young again, like you, I wouldn't care if I never got a new anything. Just so I was young again like you."

Chapter 15

He gave her a wrist watch when her birthday came round in June. Now she had something precious to remove and place on the washstand with the admonition to Reenie: "Don't let me go and forget my watch, now."

Ruthie told Margy that the gift meant Frankie was serious because *her* friend had given *her* a wrist watch on *her* first birthday after they started keeping company. She confided that she got the ring the Christmas following and now there'd be a wedding ring in a few weeks.

Marie, the office beauty, stood next to Margy at the mirrors the first day of the watch. Margy hoped she was impressed. She looked into the mirror to find the green eyes meeting her own. There was a kind of contemptuous pity in the green eyes. No wonder! For the first time, Margy noticed that Marie was wearing a watch, a watch with a smaller face and gold links instead of a black grosgrain ribbon strap. Marie did not remove it while washing her hands as if to prove that a watch was nothing in *her* life.

Margy wondered who had given it to her. Mr. Prentiss? An intense feeling of jealousy went through her at the thought. She was pleasantly shocked. After all, she'd probably marry Frankie if ever he asked her. She had no right to be romantic about Mr. Prentiss just because he gave her a smile and a considerate word now and then. But she did feel hopelessly romantic about her boss and she was jealous and that's the way it was.

The next day, Mr. Prentiss noticed the new watch and made a little occasion of it. "Do you have the correct time, Miss Shannon?" he asked.

In all seriousness, she consulted her watch and told him

the time. She looked up to catch his smile. Only then did she recall that there was a large clock hanging on the wall behind his desk. The clock kept accurate electrical time.

The watch was Margy's first piece of jewelry. She was so proud of it. She wore it with the dial on the inside of her wrist. She liked the gesture of turning her hand over to see the time. She liked to see the dial and the palm of her hand' simultaneously. Time seemed more important—more personal that way.

Sometimes she'd study the tiny watch face and muse that time had always been and always would be. Seconds, minutes, hours, days, weeks, months, years and centuries had flowed by inexorably up to the hour of her birth. And time had not broken its eternal rhythm for her birth hour and would not falter in its rhythm for her death hour. After looking at the watch face, she'd study the lines in her left palm and wonder what she was; how she figured in the cosmic plan of birth, growth and death and what her destiny was to be.

Yes, the watch meant a great deal to Margy.

She kept the watch a secret from her parents, putting it in her purse each time before she entered the flat. She wasn't deceitful but she wasn't quite prepared to tell her mother about Frankie.

But there had to come a time. One Wednesday night after Frankie had taken Margy to the Bushwick Theater, they lingered in the vestibule to embrace before the final good-night kiss. It was an important night. It was the night he proposed.

"Margy, let me give you a ring," was his way of asking her.

"An engagement ring?" she asked, trying not to tremble with excitement.

"An engagement ring. It won't be a large stone but . . ."

"But this is kind of sudden."

"No, it isn't. You've been expecting me to ask you and you know it."

She knew he was right. What she really meant by sudden was that she'd have to have time to make up her mind about Frankie. She enjoyed romancing with him. But marriage . . .

"I don't know," she temporized.

"You love me, don't you?"

She wanted to say the easy yes, but somehow it wouldn't come out. "Of course!" she said, a little too emphatically.

"That's all there is to it, then. Let's get married right away."

"Right away?" The idea of actually marrying Frankie filled her with a kind of panic.

"Why not?" he argued. "We'll be married sooner or later and sooner suits me better. How about a month?"

He kissed her lingeringly. Margy found the kiss pleasant. She fought down her panic. Why not? she reasoned to herself. I got to get married sometime and we get along. And I'll have a home of my own. Of course, there isn't the thrill about it . . . the way they write about it in the books. But how do I know the books are right? Maybe this is the real way—just liking someone and getting along with him. She said:

"A month's not long enough. We have to get a flat first . . . furniture. I ought to get things . . . clothes."

"I've got some money saved up," he said. "I can swing it. We'll find rooms and Batterman's has a sale on furniture. You can take time off from work and get your clothes and stuff."

"But we ought to be engaged a little while before . . ."

"I hate engagements," he burst out. "People knowing you're hanging out together waiting to get married—making remarks on the side about whether you're beating the gong or not. Everybody in on the love affair."

"But when a girl marries suddenly, there's talk."

"Let there be talk. They'll talk anyhow, no matter what."

"It will take three weeks for the banns."

"All right. Say two months from now, then," he conceded impatiently.

"I wouldn't want to say until after my folks met you. I've *got* to let them know."

"They won't like me."

"They will! And even if they don't, it won't make any difference. But they are my folks and I've got to tell them."

"I see your point," he said. "My folks are about the same as yours. My mother's going to carry on when she knows she's going to lose me—or my pay," he amended. "But my folks got to take it whether they like it or not." He put an arm around her. "We got a right to do as we please. Our folks should be happy just so long as we're happy. But it's not going to be that way."

"Oh, Frankie," she cried out. "When we have children . . ."

"Aren't you being a little bit previous?" he asked with a smile.

"No. I mean it. If a girl of ours gets old enough to have boy friends, let's welcome them in our home. We won't let it be like this: Standing in vestibules—talking in whispers like we were doing something wrong."

"As though we had no right to be even *thinking* of getting married," he said.

"If ever I have a daughter," vowed Margy, "the house, no matter how plain, will be for her. Her friends will be my friends and I'll try to remember how I felt when I was a young girl so I can understand how she feels. That's the important thing—to remember, when you get mad at kids, how it was with you when you were a kid."

"Check!" he agreed. "But Margy, like I said, don't be so previous. Let's not have kids till we're on our feet."

She looked at him wide-eyed. "But what's the sense of getting married if you're not thinking of children?"

"Let's figure on children after we've been married a while. How about setting a date?"

Again she evaded him without quite knowing why. "Here you want to marry me," she said. "But you never told me you loved me."

"Margy, I'm a dope in a good many ways. Like I can't come right out and say I love you the way they do on the stage. It would make me feel silly. But you've got sense. You know how I feel about you. What've I been going out with you for? Why do I want to marry you?

"Look, Margy. I been working since I was seventeen. I never lost a day except once two years ago when I took off to see the Dodgers' opening game. My bosses think well of me. I'm not a drinker and I don't hang out in pool-rooms. I go to church regular—that is, regular for a feller. I never talk back to my mother. I'm earning twenty-two a week and I've got nearly two hundred dollars in the Bushwick Savings Bank. And," he added, "I've never horsed around with women. You're the first girl I was ever serious about. Maybe you could do better—a girl like you. But you could do a lot worse than taking me. And like I told you the night we went to that dance, I have intentions of being somebody someday."

Thus he laid his meager shining life before her and she was touched by the gift of himself that he offered. Yet, perversely feminine, she wanted the three words.

"Say you love me," she whispered.

"You know."

"But say it!"

"I need you, Margy. I don't see how I could get along without you."

And she had to be content with that.

After the last lingering good-night kiss, she ran up the stairs so excited about the idea of getting married that she forgot to take off her watch. Her mother was sitting up waiting. She saw the watch when Margy took off her coat. So Margy had to tell her.

Chapter 16

It was the night that Frankie was coming to meet her folks. Margy was on her feet two blocks before Maujer Street in agony as to whether the motorman would stop at that corner. For once, she wanted to save time. Fortunately, another passenger wanted to get off at that block and while the motorman might ignore one passenger's desires, he couldn't possibly ignore two.

She got home ten minutes earlier than usual. She needn't have hurried. Flo had everything under control. The chopped meat, onions and potatoes were in the frying pan. The flat was immaculate.

"Oh, everything looks so nice, Mama," said Margy. "And you look nice, too."

Indeed, Flo looked nice. She had on a freshly laundered house dress and she had shampooed her hair that morning. Flo was only thirty-nine and still slender and shapely. She would have looked young and pretty if it hadn't been for the bitter look on her face.

"And that ain't all," said Flo. "Look!" She opened the icebox. Alone on the top shelf was a small, round, high, creamy cheesecake and a half-pint bottle of coffee cream. "Real cream for coffee when he comes."

"You shouldn't've," protested Margy. "Frankie's used to condensed milk in his coffee just like us."

"If he's coming here with the idea that we're shanty Irish trash, he's going to find himself mistaken," said Flo.

"Why, Mama, he never had any such idea."

"What other idea could he have? A girl lets him meet her on the sly without her parents knowing. She takes jewelry from him when she hardly knows him and keeps it from her mother. So he can't have much of an opinion of her and her family."

"I would've brought him home to meet you long ago only I was afraid you'd carry on."

"Am I carrying on now that I know he's coming?" asked Flo.

Yes! Margy wanted to shout. Instead she said, "Aw, Mama, you got everything fixed so nice and you're so swell about entertaining him, don't spoil it all now." Somehow, this got to Flo and she said nothing more.

Henny got home early. He had saved time by doing the opposite of Margy, riding a block past his corner, which saved some minutes spent in futile argument with the motorman. He ate quickly, ignoring the newspaper for once, and then put on a clean shirt, collar and tie. He got his vest out of the closet, brushed it and hung it on the back of a chair.

Margy washed, put on fresh makeup and a new white Georgette blouse. By eight o'clock the three clean Shannons were sitting stiffly and silently in their kitchen waiting to receive the suitor. When the bell rang at a quarter-past eight, the Shannons as one got to their feet, and while Margy pressed the button that opened the downstairs door, Henny got into his vest and Flo led the way to the parlor.

Margy, watching Frankie come up the stairs, saw him through her parents' critical eyes and decided that he'd do. He had had his suit pressed and a bay-rum barber-shop smell preceded his entrance.

She introduced him self-consciously before she took his hat and placed it in the exact middle of the bed in the adjoining room. Frankie came with gifts: a box of peanut brittle for his future mother-in-law, a couple of two-for-a-quarter cigars for Henny and a corsage of lavender sweet peas tied with tinsel ribbon for Margy.

Flo thanked him stiffly but Margy knew she was pleased. Henny made much of the cigars, assuring Frankie that he was a young man who certainly knew his tobacco. But Henny didn't smoke cigars. He placed them in his vest pocket, intending to present them to his foreman in hope of gaining some small concession in exchange. Margy beamed with pride as she pinned the corsage to the left shoulder of her blouse. Flo passed the box of candy around.

The peanut brittle came in for sprightly praise. They talked about the gifts as long as they could. Then the conversation died. No one said anything for a long time.

Henny, knowing it was his duty as host to keep the talk flowing, put his stiff curved hands on his knees, leaned forward, cleared his throat, looked directly into Frankie's eyes and asked:

"Do you think light wines and beer will ever come back?" It was a frequent question in those days. Frankie looked confused but pulled himself together.

"You can search me," was his considered opinion.

Flo put in her two-cents' worth. "Maybe the young man ain't interested in blind tigers."

"Pigs," corrected Henny.

"Saloons, tigers, speakeasies, cider stores, call them blind pigs, even," conceded Flo. "All mean the same thing —a place where a man gets drunk and spends his hard-earned money." She looked directly at her husband.

His eyes fell. He wanted to explain that *he* never got drunk; that he spent very little money in saloons; that he went there merely to relax in talk with other men. But out of consideration for their guest, he said nothing. He tried a different conversational approach.

"Me, I'm all for keeping the law. But they got no right to take a workingman's beer away from him. Prohibition was put over on us while our boys was dying in the trenches. That reminds me: Was you with the Rainbow Division, Mr. Malone?"

"I never saw action," admitted Frankie. "I happened to be in second-year High when the war broke out."

"You should have known," Flo reproached her husband.

"I only thought . . . so many of our Brooklyn boys was with the Rainbow Division," apologized Henny, "that I thought you was one of them."

"I was only a kid myself," put in Margy brightly. "So dumb, I hardly knew there was a war on. But I saw Rudolph Valentino in *The Four Horsemen of the Apocalypse* and that showed that war is a terrible thing."

All agreed that war was a terrible thing and again the talk died out. Margy revived it. "Still and all," she said, "there were the poems that came out of the war. I love the one about the poppies growing between the crosses row on row."

"My favorite," said Frankie, "is, 'I Have a Rendezvous With Death.'"

They urged him to recite it but he begged off, saying he didn't know all the words. Henny came out of a deep study.

"Rondy-voo?" he asked, puzzled.

"It means a date," said Margy.

"It means we all got to go someday," amplified Flo.

"Knock wood," suggested Frankie.

The quartet beat a brief tattoo on the arms of their chairs. There was a solemn pause—the pause that precedes a dissertation on death. Henny took matters into his own hands and rejected death as a conversational theme. He brought the talk back to poetry.

"There's a piece, not about the war exactly, but I like it anyway. It goes something like this:

> *In all my life, I've got to see*
> *A poem as lovely as a tree.*

His wife and daughter looked at him in blank astonishment. They had never heard the word, lovely, come from his lips. They looked at him so strangely that he felt he had to apologize.

"Only reason I read it when it was in the Brooklyn *Eagle* was that the feller what wrote it was a Brooklyn boy what got killed in the war. They got a legion post named after him, now: The Joyce Kilmer Post they call it."

Margy was proud of her father for knowing that. "You know a lot of things, Papa," she said.

"Oh, I get around," said Henny debonairly.

Flo pressed her lips together so that she wouldn't say, Yes, around to saloons and wherever else bums hang out.

"Brooklyn is a wonderful place in many ways," expanded Henny, heady with his daughter's compliment. "There's many a famous person come from Brooklyn."

"And most of them are ashamed of it, too," said Flo, making ashes out of his pride.

"That's because some dumb people don't realize Brooklyn's a fine city."

"This part of Brooklyn ain't fine," said Flo, "the way the neighborhood's run down."

"This neighborhood ain't all of Brooklyn, I'll let you know," said loyal Henny.

"Well, it's all the Brooklyn we'll ever know," said Flo. She stood up and asked to be excused and left the room abruptly. Frankie looked puzzled.

"Mama went out to make coffee," explained Margy.

"Oh! For a minute I thought something out of the way was said," said Frankie.

They had about run the gamut of conversational topics. They had discussed the fiery question of the day. The right of a strong minority to inflict prohibition on an unwilling majority. Henny had made a brief statement concerning the rights of the workingman. They had acknowledged the horrors of war and the beauty of poetry; the inevitability of death; and had skirmished briefly with the subject of civic pride. There remained three more general topics of conversation to get them through the rest of the evening: Religion, politics and the weather. Henny tackled politics.

"If it's not a personal question, Mr. Malone," he asked politely, "I'd like to know whether you're a Republican or whether you vote the Democrat ticket." His voice capitalized *Democrat* but put *Republican* in the lower case.

"I cast my first vote this coming election," said Frankie proudly, "and of course, I'll vote the straight Democratic ticket."

"That's fine," approved Henny. "Then I take it that you got no use for that man in the White House—Harding."

"No use at all," pronounced Frankie.

Henny got up and shook the boy's hand. They were one against the Republican party. After a while Flo appeared in the alcove.

"There's coffee," she announced.

They went out into the kitchen. There was a fresh cloth on the table. Instead of the usual custom of placing the cut cake in the center of the table where all could reach for a piece to eat with their hands, Flo had set out cake plates and forks. Margy was proud of her mother for knowing and doing the right thing. Frankie stood in the middle of the kitchen and looked around.

"May I wash my hands?" he asked politely.

Margy, knowing that his request was a delicate way of

asking where the bathroom was, was filled with consternation. They had no bathroom! Literal Flo produced a small enameled basin which she placed in the sink, handed the boy a clean towel and told him there was hot water in the kettle.

Frankie held the towel in his hands and looked frustrated. Henny drew him into the bedroom next to the kitchen.

"The toilet's in the hall," said Henny in a hoarse whisper heard by the two women in the kitchen. "I'll get you the key."

"I just want to wash my hands," lied Frankie in a clear loud voice.

The two men came out of the bedroom. Frankie's face was brick red with embarrassment. He washed his clean hands at the sink and dried them thoroughly. They sat down to coffee and cake.

Frankie, trying desperately to ingratiate himself with Margy's parents, praised the cheesecake, claiming it was creamier than the kind sold on his block. He asked where the bakery store was, saying he intended to buy a duplicate cake to take home to his mother.

Flo was anxious to know the boy's religion. To that end, she asked him bluntly what church he attended. He told her St. Cecelia's.

"We go to St. Catherine's ourselves," she said, implying that people who went elsewhere just didn't count. "I mean, Margy and me go," she added, giving her husband a bitter look.

"Sunday's the one day in the week when a workingman can sleep late," said Henny defensively.

"You could go to twelve-o'clock Mass," said his wife.

"That's High Mass and too long."

Before Flo and Henny could get off on an argument, Frankie announced his impending departure.

"I guess I better make a break," he said, "and not wear out my welcome by staying too long."

They trooped back to the parlor. Margy held his hat while he made his polite farewells.

"I enjoyed the conversation," he said, "and the coffee and cake." Feeling that this was inadequate, he added, "You certainly have a nice home here, Mrs. Shannon."

Then it came!

"I'm glad you realize that, Mr. Malone," said Flo. "You can understand, then, that Margy's in no hurry to leave her home and get married until she can have even a nicer home than this."

Frankie's face colored quickly. "I happen to come from a pretty nice home myself, Mrs. Shannon," he said with dignity.

Margy, trying desperately to change the conversation called out: "Look! It's beginning to sprinkle." All went to look out of the window at the light rain which had begun to fall.

"What's a little rain?" asked Frankie.

"But you'll ruin your press," she said.

"I happen to have another suit home, strange as it may seem," said Frankie coldly.

Stiff good-nights were exchanged. Margy walked down the stairs with Frankie. As they reached the bottom, Mrs. Shannon called over the banister:

"Thanks for the peanut brittle and all."

"You're welcome, I'm sure," he called back.

When they reached the vestibule he would have left her without a good-night kiss but she held him there in the dark cubicle. All doubt of her love for the boy vanished when she realized how vulnerable he was to hurt and how she had hurt him indirectly through her parents. She decided that she wanted to stand between him and hurt for the rest of their lives.

"It doesn't matter, it doesn't matter," she soothed him. "Mama's that way to everyone."

"That crack about taking you out of your rich home," he said.

"She didn't mean anything."

"Oh, no?"

"Well, even if she did, what does it matter? I'm the one you're marrying, not her. And I think you're wonderful."

"Thanks for nothing."

She held him tightly, murmuring comforting words. He stood unyielding in her arms. Finally she said:

"And we'll be married very soon."

That won him over. His arms went around her and he whispered against her hair, "I'll show them! I'll show them all someday."

"I know. I know you will," she whispered back in fierce faith.

They gave promises to each other.

He finished off the evening by passing fair judgment on Margy's parents. "Your old man's not a bad guy," he said. "But your mother . . ." He decided to be charitable. "Well I guess she's got her troubles," he conceded.

"They're really all right," she said. "It's just that you have to get used to their ways."

"It was sure hard talking to them," he said. "I don't mind saying I was nervous."

"You know," said Margy, "I was wondering when we'd get around to talking about the weather."

"You had a hell of a time bringing it in, all right."

"I thought I'd die."

"Come to think of it, we all had a hell of a time, didn't we?"

Suddenly the strain of the evening was lifted and they started to snicker as they recalled the more humorous aspects of the visit. The snickers changed to giggles and the giggles to laughter. Margy laughed so hard that she became weak and had to hold on to Frankie. They laughed until they cried.

The laughter came up the stairs—through the closed doors of the flat. The father and mother, hearing the young laughter, exchanged a slow look of defeat.

Chapter 17

A visit to Frankie's folks was in order but they kept putting it off. Frankie said he didn't want Margy to go through what he went through the first time he met her folks. Margy said she was willing to get it over with but secretly she was relieved at putting it off. They talked about it and exchanged wondering conjectures as to why they should have any backwardness about announcing their engagement to Frankie's people. Both agreed they were doing nothing wrong; it was right and normal to fall in love and marry. They analyzed their dread of each other's folks and came to the conclusion that they really weren't afraid of their parents only all the talk and antagonism darkened their happiness.

Now that they were engaged, with Margy wearing a diamond-chip ring to prove it, they settled into the routine of many another Brooklyn couple. They eased up on shows and chop-suey suppers, agreeing to save the money to put into a home. Frankie came to see her each Wednesday night and she entertained him in the parlor while her mother sat in the kitchen straining her ears.

The phonograph was giving out music again. Frankie had found a handle in a junky store on Canal Street. When talk ran out, they put a record on and danced. It was a form of love-making that her mother couldn't find a way to object to.

*And sunshine I'd bring every day,**

** From *If I Had My Way*, by James Kendis and Lou Klein, copyright 1913, renewed and assigned 1940 to the Paull-Pioneer Music Corporation, New York 19, N. Y., used by permisson.

he'd croon as they danced cheek to cheek.

> You would reign all alone
> Like a queen on a thro-ohn,
> If I had my way.

At ten o'clock Flo appeared to announce that she had made coffee, thus fulfilling her obligation to a guest in the house and letting that guest know that the intimate part of the evening was over.

He came late Sunday afternoons and stayed for a delicatessen supper. At five he and Margy went out to the Kosher delicatessen and bought a quarter-pound of pastrami and a loaf of rye bread. Also some salami to piece out the more expensive pastrami. They got slivers of juicy pickle and cornucopias of mustard free with their purchase. They bought potato salad at the German delicatessen and a coffee ring at the bakery, which obligingly opened up for the supper hour on Sundays. Frankie paid for the food. That was the custom.

Nights when Frankie didn't show up Margy stayed home and embroidered stamped bits of cloth which would turn out to be "runners" and doilies. Her parents kept her company in the kitchen. Henny read his paper and Flo crocheted squares for a bedspread for Margy.

Flo tried to do better. She was ingratiatingly nice to Frankie, as though she wanted to make him like her so much that he wouldn't think of taking her only child away from her. Too late, Flo tried to make the home pleasant for Margy. She urged her to bring all her friends to the house. But Margy had no friends save Reenie and Frankie.

Reenie came over and brought her embroidery. She too was filling a hope chest only she called it her hopeless chest because her marriage to Sal seemed more hopeless than ever. Margy asked how things were coming.

"Oh," sighed Reenie, "it's still the same old coffin argument. His mother says the day he marries a Protestant is the day she'll be lying dead in her coffin and my mother says the day I marry a Catholic she won't be there to see it because she'll be buried in her grave. Sal and I sort of took things into our own hands," hinted Reenie.

"You mustn't do anything you'd be ashamed of after," said Margy.

"God knows we tried our best to be decent and get married," said Reenie. "But they put too many things in our way. So we figured it out we got to live while we're still young. How many years is a person young?" asked Reenie wistfully. It was a frequent question with her.

"You wouldn't want to get into any trouble," cautioned Margy as tactfully as she could.

"We won't. We know our way around." Reenie dropped her voice to a whisper. "Aren't parents fierce?" she asked.

"I don't know," said Margy, trying to be fair. "They mean well, I guess. Maybe time passes too quick for them and they don't realize that kids grow up. Now you take Mr. Prentiss' mother."

"*You* take her," suggested Reenie. "I'd rather take a dose of salts."

"*Reenie!*" As always, Margy was shocked by Reenie's earthiness. Yet she envied it, too, and wished she could get away with remarks like that.

Margy didn't invite Reenie to the house often because her mother didn't like her. Flo was polite enough to the girl while she was there but in the post-mortem session afterward she couldn't resist running her down. Flo said Reenie was too flip and flashy and predicted that she'd come to no good end. She advised Margy to be more careful in her choice of friends.

The girls in the office took the news of Margy's coming marriage with typical reactions. They felt she was lucky—anything was better than being an old maid and slaving your life away in an office. On the other hand, without ever having seen Frankie, they insisted that Margy was too good for him—that any woman was too good for any man. (The men had all the fun and the women had to bear the children.) They seemed to regard marriage as a tug of war in which the woman had to get the best grip. The youngsters gave her washroom advice based on what their mothers and other women had told them and on their own conclusions and observations.

"Don't take no lip off your mother-in-law," said a frank, perky eighteen-year-old. "If she gets an edge in, you're sunk."

"Make him turn over all his pay to you," advised an older girl. (Flo had said that and *her* mother before her.)

"Go wherever he goes. No matter where," counseled Ruthie. "Even ball games. Even if they kill you."

"Don't have children right off," suggested an engaged girl. "Wait a while and enjoy yourself first. But then I'm talking to the air," she decided. "You're Catholic. You'll have one before you're married a year."

"Don't kill yourself washing," was Reenie's contribution to the manual of marriage. "Send your laundry out to the wet wash. So you lose a towel once in a while. What's a towel compared to your health?"

Even the aloof, luscious, red-haired Marie came through with something. "Don't let yourself run down after you're married," she said. "Keep your hair curled and dress up every night like you had a date."

Mr. Prentiss caught the fever of advice-giving and contributed a thought. "I understand you're going to take the plunge," he said in his likable unoriginal way. "Well, look before you leap," he advised. "But on the other hand he who hesitates is lost." He took off his glasses. "Sometimes I think it's better," he looked away from her as he talked, "to shut your eyes, take the plunge and hope for the best. Only I wish you weren't leaving," he blurted out.

The look of pleasure that spread over her face frightened him into thinking he had said too much. His mother would consider that too personal a remark to address to an employee. "What I mean," he amended, "is that I hate to see any of my girls leave. It's so hard to break in new ones."

He didn't fool Margy. She knew he was sorry she was being married. He had to be because that worked in with her dreams. She had a romantic feeling about him. Now that she was soon to marry another man the romantic feeling seemed sinful and more exciting. She thought again of that poem of grammar-school days—the girl raking hay on a summer day and the rich judge riding by and the refrain: "It might have been."

Listen to me! Margy chided herself scornfully. It could never be. Only in books do girls marry the boss. He's way above me—college and all. Besides, he's too old; past thirty. Then there's always his mother. But it's nice the way he has a saying for everything. That's the benefit of a good education. (And if I have a son, he's going to Fordham.) Mr. Prentiss would be a good father, I guess—

127

the way he's so patient. He'll make the right girl a good husband someday—providing he doesn't wait too long. He'd be the first to say that time and tide waits for no man. He sure makes it wait for him, though. Poor Mr. Prentiss! He's so darn decent.

Chapter 18

The Malones made no special preparation for Margy's visit. Frankie had mentioned that he knew a girl he'd like to bring to the house. His mother looked at him sharply but said nothing. Patsy urged his son to bring the girl around so's he could give her the once-over. "Don't bring her if she's bow-legged, though," he said. Everyone in the family thought this was very funny except Frankie.

The night of her visit, the house was the same as usual; helter-skelter, everyone rushing around and Malone studying the undertaking business. Frankie had asked his mother whether she was going to fix up the house a little for the visit and she had asked: "What for? It isn't as though you were going to marry the girl." She waited. It was his chance to tell he was engaged. But he just didn't have the nerve.

They were not at all constrained in their greetings of Margy. The old man gave her a slow looking over and decided she had a nice shape—or would have if she ever filled out. Mrs. Malone took one look at her, settled herself more firmly in her corsets and prepared to do battle for her only son. After the pleased-to-meet-you's and the like-wises of the introductions, the sisters went about their preparation for the evening. Cathleen kept running into the parlor and asking Frankie whether her slip showed and Noreen asked him to "button her up in the back."

"How come I rate all this?" asked Frankie. "Other days they pass me up like a bundle of dirty wash. But now, all of a sudden, I'm important around here. How come?"

Margy knew how come. The Malones were letting her know that Frankie was their property and no outsider stood a chance. The conversation consisted mostly of Mrs.

Malone reminiscing with her son, with explanatory asides to Margy.

"Remember that time, Frankie, when you and me went to St. John's to plant geraniums on your grandfather's plot?" In an aside to Margy: "He always goes with me no matter where I want to go."

"Don't let's get off on me, Ma," protested Frankie.

"He don't want me to tell certain things," hinted his mother. She turned on him again. "Frankie, whatever became of that pretty little girl you was so crazy about?" she asked. Aside to Margy: "He's very fickle."

"Love 'em and leave 'em is his motter," said Mr. Malone.

"And that other girl," she went on, "the one whose father had means. She was the athletic type. I really worried over that one. She got very serious about Frankie."

"Now, Ma, you're only saying that. I hardly knew those girls."

"And Irma! I bet you she's sitting on the stoop this minute waiting for you."

"Ma's making all this up," he explained to Margy.

Margy smiled painfully but said gaily, "My! I didn't know you were so popular."

"I'm not! I don't like girls," he blurted out.

"I don't see Miss Shannon wearing pants," observed Malone. "Or maybe I'm not supposed to see." He laughed heartily.

"You don't like me to give you away to your new girl friend, do you Frankie?" said Mrs. Malone. Aside to Margy: "He wants you to think that you're the one and only."

This is what Reenie would call getting needled, thought Margy. She knew that Frankie had not yet told his mother of their plans. She put her left hand on Frankie's knee intending that Mrs. Malone notice the engagement ring. Mrs. Malone's eyes flicked to the ring and back again to Frankie's face.

"Frankie, tell her about that time you was almost engaged to that girl what was older than you," suggested Mrs. Malone.

Frankie lifted Margy's hand and drew her left arm through his as they sat on the davenport side by side. He gripped her hand tightly. "Ma, Margy and I are thinking of . . ." he swallowed hard.

"Frankie and I are going to be married," said Margy clearly and suddenly.

"No!" exploded Mr. Malone.

"Yes!" said Frankie. "I hope there's no law against it."

"Keep your teeth in your mouth," threatened Malone casually. By this time, Mrs. Malone had recovered somewhat from the announcement.

"Married?" repeated Mrs. Malone. She laughed heartily. "What could he gain by getting married?"

"*You* know," suggested Malone slyly. His wife ignored him.

"Why should he tie himself down?" she continued. "Home, he has his own room. A married man has to share a room with his wife."

"And bed," added Malone, his thoughts turning easily to the salacious.

"I cook what he likes. A wife would cook what she likes and he'd have to eat it even if it killed him. Here he can stay out till all hours of the night. A wife wouldn't let him get away with that. And he'd have to hand over all his pay, too. Here he gives me just so much and keeps the rest to spend on hisself."

"How much did the ring cost?" asked Malone. But as usual, he was ignored.

"I cook for him," summed up his mother, "wash for him, ask no questions about where he goes. What does he want a wife for? What can a wife give him that I can't give him? Answer me that, Miss Shannon."

"I will," said Margy obligingly. "She can give him children."

"Good for you!" boomed Malone. "That's one on you, Nora," he told his wife.

Suddenly Mrs. Malone's eyes filled with tears. She got up and left the parlor without the conventional "Excuse me." Malone got up and shook hands with his future daughter-in-law. The visit was over.

Her mother asked her how the Malones had taken it. "Well, they were kind of surprised," said Margy. "But they were all right."

However when Reenie asked her about it she said: "It was murder!"

Chapter 19

Flo did no carrying-on as the time for the marriage came near. However she became more quiet and thoughtful and the bitter look on her face subtly changed to a tragic look. Once she urged Margy to wait another year. (You're young, yet. You have your whole life before you.) But Margy didn't want to wait. She was anxious to get started on her new life.

Flo tried to make up for all her sins of omission in those last two months. Painstakingly, she laundered the girl's clothes and foraged far out of her neighborhood for food that was "different" and yet within her means. In a way, Margy longed for the routine meals of ground steak or eggs. They'd make supper seem less sad.

Henny took to staying home nights because Flo almost convinced him that it had been his going out in the evenings that made Margy decide to marry so young. Both parents avoided quarreling in the presence of their daughter. Only hissing whispers in the night behind their closed bedroom door indicated that they pursued the familiar tenor of their lives in private.

They had always meant to be good parents; to make their girl happy. But they had kept putting off the time to start. This is only for now, Flo thought. Someday next week, I'll take time and make something good to eat. Next month I'll buy a new spread for her bed. She's been asking for a pink one for so long. Sometime I must ask her if she has any friends—she must have some—and I'll fix up the house and ask her wouldn't she like to have them here. Next year maybe I can let her get that new winter coat. Maybe Henny might get a raise, then I could let her keep more of her pay.

Tomorrow—next month—next year. Everything was always going to be better in the future. And suddenly the future had come. It was a brief present. Too soon it would merge into a past to be remembered. And now there were two months of the present left. She tried to do everything in that time. She couldn't manage the new coat but she dyed Margy's white seersucker bedspread a pale pink.

December, the month set for the wedding, began to draw in. According to the books Margy read this should have been a happy time; full of anticipation of the ultimate consummation of love, heady with hopes for the future, plans for children, tender with thoughts of how two people who could not live without each other would have each other until life's end.

But it wasn't that way. It was a time of sadness and foreboding. The parents on both sides were unhappy. Both families would miss the financial help of their children. But they were used to economic deprivation and would adjust themselves to it. What saddened most was that the families had counted on marriage lifting their children up out of the environment in which they had been born and reared. Marriage was one of the few chances in the world that the poor had to better themselves.

Flo had no dreams of a knight in shining armor riding by on a white horse to scoop up Margy and set her upon his saddle's pommel with her white chiffon robes floating back in the breeze. She had no such dreams because she had never heard of knights and didn't know what shining armor was. But she had had dreams of the knight's equivalent; a decent man of a better family; a professional man or one in business for himself; one who would set up her daughter in a little house which he owned on Long Island or somewhere not too far from Brooklyn; a house with all the modern conveniences. He would be someone who would give Margy not the luxuries of life but lifelong freedom from grinding want for herself and her children.

Henny felt as Flo did—that Margy should have married someone who'd improve her life. But marriage to Frankie being inevitable, Henny began to have hopeful thoughts about the boy. The Great American Dream had betrayed Henny. But why couldn't it work for Frankie? Henny began to dream of Frankie becoming indispensable to his firm; getting steady increases in salary; working himself up to be one of the bosses. Why not? It had happened before. It could happen again.

Yes, the Great American Dream had betrayed Henny. Sometimes he wondered whether it had ever existed in the first place. But it must have existed sometime in America. There were records—there was history to prove it.

The Dream was this: The important ingredients of wealth, fame and success were backgrounds of poverty, hard work, ambition, rigid honesty and systematic saving. Henny had had the correct ingredients. His folks had been desperately poor; he himself had worked at hard labor since he was a child of twelve. He had been ambitious—had thought of going to night school after the laboring day was over. He had even saved a little money before he married. He had lived as honestly as possible, cheating no fellow-man and giving sixty full minutes of work for every hour's pay he received.

And he had become neither successful, famous or wealthy. In fact, he had become poorer and more obscure with each passing year. So he concluded that the American Dream had faded away into the mists of legends. The Dream had had its heyday, reasoned Henny, about the time of Horatio Alger, the favorite author of his boyhood. The Alger book titles were subtitles of the Dream. *From Rags to Riches*.

And there was the true and golden chronicle of Abraham Lincoln, who had been the poorest of poor boys.

Once in the first days of his marriage he had discussed the Dream with Flo. "What does a man have to do in America," he had asked, half jokingly, "so that he has a chance to turn out like—say Lincoln?"

"He has to sit in a box at the theater and be shot dead by an actor on the stage." They had laughed over the remark. Then Henny had said:

"I'm sunk. I can't afford to buy a box seat at the theater."

It had seemed funny then. But often recalling the little dialogue in later years, he realized how bitter it had been.

But he still believed that Frankie would make good and his daughter would have a comfortable life. He had to believe in *something*, otherwise he would have found the going hard.

Chapter 20

Margy quit her job a week before her wedding. The girls gave her a little party during the lunch hour of her last day. Reenie had started a collection and a committee had spent a Saturday afternoon choosing and buying a box of Rogers' Silverware for a wedding gift. With Miss Barnick's co-operation, Reenie got Margy out of the office while the girls decorated her desk with a white crepe-paper tablecloth and blue crepe-paper swags. A cake with a papier-mâché bride and groom atop was placed on the desk next to the open box of silverware. The crack typist of the office had typed the names of the contributors in red on a wide white satin ribbon which lay, with its notched ends, across the box.

Margy had a hard time acting surprised—having served on a similar committee for Ruthie some months before. But she was genuinely moved and tears flooded her eyes at the thought of leaving the only friends she had ever had.

Mr. Prentiss came to the party—pulling off his glasses as he crossed the room. He declined a piece of cake saying that he seldom indulged in sweets, but he was induced to take a piece home to place under his pillow to dream on.

The publicity department sent a photographer. He took a picture of Margy standing behind her desk cutting the cake, Miss Barnick on her right, Mr. Prentiss, sans glasses, on her left and all the girls grouped behind. The picture was for the house organ but they promised Margy a print.

Half an hour before closing time, Mr. Prentiss told Margy she was "fired." That was the traditional way of giving an employee who left in good standing time for individual farewells. Margy went to each girl's desk and the good-by was the same with each as it had been with former office brides and Margy.

"So you're leaving us, Margy?"

"Yes."

"I don't blame you. This dump!"

"Oh, I like the office. It's just that I'm getting married."

"I know!" Sigh. "Well, I wish you luck."

"Maybe I'll need it." Margy smiled.

"There's many a true word spoken in a joke."

"Gloomy Gus. That's you."

"I suppose we'll never see you here again."

"Oh, sure. I'm coming back to see you girls."

"Yeah? They all say that but they never come back."

"But I mean it," vowed Margy. "And you must come see me when I'm settled."

"It's a promise!"

"Well . . ." There was a clumsy pause.

"See you in church," promised the girl.

"That's no lie," said Margy. "I expect you to come see me married."

"I'll be there with my hair in a braid."

Again the pause. Something more needed to be said—something important; something that could be remembered for always. But neither had the words.

"Well, it was nice knowing you," said Margy.

"What do you mean *was*? You still know me."

"I mean . . ."

"Sure, I know what you mean, Margy. Likewise."

"Well . . . good-by."

"Don't say good-by."

"So long, then."

"So long. I'll be seeing you."

So many brides had promised to come back for a visit but few did. Occasionally one would come back after the honeymoon, glowing and happy, and dressed in trousseau finery. She never repeated the visit. A year later, the girl who had been her closest friend at the office might receive a birth announcement. The friend would collect nickels and dimes from the other girls and a silver-plated baby spoon would be sent to the infant. No announcements came of subsequent babies. Years later in the washroom, one of the older girls would muse:

"Whatever became of Ray?"

"Didn't you ever hear?" another girl would reply. "She's living in Elmhurst. I heard they have three children and are paying on their home."

"Well I'm glad it turned out all right." Then the girl was forgotten.

Margy's farewell with Marie the office beauty was brief.

"You can always get your old job back if things don't turn out right," suggested Marie. "Let me know and I'll put in a good word for you with Prentiss."

"Things will turn out fine," said Margy.

"I hope so," said the beauty without conviction. "I certainly hope so."

Margy, made important by her coming status of matron, dared to speak intimately to Marie. "I'm surprised," she said, "that we didn't lose you long ago—with your looks and all."

"I'm not in any hurry," said Marie. "I'm waiting for Mr. Right to come along."

"I thought Mr. Prentiss was Mr. Right," said Margy daringly.

"Don't be sil'," drawled Marie.

Margy felt very happy. Of course she knew she was nothing to Mr. Prentiss but she had his interests at heart and she'd certainly hate to see such a nice man married to such a cold, conceited girl like Marie.

Mr. Prentiss shook hands warmly. He told Margy that Welcome was written on the mat for her and that the latchstring was always out. Finally he admonished her not to buy any wooden nutmegs. Margy could tell the parting affected him. He had used three sayings in one sentence!

Since Reenie was to be bridesmaid, there was no farewell scene with her. Margy folded the ribbon with the names typed on it and put it in the box with the silverware. She took home three pieces of cake for Frankie and her parents and the girls let her have the papier-mâché bridal couple.

Chapter 21

Wayne Prentiss did not sleep on the cake. But he dreamed. He woke up in the middle of the night out of the dream. It had been a nice dream. He couldn't understand why he woke up feeling uneasy.

In his dream, his mother was a different kind of woman. She was strong, not frail. And she was wise instead of cute. In the dream, she was friend and mother to Margy, Reenie, Marie and Ruthie and the other girls in his office. There was always one or the other, usually Marie or Margy, in the house. His mother brooded over them and tried to solve their little problems. And the girls loved her and confided in her. And he felt happy and unbound.

Yes, it had been a pleasant dream. He couldn't understand why he was so disturbed about it. He switched on his bedside light, got up, went over to the closet and got his cigarettes out of his coat. He went to the window and stood there smoking. He looked down on the deserted tree-lined street. In the nighttime it had a glamor and a mystery that it never held in the daytime.

He finished the cigarette and went back to his bed. As his hand went out to the light chain, he heard the click of the light going on in his mother's room across the hall. His first instinct was to complete the act of turning off his light, getting back into bed and pretending to be asleep. But he didn't have it in him to deceive anyone.

He was again at the window when she came in. He had moved as far away from his bed as he could simply because he didn't want to have a sitting-side-by-side-on-the-bed talk. She wore a lavender flower-sprigged dimity dressing gown with lace at the neck and wrists. All her clothes were made by an old-time neighborhood dressmaker according to Mrs. Prentiss' designs. All carried out the mood of a lovely and gracious lady of a bygone time.

"What is it, son?"

"Nothing."

"But you can't sleep."

"I slept."

"A dream wakened you."

"Yes."

"Was it a bad dream?"

"No. It was a very nice dream."

"Tell me."

"I've already forgotten it," he lied. She sat on his bed. "Remember," she said, "when you were a little boy and cried out in your sleep I'd come to you and tell you a story?"

"I remember."

"It was a story of a boy with a selfish sweetheart. The sweetheart demanded that the boy bring her his mother's heart as a proof of love. And the foolish boy cut out his mother's heart and ran with it to his sweetheart. But he stumbled and fell and the mother heart spoke and said: 'Are you hurt, my son?' "

"Yes, I remember the story."

"But you're too grown up now to be soothed by a story."

"Yes."

Yes! Yes, yes, yes. Always yes. Everything she asks me, he thought, I answer, yes.

"There's *something* wrong," she said. "I won't be able to sleep all night worrying about you."

"It's nothing, Mother. I had a heavy day at the office, I guess. I thought a cigarette would calm me down. That's all."

"You're keeping something from me."

"Nonsense!" he said firmly. He took her hand. "Come now. I want you to get your beauty sleep." He took her to the door of her room and kissed her cheek.

He went back to bed and turned out the light. He lay awake a long time. Then he began drifting into sleep. He lay face down and spoke into his pillow. "I hate you, Mother," he whispered fiercely. "I hate you!"

And in the morning, he couldn't remember whether he had actually said that horrible thing or whether he had dreamed he said it.

Chapter 22

Frankie and Margy rented a one-room, bath and kitchenette apartment on Bushwick Avenue. It had a Murphy bed which was a break as it saved them the cost of buying a bed. It upset Flo's plans, however. The bedspread she was working on would not be needed since the Murphy bed folded into the wall. So she took her many years' collection of Lion Brand Condensed Milk wrappers, tied with thread in rolls of fifty, and redeemed them for a set of dishes—with violet sprays and a gold band around the edge of the plates. The china looked beautiful on the kitchenette shelf.

They missed the furniture sale at Batterman's but a store on Graham Avenue sold them a three-piece livingroom suite on time—dark green wicker with bright cretonne cushions. They bought a gate-legged table painted to look like mahogany and two straight chairs to match. Margy set a black glass bowl on the center of the table and filled it with artificial red roses. She thought it looked beautiful. Flo let Margy have the dresser from her bedroom at home. A secondhand porcelain-topped kitchen table and two white chairs completed the furnishings.

Aside from the black bowl there were a few other artistic touches. Margy's pride was a fringed tapestry, the newest thing in home decorations, tacked up on the wall behind the table. It was a medieval hunting scene. It was a nice tapestry only the seam down the center was not quite straight which made the upper half of the huntsman's hand an inch forward from the lower part. Flo pointed out the defect saying: "You got skinned." Margy explained that the defect had been brought to her attention before purchase and the price reduced accordingly.

Two pictures hung on the wall; a framed lithograph of

the "Weeping Magdalene" with her Titian hair and blue robe, and Gainsborough's "Blue Boy." Margy loved blue.

A cedar hope chest, the gift of Frankie, stood between the two windows. Reenie's wedding present, a French doll, with its exaggerated legs tied in knots, sat on the hope chest propped against cushions that almost matched the furniture upholstery. When asked, Flo agreed that the chest *could* pass for a window seat.

After a thorough inspection of the apartment and a dire prophecy that cockroaches would come in from the people upstairs and bedbugs from the people downstairs, Flo pronounced the apartment "very mod-dren and up-to-date in the bargain." Henny said nothing. But he was proud. Already Margy was doing better. An apartment was a step up from the flat.

Margy spent her evenings there that last week, fixing it up. Reenie and Ruthie met her there one night by appointment. The girls examined the place with squeals of delight.

"It's the nuts," was Reenie's judgment. "I wish it was Sal's and mine."

"Someday," soothed Margy. "Someday."

"And a private bath!" Ruthie exclaimed. "Your intended must be coining money."

"I intend to *live* in that bathtub," said Margy.

". . . and soak your troubles away," sang Reenie.

"It's smoke your troubles away," corrected Ruthie.

"I think it's sing your troubles away."

"It's soak!"

"It's smoke!"

"It's hoke!" clinched Margy.

They started to laugh. They laughed and laughed and couldn't stop. "What are we laughing at?" they asked each other gaspingly. They didn't know. They were too young to know that they were laughing for no other reason than that they *were* young.

Chapter 23

A few nights before the wedding, Flo spoke to her daughter in the dubious privacy of Margy's bedroom. She said, "Being as you're getting married, there is things you ought to know." Then she blushed painfully.

"I know them, Mama," said Margy gently.

"Oh, you do, do you?" Suspicion flared up in Flo like excelsior to which a match had been applied. "So you've been running around," came the instant accusation. "And all the while I'm sitting home alone thinking you're a good girl, and all the while behind my back . . ."

"No. It's just that the girls at the office . . . well, we talk about those things."

"Fine company you keep! Telling dirty stories when you should be tending to your work. When I was a girl . . ."

"Mama, I'd drop dead if you ever stopped scolding me. I'd be that surprised. So save my life and don't ever change."

"All I was trying to do was what a mother should do—see that her daughter keeps out of trouble . . . tell her things."

"I know. And it's all right, Mom." She kissed her mother on the cheek.

Both were intensely relieved; the mother to sidestep a painful duty and the daughter to be spared the embarrassment of her mother's fumbling sex instructions.

Margy bought a long-sleeved white dress. "A fine wedding dress it will make," the saleswoman assured her. "And after, you can shorten the skirt and dye it navy blue and wear it for everyday."

Margy shuddered. She had had enough of navy blue to

last a lifetime and, God willing, hoped she'd have no more of it.

She couldn't afford to buy a veil. Reenie went with her to rent one. There was a store on Moore Street whose brightly lighted window displayed wax dummies dressed in bridal garb. A life-sized, tuxedo-dressed dummy, whose doll's face sported a smirking mustache, linked arms stiffly with a waxen bride. A bridesmaid who had lost a wooden foot—the loss concealed by her long pink tulle dress—leaned drunkenly against a cardboard facsimile of an altar.

The girls stared at the display like two little kids staring at Christmas dolls. "That's for me," said Reenie, "when—I mean if—I marry Sal." She referred to the bridal gown. "With a train and all. You could have rented that, Margy."

"I want to own the dress I get married in," said Margy. "I want to keep it for remembrance. It will be nice for when my daughter marries. It will be cute and old fashioned when she marries."

"Listen to her!" said Reenie to an imaginary companion. "A daughter already and she's not even married yet."

"A person has to look ahead," said Margy. "No sin in that. And you can be godmother."

"Remember now. You promised!"

Margy and Frankie went to their prenuptial confession late Saturday afternoon. After supper, Frankie brought his parents and oldest sister, Cathleen, over to meet the Shannons. (Malone was in his civilian clothes.) Frankie brought Marty along, too. Marty was Cathleen's fiancé and would be Frankie's best man at the wedding.

After the boisterous, falsely gay flush of introductions and acknowledgments, the menfolk went out together to rent their outfits for the morrow's wedding. Then Reenie came over. After Cathleen and Mrs. Malone had grudgingly made her acquaintance, Reenie went out with Margy to do some last-minute shopping. Flo was left alone with the two Malone women.

She didn't like either one of them. Cathleen Malone, irritatingly called "Cat'leen" by her mother, was gaudily dressed, heavily made up, sullen and unsociable. Flo classified her as a skinny, snappy flapper.

Poor Cat'leen had reason to brood. Not only did she resent the loss of Marty's company for the evening but she was furious because she had not been asked to stand up for the bride in company with Marty. But Margy had to pick out that Reenie! She hated Reenie. It often happened that the best man and bridesmaid started going around together—their romance getting off to a head start in the hothouse intimacy of a wedding meeting. If Reenie so much as smiled at Marty tomorrow. . . . Cat'leen clenched her hands. And that Margy! She had deliberately arranged the whole thing to get Marty for Reenie. So Cat'leen sulked the evening away.

The future mothers-in-law had hated each other before they met. They engaged in many little skirmishes throughout the evening but blood was drawn only once.

"Your girl is certainly getting a good man."

"And what do you think your boy is getting?" asked Mrs. Shannon. "I'd say he was lucky."

"I didn't mean nothing out of the way," said Mrs. Malone. "But you don't know how a mother feels."

"Why don't I? I happen to be a mother myself," said Flo.

Mrs. Malone tried to explain. "Here's the way it is: Your daughter might be a good girl for all I know."

"She *is* a good girl," said Mrs. Shannon. "And you know it."

"I have nothing against your daughter. I would feel the same no matter who my son married. Even if she had a million dollars in her own name."

"I wouldn't," said Flo. "I'd feel a whole lot different if my daughter married a millionaire. Not that I have anything against Frankie. But you're a mother—like you said. And you can understand how another mother feels."

Cat'leen yawned.

Marty, taking his job as best man seriously, took charge of the costume-renting expedition. He steered the three men to a store on Seigel Street which had a sign in the window: COSTUMES SUPPLIED FOR THEATRICALS, MASQUERADES AND WEDDINGS. In no time flat, the overanxious proprietor got the boys into satin-lapelled tuxedos and the two fathers into striped pants, swallow-tailed coats and ready-made, on-an-elastic, black, satin, puff ties.

The boys looked handsome in their tuxedos but Frankie

demurred at the white lawn tie supplied, insisting that black ties went with tuxedos. The merchant had an answer to that.

"You are a smart fellow to know that," he granted. "But you're not smart enough to know that weddings is different. White ties is the style. You want people should laugh when you stand up in your church in a black tie? No, my friend. For funerals is black ties the style. But not for weddings."

The fit of Henny's suit was far from perfect. The trouser bottoms hardly came an inch below the tops of his high laced shoes. The sleeves exposed his wristbones and made the hands coming out of the smooth, pressed, black cloth seem alien. The man assured Henny that the stiff detachable cuffs supplied with each "rental" would fix that up. Henny asked what would fix up the shortness of the pants. The man said the pants were of the right length to give him "hi'th."

Derby hats went with the rentals. The boys drew hats that fitted well enough but Malone's was too small for his big head and Henny's was too round for his narrow oval head. The resourceful proprietor made Henny's hat fit by inserting strips of toilet tissue under the sweatband—he kept a roll under the counter for such emergencies. He couldn't stretch Malone's hat. So he told him that he surmised men didn't wear hats in *their* church. "And on the street, who looks? And if they look, you can carry the hat in your hand."

The four stared at themselves in the triple mirror. "The Harmony Four," decided Malone. "We look like a goddamned quartet.

"All together now, fellers. Let's harmonize," he suggested. "Mee—mee," he ventured tentatively, then broke into the opening lines of "Shine on, Harvest Moon." Marty and Frankie joined in. Henny stood silent. He always felt ill at ease in the presence of exuberance or exhibitionism.

The costume renter beamed. "Good times I like to see in my store," he said.

While the three were harmonizing, Henny came to his decision. He announced it at the end of the song. "I ain't going to do it," he stated flatly.

"What? Do what?" asked Frankie, worried.

"Wear this monkey suit tomorrow."

"You look swell in it," boomed Mr. Malone. "Like J. P. Vanderbilt himself."

"That's a lie."

"What are you kicking about?" asked Malone, surveying his bulk in the mirrors. "We're all in the same boat. I don't look so hot myself. But who gives a damn?"

Henny was adamant to begging, threatening and coaxing. He had made up his mind that he wouldn't be found dead in that outfit. He formulated a personal declaration of independence. "I was born a workingman," he said, "and I'll die a workingman."

"I'm a workingman, myself," admitted Malone. "And I don't see what that's got to do with anything."

"As a workingman I've been shoved around a lot in my time but nobody's going to shove me into that outfit tomorrow. I won't dress up like no horse's ass for nobody."

The simile was so terrifying in its finality that they gave up trying to persuade him. Malone decided that Shannon was shy a few marbles and he felt sorry for his son, getting into that kind of a family.

Henny changed his mind as the outfits were being boxed. He had a thought of how upset Margy would be if he wasn't dressed properly for the wedding. He thought of his wife's reproaches. He decided it was better to look like a fool than to go through a lot of emotionalism. He told the man to wrap up his outfit, too. The three men took turns pounding him on the back in gratitude.

The rental fee was exacted in advance and a deposit collected—"So that you should return the garments in good condition and not spill nothing on them." Henny insisted that they get a receipt for their money. (He was receipt conscious ever since he lost that victrola handle years ago.) As the proprietor complied, Frankie complimented Henny on his business acumen and Marty said that Mr. Shannon sure knew his onions all right. Henny modestly replied that all he knew was what his rights were.

The quartet adjourned to a chain shoe store on Broadway where the two young men were effectively shod in paper-thin, patent-leather oxfords at three ninety-eight a pair.

"They're the cat's meow," said Marty, admiring his outthrust twinkling feet.

"You said it," agreed Frankie.

"Very, very snappy," was Mr. Malone's comment.

"But can you wear them for work after?" asked Henny.

The boys tried to inviegle Mr. Shannon into buying a pair but he said, "I got a pair of black oxfor' ties will do in a pinch and boy, do they pinch!" He laughed heartily.

On the way home they came to a store with a curtain across the window but with lights behind the curtain glowing through the dull red stuff and making it look gypsyish. A neatly printed sign said: CIDER STORE. NOTHING STRONGER. DON'T ASK FOR IT! Malone interpreted the sign correctly. "Let's go in for a beer," he said.

They walked through the store proper where a lot of flappers and cake eaters were sitting at round tables covered with rumpled red-checked tablecloths and drinking mugs of cider through straws. A nickel-in-the-slot piano was tinkling out, "Yes, We Have No Bananas." They went through a door into a large back room equipped with round saloon tables and chairs to match, a bar with a soaped-mirror backdrop, and a white-aproned, shirt-sleeved bartender.

Over the mirror was a sign which read: IN GOD WE TRUST. ALL OTHERS PAY CASH. Under the sign were two hairy coconuts tied together with a neatly lettered card crediting Brigham Young with ownership.

Mr. Malone stared at the display and Frankie cringed when his father went closer to read the card under the coconuts. Frankie tensed himself in preparation for some dirty remark from his father. But all that Patsy said was:

"Guy runs this place is losing time. He could be an expert sign writer."

"You said it," agreed Henny.

They had four needle beers at a quarter a glass. Malone laid down a dollar and after waiting a second to see if his father would add a tip, Frankie put a dime on the bill. They toasted the bride and groom in the beer. Malone waited for Henny to treat to the next round. Henny had his next week's carfare and lunch money in his pocket. He held back a while. Then he decided what the hell, let next week take care of itself. He bought the second round and gave the bartender a quarter tip. Frankie bought the third and they looked to Marty to buy the fourth, but he had spent all his money accumulating his best-man outfit. He rapped on the table and said, "I pass." Malone thought that was very comical.

When the bartender came over, thinking the rap was a call, Patsy Malone asked him whether he had anything stronger than doped-up beer. As the bartender hesitated, Malone added: "This here young feller's putting his head in the rope tomorrow and we'd like to cheer him up."

Henny turned that remark over in his mind. He was in a pleasant glow from the beers. He knew he should resent the remark but he decided to be broad-minded and let it pass.

The bartender produced a pint of dark turgid liquor "just off the boat." They drank it with beer chasers. Henny started to brood over the rope remark. He decided instantly that the wedding was entirely on Margy's side with the Malones a necessary evil attached to it. Margy was the one putting her neck in the noose if you asked him.

Malone got a little high and began telling dirty premarital jokes. Henny got more resentful. Like many fathers to whom a loved daughter still seemed an innocent little girl child, he was revolted by the thought of her in physical intimacy with a man.

Frankie resented the jokes, too, but for a different reason. Since the time when as a child he had been told by some boys on the street that he owed his being on earth to physical relations between his father and mother, sex talk coming from either of his parents had nauseated him.

Marty was the only one who laughed at the jokes. He tried to top one of them out of his own meager experience. While Malone laughed loudly at Marty's anecdote, he filed away the conclusion in the back of his mind that Marty was too dirty minded to be allowed to go around with his innocent daughter, Cat'leen.

Frankie suggested that what they all needed was a brisk walk home in the frosty air to sober them up. They left the place, but the flighty Marty had to go back after a block because he had left his outfit in the speakeasy. They walked slowly, waiting for Marty to catch up to them. Henny kept brooding over the impropriety of the rope remark and getting angrier at the dirty stories Malone had told with Margy in mind. He boiled over while they waited at a street intersection for Marty.

"Malone, you got a big mouth," he announced out of a clear sky.

"Come again?" requested Patsy Malone politely. By this time Marty had joined them. "He said I had a big mouth," Malone told Marty, as though anxious that the boy not be left out of anything.

"A big, *dirty* mouth," amended Henny.

"Shannon, you asked for it," said Malone and swung. He missed by a mile. His fist swung in a circle and hit his own shoulder. The two boys caught him to prevent his falling as he went off balance.

Henny put his box down on the sidewalk. He took off his overcoat, folded it neatly, put his hat on top of it and took a fighting stance. Marty grabbed Henny's arm while Frankie held his father back. Malone was glad to be held back.

Marty got out oil for the troubled waters. "Now, Mr. Shannon, you wouldn't go and hit an old man, would you?"

"No, I would't hit him," said Henny mildly, "I'd just beat the b'Jesus out of him."

"You'd beat an old man with kidney trouble?" asked Malone incredulously.

"You wouldn't be on the force with kidney trouble," said Henny.

"I'm retiring next year," said Patsy quickly.

Henny decided to be fair. "Which side is your bum kidney on?" he asked. "So's I can wallop you on the other side."

"Now, Shannon," said Patsy calmly, "if I said anything out of the way, I'm sorry I said it."

"If!" sneered Henny. "*If!* You know damned well you said plenty out of the way."

Malone rearranged his apology. "If I said anything that you could take up to be out of the way, I'm sorry."

"I didn't have to take up nothing. It *was* out of the way. My daughter's an innocent, decent girl and no man's going to tell dirty jokes with her in mind while I'm around."

"So I'm a son-of-a-bitch," acknowledged Malone graciously. "And I don't blame you for trying to take a swipe at me. I'd do the same if it was my daughter, Cat'leen. Let me tell you a purer girl never. . . ." He stopped.

149

Suddenly he remembered the dirty story Marty had told. He was sure that the boy had Cat'leen in mind at the time. His eyes sought out Marty.

"You sow," he said. "You holy sow!" He lunged at the boy.

The astonished groomsman jumped behind Henny for protection. "What's biting you?" he asked of his future father-in-law.

Frankie, taking a firmer grip on his father's arm, now spoke up. "Thanks," he said bitterly. "Thanks for the swell send-off you're giving me on my wedding eve."

Malone came to his senses. "Excuse me, son," he said. "I guess I got a little out of line. But I didn't mean nothing by it."

Henny was instantly ashamed. He sort of liked Frankie and he figured the boy wasn't to blame for what his father said and did. "I'm too hot headed, myself," he apologized. He held out his hand grudgingly. Malone shook it warmly.

Henny was cold sober when he got home. After putting his cutaway and striped pants on a hanger, he went into his sleeping daughter's bedroom. He stood looking down on her in the faint light from the street lamp. He wished that they had the habit of talking intimately together; that he had the gift of articulation; that he could tell her what he thought in such a way that she'd know he spoke the truth purely. If only there was that communication between them he could wake her up and tell her not to marry on the morrow; that somehow there would be a miracle in the home; it would change into something wonderful that she couldn't bear to leave while she was still so young; that a man more mature, more tender, wiser, more worthy of her would materialize someday.

Still, if he could, he wouldn't tell her those things because he knew in his heart they could never happen.

Her white wedding dress, luminous in the faint light, hung on its wire hanger from the central light fixture. The veil was neatly folded on a chair and the little white satin slippers peeped in eager readiness from under the bed. His eyes went to the dresser top and clung to the objects arranged in an orderly row there; the white prayer book (he recalled buying it for her when she had made her first communion); the small white-beaded child's rosary; a beruffled and beribboned blue garter; a lace-edged handkerchief.

> *Something old, something new;*
> *Something borrowed, something blue.*

The aged incantation was meant to ensure a happy marriage. The old prayer book, the new dress, the borrowed handkerchief and the garter of clearest blue—she had gathered the sacrificial items to appease whatever pagan god of marriage might still ride the winds of night. (Only she called it being superstitious.)

She slept peacefully, the carefully made waves of her freshly washed hair protected by a blue net. (She always liked blue, Henny thought in the past tense.) Her cold-creamed hands were growing softer and smoother through the night in the old kid gloves she wore. He looked at her closely.

The father saw only a bright-haired child playing with clothespins.

He went out and sat in the dark kitchen. After a while Flo came and sat with him. She sat quietly, saying nothing. Clumsily and fearing a rebuff, he reached out and took her hand in his.

She did not pull it away.

Chapter 24

Margy stuffed the pillows and blanket away in the closet and smoothed the sheets on the Murphy bed in order to lay out Frankie's clothes on the bed. She unfolded a white shirt and looked at it ruefully as she smoothed it out. She had put in a lot of time ironing that shirt and still it didn't look right.

"I wish I could get a job in a laundry for a while," she said.

"What?" asked Frankie from the bathroom where he was shaving.

"I mean just long enough to get on to the secret of ironing shirts."

The running water stopped. Frankie appeared in the bathroom doorway. His face was neatly lathered with a dark O in the middle of the white foam. This was his mouth.

"What'd you say?" he asked.

"Nothing," she answered.

He waited. He thought he looked comical with his face lathered and he waited for Margy to tell him he looked just like Santa Claus. His mother always made that remark when she saw his face that way and the family laughed. But Margy's mind was on the ineptly ironed shirt. She was deciding to let the Chinese laundry do up one shirt and she'd use it as a model in ironing. It would be ten cents well spent, she figured, and she could enter it into her little budget book under "Educational Purposes." She looked up and wondered what he was waiting for.

"Red or blue tie today?" she asked.

"What? Oh, I don't care." He went back into the bathroom.

She laid out her favorite tie, navy blue with white polka dots, and two fresh handkerchiefs—a white one for his pants pocket and a blue-and-white-striped-border one for his coat pocket. She added a pair of socks that almost matched the color of the border of the handkerchief. She surveyed the neat display. Something was missing.

"Did you put on clean shorts this morning?" she called.

The water turned on suddenly in the middle of the sentence and she knew he hadn't heard. She stepped into the bathroom and noticed that he had put on yesterday's shorts. She raised her voice above the sound of the water. "I'll lay out clean shorts for you."

"What?" he asked. She didn't repeat the remark, knowing that he had heard and that his "what?" before answering was a nervous habit. He said:

"These are clean. I only put them on yesterday."

"Put fresh ones on, anyway."

"Why? Who sees?"

"Nobody"—with a grin—"I hope." She waited until he returned her grin. "It's only that it will make you feel like a better man."

"But it makes extra washing for you."

"So what? I like to have a lot to do. The day doesn't seem so long, then."

"Now don't start that about going back to work," he warned.

"Why I never said . . . all right, Frankie, I won't."

"I'll put on clean shorts," he conceded.

He bent over the washbasin to lave cool water on his freshly shaven face. His thin bent back, showing a row of small spine bones, made him look helpless and vulnerable. Impulsively she put an arm about his waist and placed a kiss on his back. He straightened up. She looked at him in the mirror and saw that his face had an embarrassed, uneasy look on it.

"Now, Margy," he said in apprehensive protest.

"Let me," she murmured. She put her other arm about his waist, held him tightly and laid her cheek against his bare back.

He stood rigidly suffering the embrace. Finally he said, "I'll be late for work." She released him then and he went into the living room and got into his shirt.

She often wondered why he was so embarrassed by a

caress; why his lovemaking had to be done in the deep of the night and in furtive whispers. Sometimes she'd ask, "But who can hear us?" He'd put his hand over her mouth and whisper, "Sh!" In the daytime if she so much as kissed his cheek, he looked around uneasily as though the walls of the room had eyes to see and lips to jeer.

Ah, well, thought Margy, turning her head away as he got into clean shorts (because he didn't like her to see him wholly or semi-naked), there's always a reason for the way a person is. When he was a child his father and mother must have acted funny about love—like it was only something to make sly, off-color jokes about. Yes, I can imagine. Because Mr. Malone is still that way. And then, I guess that the kids he played with on the street talked about people being married as though it was something dirty.

Of course, she reasoned, most kids hear the same kind of talk on the streets. Some it doesn't affect. Others grow up always feeling there's something nasty. . . .

Frankie broke into her thoughts. "I wouldn't want to be late now," he said.

"You won't be," she assured him. "I'm going to the baker's right now for the buns."

"Well, Mrs. Malone, what can I do for you this morning?" inquired the cheerful baker.

"Let's see: I'll have three buns, a crumb, a coconut and, yes, a jelly doughnut."

He put the crumb bun and the doughnut in the bag. "The coconut. Is for you?" he inquired. She nodded. He made a careful choice of a round bun with shreds of toasted coconut imbedded in the icing. "Always it's that way," he remarked. "Two for the husband, one for the woman."

She stopped at the corner delicatessen for a pint of milk. "You didn't bring no empty bottle," said the woman.

"I forgot."

"So I got to charge you two cents deposit."

"Okay. I'll bring two bottles back tomorrow."

"And make sure they're from this store."

Why does she have to be so fresh about it, thought Margy.

When she got back the bed was folded up in the wall and Frankie, dressed, was pacing the floor nervously.

"I'll be late."

"You've got time. Table's set, coffee's done."

He sat down. She placed the buns on a plate and started to spoon off the inch of cream from the top of the bottle of milk.

"I'd as soon have condensed milk," he said.

She got the can from the icebox and removed the paper plugs from the two holes.

"Don't bother putting it in a pitcher. I'm late enough as it is," he fretted. He poured the thick stuff direct from the can into his coffee.

"It's only that I want us to live nice," explained Margy.

"I know. But I got no time to wait."

Margy, waiting for her coffee to cool, pulled the label off the can and put it in the table drawer. Soon she'd have enough labels for something.

"Don't you want me to fry you an egg?" she asked. "You work hard all day and only a sandwich for lunch."

"Coffee and rolls is all I want." He ate rapidly, she ate slowly. "My mother made oatmeal every morning," he said.

"Would you like me to fix you some oatmeal tomorrow morning?"

"No. I didn't say I liked oatmeal. I just said my mother made it."

"Oh!"

He got up to put on his coat. She swallowed the last of her coffee and stood up to tuck the handkerchief in his breast pocket.

"Got your money?" she asked. He jingled a few coins in his pocket to prove it.

"See you tonight," he said, as he made for the door.

"You forgot something."

"What?" He looked around the room while he patted his pockets and felt for his handkerchief.

"You forgot to kiss me good-by."

"Oh, Margy," he groaned.

"Suppose one of us died during the day," she said.

He put his arms around her then and pressed his cheek to hers. She held him tightly.

"Please say you love me," she whispered.

"Now don't start that again," he said apprehensively, trying to back away from her, "or I'll be late for sure."

"I was only teasing," she said.

He was touched by the wistful look on her face. "You know I do," he said, and kissed her quickly. "I've got to run now."

"Take good care of yourself—for me," she called down the stairs after him.

Margy had another cup of coffee before she washed and dried the breakfast dishes. She considered mopping the kitchen linoleum but it was clean from the mopping the day before. The cupboard shelves were in perfect order. There was nothing more to do in the kitchenette. She swept and dusted the living room; did her daily laundry in the bathroom—the shirt, shorts, socks and handkerchiefs that Frankie had used the day before, and a slip, brassière, step-ins, handkerchief and pair of stockings of her own. She set the bathroom in order. She looped up a toy clothesline over the tub and pinned up her wash with toy clothespins, thinking how some little girl would go crazy over the line and pins. She repinned a handkerchief to make it hang more evenly. It bothered her when hung-up wash was out of alignment.

It was a quarter to nine and her day's work was done. How could she fill in the rest of the day? She planned her marketing; three lamb chops, two for Frankie, one for her. Three water rolls apportioned in the same way, and a quarter-pound of butter and bunch of carrots. But she wouldn't do her marketing until just before supper. Might as well let the butcher keep my meat on his ice instead of mine, she thought.

Impatient to be doing something, she put up some potatoes to boil. She'd let them get half done, put them in the icebox and cube and fry them for supper the way her mother did. She made a cupful of pastry dough, rolled and trimmed it into three squares and heaped a mince of chopped apple, raisins, cinnamon and sugar on each square, folded them to make bumpy triangles and with a fork, pricked out an F on two and an M on one. Again she thought of a child; how pleased it'd be to have its initial on a turnover. She put them in the icebox planning to pop them into the oven just before Frankie was due home.

The icebox was bare enough; a pint of milk, two tomatoes, a dab of butter, the milk can and ketchup bottle. She wished she could keep it filled but there wasn't enough money to stock up things. She had to buy as she needed. She could save money if she bought in bulk. That much she had learned in the Home Economics course at High. Only the course hadn't taught her how to get enough money ahead to buy in quantity.

She did some figuring on a paper bag. (She often passed time that way as some people do working crossword puzzles or playing solitaire.) Let's see now, she instructed herself. Frankie earns eighty-five a month. Make believe he gets it all at once. Instead of twenty-one something a week. In the first place he could buy a six-dollar meal ticket for five where he eats lunch. That would save two dollars a month. I could buy a bushel of potatoes instead of a dime's worth at a time. Dollar a month saved. Butter is two cents a quarter-pound extra when you don't buy a whole pound. And so on. She totaled her savings on food.

She figured on the insurance. She knew that if she could pay up for a whole year at once it would be cheaper than a quarter a week. The same with the furniture. They could save the carrying charges if they paid it all at once instead of two dollars a week.

Her final figures showed that she could save eight dollars a month if only she had a large enough sum, say a hundred dollars, to start with—enough to live on for a month so that the next month's salary would make another large sum.

Eight a month added up to ninety-six a year. Say nearly a hundred with bank interest. Why they could go to the Catskills when Frankie got his two-weeks' vacation in August. But wait. Suppose they saved that. Why in five years' time they'd have enough to make a down payment on a little semidetached house out in Queens somewhere and they could pay off the rest like rent.

I'll make yellow dotted-Swiss curtains for the kitchen windows, she decided, and paint the cupboards a kind of delft blue.

Listen to me, she admonished herself wryly, furnishing a house I might never have. Still and all, there's no harm in dreaming.

It was ten-thirty and the clothes weren't dry enough to iron. Margy wondered desperately how she could fill up her day. If Frankie would let her go back to work . . . But he got so angry when she suggested it— What? And have people say I can't support my wife? She sighed. She missed the office. Right now the mail would be coming in heavy and the girls would be keyed up but managing to exchange whispers when Miss Barnick was at the other end of the room. The office wedding-party picture hung on the wall next to the cabinet photo of herself and Frankie in their wedding finery. How familiar they all seemed! And how happy she looked standing between the supervisor and Mr. Prentiss and Reenie smiling over her shoulder. Reenie! Suddenly, Margy put her palm over Reenie's pictured face. She wanted to blot out the thought of her for a moment. Reenie and Sal had been living as man and wife for some time now. Margy had a shiver of terror as she wondered what would become of Reenie if she got pregnant and Sal wouldn't marry her.

Eleven o'clock. Margy groaned. No work to do, nothing to read in the house. She had finished *So Big* yesterday. She could return it and get a new book from the library but the library was something for the evening. Frankie liked to go with her and look through back numbers of *Popular Mechanics* while she chose a book.

Earlier in the morning she had wanted to do something but she couldn't remember what. She did remember the warm, excited feeling she'd had about it. She'd been standing by the bed when the idea came to her. She pulled the bed down and pantomimed her morning's activities, hoping to conjure back the memory. Now! I was laying out Frankie's shirt. Shirt! That's it! I was going to take one to the laundry so's I could have a model to iron by. She took the more ineptly ironed shirt from the two in the drawer and took it around to the Chinese Laundry.

"Charlie," she said (his name was really Sing Fung Lee, written as plain as anything on his store window, but everyone called him Charlie). "Charlie, can you get this shirt done for me by Wednesday?"

He examined the shirt carefully as though his answer depended on its texture. Finally he looked up, shook his head sadly and murmured, "Tsch! Tsch!"

"No can do?" she asked loudly in the mistaken belief that a person had to talk loud pidgin English to a Chinese.

"Yiss, mimm," he answered politely. "Can do. But you, no can do. Come. I show."

He opened the door at the back of his store and stood aside to let Margy precede him. She had a quick sensation of terror. All during childhood she had heard stories of how Chinese laundries were fronts for white-slave activities in back rooms. She took a tighter clutch on her loaded purse, ready to use it as a lethal weapon in case of attack, and walked into the back room.

Instantly she felt ashamed of her foolish fears. Two middle-aged Polish matrons were hard at work. One fed collars through the rollers of a machine and the other was ironing a shirt on an oversized ironing board.

She waited with Charlie while he, with timeless patience, stood by the ironing board waiting for the Polish woman to finish the shirt she was working on. He took the finished shirt and with an authoritative nod turned over the shirt that Margy had brought to the ironer. The Polish woman looked up—first at him, then at the girl— and returned the nod. She understood she was to iron the shirt immediately. Margy followed the Chinese to a long, smooth table with pigeonholes of various sizes built above it. He placed the freshly ironed shirt on the table.

"You see how now," he told her.

He put a wooden collar button in the neckband. He buttoned the shirt, skipping the second button, and then turned it bosom side down on the table. He took a piece of cardboard from one of the pigeonholes, placed it on the back of the shirt and folded the shirt over it. He folded the sleeves, drew up the shirttails, tucked in the ends and pinned it to the shoulders.

His movements were slow and precise. He worked with his fingers bent in to his palms and he used his knuckles the way other people used their fingertips. She wondered whether all Chinese used knuckles for fingers or whether

Charlie was the only one. He turned the shirt over, took a narrow strip of blue paper from another pigeonhole, placed it around the shirt, licked a gummed edge to fasten the ends of the blue strip and turned the shirt right side up.

"Perfect!" exclaimed Margy. He bowed. She thought: It's not in the ironing, it's in the folding.

The Polish woman came over and gave him Frankie's shirt—now expertly ironed—and the Chinese went to work on it. This time his movements were so rapid that the whole process of folding was a magician's sleight-of-hand trick. He presented the finished shirt to her and she held it in the crook of her arm as though it were a sheaf of lilies.

"It's beautiful! Just beautiful," she said. Then she asked timidly, "How much?"

"Please," he answered deprecatingly, meaning it would cost nothing.

"But I couldn't let you . . ."

"Please!" he repeated in the same way.

He gave her two of his cardboards and two strips of blue paper. He dropped six wooden collar buttons in her hand. She was pleased and grateful. She wanted to do something for him. She got a dime out of her purse and held it toward him meaning it as a tip. He folded his hands in his wide sleeves and shook his head sadly.

"It was my pleasure," he said, in perfect, unaccented English.

This gave her a shock which changed to acute embarrassment. She was ashamed that she had blundered in offering him a tip. She was embarrassed that she had assumed he knew so little English. She guessed he spoke a pidgin English only because people expected it of him. Flushing, she returned the dime to her purse.

"Well, anyhow, thank you . . ." She tried desperately to remember the name on the window but couldn't recall it. So she compromised with, "Thank you, Mister Charlie. Thank you a whole lot."

He nodded, indicating that she precede him out of the room. She called back a "Thanks" over her shoulder to the Polish woman who had ironed Frankie's shirt. The woman looked up and stared at her heavily but did not give the conventional, "You're welcome," in return. Maybe, thought

Margy, she's the one I should have given the tip to. Oh, well, a person can't know *everything*.

When she got home she pressed the shirt hanging on the line and re-pressed the one left in the drawer. She tried to fold them the way the Chinese had done and after several failures she got the hang of it. She looked at the three shirts in the drawer, delighted at the neat array they made.

She was happy. She had learned to fold shirts just like they did at the laundry. Mixed with her happiness, though, was an alloy of embarrassment. She had tried to *pay* for a friendly favor and she had shouted pidgin English at a man who spoke better English, probably, than she did.

I'm glad I'm not a president's wife. she thought. Just think! All the time they have to decide what's the right thing to do. All the time new things are coming up for them to decide about and lots of those things don't have rules. It must be hard. Very hard. I'm glad I'm me. I'm glad I learned how to fold a shirt decently.

If I never learn anything more in my life, at least I learned that much.

Chapter 25

Margy dressed carefully for her semiweekly visit to her mother. She knew Flo's alert eye would ferret out a missing button, take notice of a baggy skirt or a wrinkled shirtwaist, and she would be quick to deduce that Margy, like so many women after marriage, was "letting herself go."

Margy took a slow walk from Bushwick Avenue over toward Maujer Street. It was a day that presaged spring. The sun shone warmly but there was a nippy wind coming in from the sea. The air smelled like hot sun shining on cold snow. The day was like an Easter Sunday that comes too early in the year. Margy had known many such Easters; sun and wind mixed with sober thoughts of Resurrection. A day too cool for a suit, too warm for a coat.

Margy enjoyed the weather. She thought: It's the feeling of the first straw hat of the season; of a corsage of three dark pink rosebuds tied with silver ribbon to wear to church. It reminds me of the wish I wished when I was very young—that I had a good-looking boy to go to Mass with me and kneel next to me as we took Communion together.

It's the smell and look of weedy Madonna lilies, twenty-five cents for each flower and a dime for each bud on the stalk, set out on the sidewalk in front of a flower store in new pots too small for them. (How I used to want to work in a flower store!) It's the clay smell of new flowerpots and if life itself had a smell, it would smell like new clay flowerpots.

And it's the passing a store window and stopping to look at the white, blue and pink hyacinths and aching all over because you can't afford to lay out fifty cents to buy a hyacinth plant. Yes, this day is like all those days mixed together.

Then there happened one of those things that make people believe in small miracles. She saw a wagon rounding the corner. It was a slow-moving platform of scent and color. It made visual a hundred times over the things she had been thinking about. Small fir trees with burlap-wrapped roots were crowded in the front part of the wagon, then came geraniums, white, rose and red. Little berry boxes holding tightly crammed pansies were on a small board extension nailed to the back of the wagon.

The shaggy horse obeyed the gentle pull on the reins and slowed down. "Want to buy a nice plant, lady?" asked the driver.

"I don't know," said Margy.

Her tentative answer so encouraged the peddler that he tugged the reins decisively. The horse seemed glad of a chance to stand still and let his head hang down for a while. The peddler turned on the wagon seat to speak to her.

"I got nice little trees only seventy-fi' cen's apiece and the bes' geraniums on the market and I'm only askin' a quarter for those."

"I was just looking at the pansies," explained Margy.

The man, pleased by a sales prospect whose interests narrowed down so easily, swung himself off the seat. "And I don' blame you for lookin'," he said feelingly. "You won' fin' no better pansies anywheres in Brooklyn."

"How much?" she asked.

The sale was coming too quickly. It was no fun. He wanted to practice more salesmanship on her. "I wan' you should examine a box first before we talk price," he said. He picked up a box and held the pansies under her eyes. "I don' have to talk up these flowers," he said. "They talk for theirselves."

And indeed they did—velvety purples, smoldering yellows, smoky garnets and the more prosaic blues and whites.

"Yes. But tell me how much," said Margy.

"So I'll tell you: I give twen'y cen's a box for'm at the market. I as' twen'y-fi' cen's when I sell'm. Is that too much?" he wanted to know. "A nickel profit, bein's that I got to get up in the dark and go down to Fulton Street to buy'm and then drive throo the streets all day sellin'm?"

He answered his own question. "No, it ain't too much."

Margy agreed it wasn't too much but admitted that she couldn't afford to lay out a quarter for flowers.

"A quarter!" he argued with suppressed passion. "What's a quarter if it buys somethin' what makes you happy if only for a minute?"

"You said it," she agreed.

And their words weren't banal because their eyes met as she spoke and she and the peddler had the same brief thought: that quickening happiness wasn't as hard to grasp as people thought.

"But I shouldn't've taken up your time," she apologized. "I was only looking for something reasonable to take to my mother. Thanks!" She started to walk away.

"Wait a minute!" She came back. "Now you don' wanna go and be so hasty," he said, "because I got just the thing for you." He reached into a secret recess under the wagon seat and brought out a box of dilapidated pansies. "Box lef' over from yesterday," he explained. "Got a little crush'. So it don' look so nice, you think? But they'll straight'n up. A little sun, a little wa'er. And you can have this box . . ." he looked intently into her face not wanting to miss the look of pleasure that he was sure would grow there, ". . . for a dime!"

He was rewarded by the instant look of happiness that leaped into her face. "I'll take it!" she said breathlessly, afraid that he might change his mind.

It was only after he had put her dime in his pocket that she noticed the plants in the middle of the basket were withered and dead. She flashed him a look of hurt disappointment and not meaning to, she spoke her instant thought aloud.

"People like us," she said, "shouldn't do things like this to each other."

He lowered his eyes and the hand in his pocket tightened on the dime an instant before he brought it out and held it out to her.

"Here," he said, ashamed. "Take your dime back an' keep the flowers." She declined the dime, shaking her head.

"A bargain's a bargain," she said. "And I've never gone back on one yet."

She pulled out the withered plants and dropped them

into the gutter. There was one perfect plant left in the box. He picked up the discarded plants and held them out to her.

"If you put these roots in wa'er when you get home they migh' freshun up and then you'd have a boxful insteada only the one plant. And they'd be good enough."

"No, I'm funny that way," she said with a slightly superior air. "I'd rather have only *one* good thing than a whole lot just good enough."

He considered her remark, then opened his hand and let the plants drop back into the gutter. He put one foot up on the hubcap of the back wagon wheel, leaned forward and rested his arm on his raised thigh. He pushed his shapeless busted-peak cap back from his beaten-down face.

"You know," he said in mellowed, measured tones, "that's jus' the way it is with me. I d'rather have one plain thing—you know—grade A, number one, than a whole lot of fancy stuff secon'han'. I always say to the wife, 'I sooner have one nice piece a crusty rye bread,' I say, 'wit fresh sweet butter on it,' I say, 'than a sir-line steak what's tough and stric'ly secon' grade.' That's what I always say to the wife."

His little speech transformed him. Gone was the shabby little peddler with the wincing eyes. His pose while he rested his foot on the hubcap gave him an attitude of debonair self-confidence. His views made him a man of personality. Margy took all this in, but the only words she was able to give him were again, "You said it!"

They had nothing more to say to each other. The little business deal that had brought two strangers together for a few moments of communication and understanding was completed. He climbed back on the wagon seat, slapped the reins on the tired horse's back and went his way bellowing out his wares to the deserted street.

The little contact added some excitement and imagination to Margy's day. She met so few people and spoke to no man outside of Frankie, her parents and the tradespeople. She got interested in trying to visualize the peddler's private life.

I bet he was quite a guy in his young days, she thought, when he was keeping company. I can just see him going to his girl's house all decked out and full of swell ideas about himself and the world. And probably she thought he was wonderful. Maybe he never told her he was a peddler but made out like he was a big shot and let her believe he was a regular florist. She must have thought that would be nice—living in back of the flower store and, between the times of minding a baby or two, helping him fix up graduation and wedding bouquets.

Probably he always wanted a flower shop himself. So he started out first with the wagon and thought that was only temporary—the wagon, and the first thing you know he'd have enough money saved up to buy a store. But I guess that never happened.

Or it could be that he started out selling bunches of flowers in a pail of water on a street corner and worked up to the wagon. Maybe he thinks owning his own horse and wagon is tops and he doesn't want to go higher. I wish I really knew. I could have asked him, I suppose, but that would have taken too much nerve.

She stopped at the corner bakery and bought two charlotte russes. She paused on the stairs out of old habit, hoping for familiar sounds; her mother's quick step behind the closed door, the thump of the lard hitting the frying pan, the smell of onions beginning to fry and the small clean sound of eggs cracked on the rim of the pan. For a moment she wanted things to be as they had been. Her days at home had not been happy but they had been full of hope. Everything good had seemed to be in hand's grasp just around the corner. In marrying she had turned a corner. While she wasn't sorry for having turned it, she was a little sad having it behind her instead of before her. She had one less thing to dream about.

"Hello, Stranger," said Flo, emphasizing the stranger.

"Now, Mom," came Margy's automatic protest.

"So you finally found the time to come see your mother."

"Why I was here a little less than a week ago."

"I could be dead and buried in my grave in a week," said Flo.

"It's such a nice day, Mama," pleaded Margy obliquely. "Almost like spring."

After considering that fact briefly, her mother said, "Sit down and stay a while." She started the kettle of water to boiling.

"I brought you some . . . I mean *a* pansy plant."

Flo accepted the box and buried her nose in the three blooms on the plant. A look of tender pleasure almost showed in her face. As if embarrassed by being pleased, she said, "You shouldn't waste your money."

"Only a dime," explained Margy.

"Dimes grow into dollars."

"Oh, no," smiled Margy. "Dollars melt down into dimes."

She watched her mother set the box on the window-sill garden where the plant looked very modest among a Boston fern, a rubber plant and a rose geranium.

"How's Papa?" asked Margy.

"Your father," said Flo, as though disclaiming all relationship to the man, "ain't doing so good. He was laid off two days last week."

"Why?"

"They didn't say. All they did was give an excuse. Times is hard, they told him."

"I wouldn't worry," soothed Margy.

"*You* wouldn't," agreed Flo. "But I got to."

"Why?"

"Because if I don't worry, who will? I imagine they're getting ready to let your father out but he's been working there so long they haven't got the nerve to fire him outright. They'll keep on laying him off more and more until finally he's laid off altogether."

"He'll get another job."

"Where? A man his age."

"Papa's still young—only forty-three."

"A workingman's old when he gets past forty. The bosses are always looking for younger men. If he'd only studied and passed Civil Service then he'd have a pension in his old age. How much did these Charley Ruches cost?"

"Ten cents."

"They're nothing but air. There's more on a coffee ring for the same money."

"All right. Next time I'll bring a coffee ring. But don't worry, Mama. If Papa loses his job maybe Frankie and I can help out."

"We're not asking help from nobody," stated Flo. "Only

we might have to move to a cheaper flat. Drink your tea while it's hot."

"It won't come to that," protested Margy, wondering how any flat could be cheaper than her parents' home.

"Now that I don't have your money coming in every week, it's hard to raise the rent. I was thinking that if you and Frankie moved in with us—you could have the front room and the bedroom next to it—we could share the rent and the cost of cooking. You and Frankie could save a lot that way. Us, too," she added honestly.

"That wouldn't work out, Mama, and you know it."

"I wouldn't interfere," said Flo humbly. "You'd be private."

"It's just that Frankie wants his own home."

"If his mother wanted you to live with them, you'd run."

"I certainly wouldn't," said Margy too quickly.

"You mean you and his mother don't get along?" asked Flo sharply.

"We get along fine," lied Margy. "It's just that every couple likes their own home. Maybe someday Frankie and I will buy a little house out on the Island," she dreamed. "And we'll live downstairs and you and Papa can live upstairs."

"No, thank you," declined Flo proudly. "I've always had my own home even though it was only a few cheap rooms. It would be terrible if I couldn't have my own home in my old age after working hard all my life. Is that too much to ask? A home of my own in my old days? No. Besides, I always said I'd never live with my daughter and son-in-law."

"But you want us to come live with you."

"That's different. I'd still be in my own home."

As Margy was leaving, Flo said, "Don't stay away so long the next time."

"I won't. But you must come see me."

"I haven't got the clothes to go anywhere."

"You don't have to dress up to see me. You ought to know me pretty well by now. I'm the girl you once gave birth to. Remember?"

Flo's heart turned over when she saw the old familiar smile of aching archness come to her daughter's face. She knew it was a time to say something memorable or tender. But all she said was: "As if I could forget. Such a hard time I had."

Her mother called after her as she went down the stairs. Margy turned and looked up. "Are you all right?" asked Flo. Margy knew she was asking whether she was pregnant.

"I guess so," she called back.

"You guess! You guess!" Her mother's voice was full of sudden panic. "Don't you *know?*"

"Of course I'm all right. Yes, I *know* I'm all right," she called up the stairs. She heard her mother expel a sigh of relief.

Walking home, Margy came to the decision that there was no use worrying about her father. He'd never liked that job anyhow. When he first took it he said it would do until something better turned up. Nothing better had turned up in fifteen years. He had never dared leave that stopgap job to look for a better one. Now if he got fired he might have a chance to find that better job. He was still young, Margy assured herself vehemently, and there was nothing at all to her mother's idea that a workingman was washed up at forty.

But somehow it didn't seem like such a nice day any more. The sun had got lost behind some clouds and the wind blew damp and chill.

Chapter 26

It was Saturday morning. As usual, Frankie was fretting about being late. Margy was dressing up to go to New York. Reenie and Sal were being married at City Hall at eleven o'clock. Margy was to be her friend's witness. Margy asked Frankie, please, as a favor, to knock off work an hour earlier since Saturday's a half-day anyway, and be best man.

Frankie refused. It wasn't only that he didn't want to take off from work, he told Margy, but he didn't like the combination; a Wop and a girl like that. By a girl like that, he meant that Reenie was already six months pregnant.

"I know it's terrible," admitted Margy. "But think how much more terrible it would be if he wouldn't marry her. That's why I think we ought to stand by; kind of make it all seem normal and ordinary so's he won't feel that he's doing her such a big favor."

"He is," said Frankie. "And she's lucky. That's all I can say. She's lucky."

"He's lucky, too."

"He's a sucker," pronounced Frankie.

"A man never gets blamed. It's always the woman who has the disgrace."

"A loose girl hasn't the guts to feel disgraced."

"Still and all, Reenie's a good girl," said Margy.

"Hah!"

"Can she help it that she loved him so much and their folks wouldn't let them marry?"

"They could have been married any time without asking anybody," he said.

"They just didn't have the nerve."

"They had the nerve for the other thing."

170

"Well, that just happens. Two people together so much. It stands to reason . . ."

"A baby three months after marriage. The poor kid will never live it down."

"Not if people like you put one strike against it before it's born. Sure, it will be hard the first year. Everyone will know and talk. But he'll be too young to know anything. Then they can move to Jersey or somewhere. So when he's, say, five years old, who'll remember, or if they remember, care? Nobody will throw it up. Only the people who should love and protect him. The family on both sides are the only ones who'll throw it up when they fight with each other."

"You know all the angles," he said. "I'm surprised you didn't get in the same fix."

"I never had that chance."

"Chance?" echoed Frankie. And his voice went into a squeal at the end of the word.

"I never had to fight off temptation," said Margy, knowing she was sticking her neck out, "because I was never cute or pretty or full of pep like Reenie."

"Lucky I came along," said Frankie, almost sarcastically.

"I thank my lucky stars every day," said Margy, almost bitterly.

"If I didn't know better . . . if I didn't know I was the first one, I'd think you were no better than your friend."

She wanted to say, Don't worry, there was never anyone I was crazy enough about. But she didn't say it. Instead she said, "Is that meant as a compliment?"

"Aw, Margy, cut it out, will you? First thing you know I'll be late for work."

"Got your money?" she asked. He jingled a few coins in his pocket to prove it and started for the door. "You forgot something."

"What?" he looked around the room.

"Forgot to kiss me."

"Oh, Margy," he moaned nervously. He put a quick kiss on her cheek. She hung on to him.

"We're so lucky, Frankie," she said. "We have the same religion and you have a job and we've got a nice home and we're young and have the future before us . . . and . . . don't be late for work, now." She pushed him out of the door.

171

Frankie was relieved that she hadn't fussed more over his refusal to attend the wedding. And he was relieved that what might have been a nasty quarrel had been averted. He wanted to reward her.

"Tell you what," he said. "Wait over in New York for me. I'll meet you outside City Hall and we'll eat at Childs'. A date?"

"Yes," she said. "Yes. Oh, Frankie, I *want* to love you so much." It was a change. Before that morning she had always said: "I love you so much." But he didn't notice.

Salvatore took his hat off the block, looked inside it, then dented in the crown with a nod of approval.

"Okay, Boss?" asked the hat blocker. Sal made a circle with his thumb and middle finger and gestured toward the blocker. The swarthy young man smiled in pleasure. "Tried to clean it good—for your wedding day," he said.

Sal climbed into the end chair. The head shoeshine boy finished thanking a customer for a tip, then came over to work on Sal's shoes. A third boy rushed in from the street holding aloft a freshly pressed suit on a wire hanger.

"Made it, Boss," panted the boy. Sal nodded his thanks and the boy hung the suit behind a curtain at the back of the store.

With the bored but alert eye of the professional, Sal watched the shoeshiner slap pungent-smelling polish on his pointed, perforated-tipped tan shoes. Then his eyes traveled to the window of his small hole-in-the-wall store and saw the lettering in reverse: SUPERIOR SHOESHINE PARLOR. HATS BLOCKED. Underneath in small letters were the words: S. DE MUCCIO. PROP.

The Prop. meant that Sal was in business for himself. True, after he paid off three boys, paid for materials and for the rent on his cubbyhole, his profits were no larger than the salary of a clerk or factory hand. The bonus was that he didn't have to take orders from anybody. He was his own boss and that was worth a lot.

The heat caused by the friction of the rapidly moving shine cloth came through his shoes. He looked down on the bent head of the shoeshine boy and noted with approval that the boy was doing a good job—polishing the heel counters of the shoes as thoroughly as he polished the toes.

Sal, himself, had started as a shoeshine boy in a hotel barbershop after years of apprenticeship on the streets of Brooklyn. He had gotten ahead because he was ambitious and because he tried to polish shoes better than any other kid. He had taught his own apprentices little touches that he had picked up—touches that made a superior shine appreciated by customers.

That's the American Way, thought Sal, who had been born in America of Italian-born parents. Do something a little better than the next guy and you're in. The American Way.

"Okay, Boss," said the boy as he untucked the bottoms of Sal's trousers and let the cuffs down.

Sal got down from the chair and smiled reassuringly at the anxious boy. The boy was only seventeen, also the son of immigrants and also wanting to make good as an American. The way to do it, thought the boy, was to emulate his boss in all things. Sal knew that emulation wasn't enough. He often told the boys, "Don't try to copy me. Try to top me. That's the way to get ahead."

Sal wanted to put his hand on the boy's head in a gesture of appreciation and affection but he killed the impulse, saying to himself: He'll only think I'm a God-damned fairy. He worked it out by pretending to swing a left to the boy's jaw. The boy, playing the game, grinned and ducked. He understood.

Funny, thought Sal, changing into his freshly pressed suit behind the curtain, how different nationalities go for different trades and how it starts with the kids. Take a Jewish kid: He buys something and resells it at a profit— like buying pretzels a cent each and selling 'em for two cents apiece in the park. A German kid sells what he makes himself—like lemonade at a ball park or pinwheels made out of wallpaper that he sells to other kids. Greek kids, now: They like to hang out in back of restaurants, waiting for a chance to deliver coffee to offices or factories. They move on up into dishwashing and then cooking. American kids, they go for selling newspapers. They like to be a part of what's going on. They like to holler out headlines, fold over a paper with a flip while they take the money at the same time. And the Irish?

The Irish had Sal buffaloed. The kids never seemed to work at anything. They were always fighting—with other kids and with each other. They fought to prove that something was true or to prove that something was a lie. That's what makes them good politicians, decided Sal.

Thinking of the Irish, he thought of Reenie. She was half Irish, her father having been the son of Irish immigrants. Her mother was second-generation German-American. But Reenie was mostly Irish the way she was so reckless, not giving much of a damn and always willing to take a chance.

He'd had other girls before Reenie, daughters of parents like his own, Italian born. But he fell in love with Reenie. She was all American and she had class. He fell in love with her but he hadn't wanted to marry her especially. She was all right to go dancing with and for "mushing," as the expression of the day had it. But for a wife?

He had dreamed of an ideal wife—a beautiful girl, passionate in lovemaking, but only so far as he was concerned, and utterly pure in heart, mind and soul. Oh, well, it had been one of those misty dreams—the kind that couldn't come true. And Reenie was all right. Maybe she had some kind of dream, too, of an ideal husband—not a shoeshining Wop.

He had put off marrying Reenie. Why, he didn't know. Unless he expected marriage to be disillusioning and humdrum and the beginning of getting ready for middle and old age. He would have liked everything to be the way it had started out: In love, dates, stolen hours of passion and utter freedom the rest of the time. He had put off marriage then, using his parents as an excuse. Sure, they wanted him to marry a Catholic. That was their religion. That was the way they'd brought him up. Certainly they wouldn't be worth a damn if they'd been able to set all that aside. However, they were humble and easily confused. They held Sal in awe and tried always not to offend him. He was American, of age, in business for himself. He could marry whom he pleased and how he pleased. His folks would come around. They were grateful as hell, he knew, that he still lived at home with them.

There had been four daughters and Sal. The girls had been born in Italy. Three had remained there when the parents—the mother pregnant with Sal—had sailed for America. They remained behind with their husbands and children. The fourth girl had married a naturalized Italian and gone out to California to live. Sal was the only one left to them. They'd agree to anything he said.

Sal enjoyed his parents' looking up to him, their American-born son in business for himself. But they don't have to look up to anyone, he thought. They got their own business, too—such as it is.

They were in the business of supplying quick full-grown lawns for newly built houses. Pasquale, the father, "rented" the grass on several vacant lots in Ozone Park for a few dollars a year. He and his wife pulled up the weeds, cut the grass short, mixed new seed in it and tended it until it was thick and springy. Then they mowed it and dug it up in two-foot squares, two inches thick, and Pasquale placed the squares side by side, like a carpet, on the strip of barren ground before a house, watered it, rolled it and lo! a lawn. All at twenty cents a square foot.

They had a sign in their window, too: DE MUCCIO. LAWNS MADE TO ORDER.

Sal stood before his three boys in his newly blocked hat, freshly pressed suit, with a white carnation in the buttonhole, in his shining shoes. The boys stood in a row and looked at him worshipfully.

"Well, do I pass?" he asked.

"You look just like Valentino," said the hat blocker. "Only not so dead pan."

There was a rattling of the doorknob. An irate customer peered through the door window. "What's the idea?" asked Sal, "locking up in the middle of the day? Are you on strike or something?"

"On strike five minutes," said the elder shoeshine boy. "To wish you a happy married life."

He and the blocker nudged the younger shoeshine boy who was standing in the middle. The boy brought out something that he had been holding behind his back and presented it to Sal, saying: "A present for you and your bride. From us."

Sal took it. It was a framed print of Mt. Vesuvius. The print had cost a quarter, maybe, but the ornate frame, filigreed and painted to look like gold, had probably cost three dollars. Sal took it, looked at it, and had to clear his throat twice before he spoke.

"You punks!" he said. "So that's how you waste the money I give you. I've a good mind to cut all your wages twenty per cent."

The boys grinned at each other. They knew their boss was tickled to death with the present.

Sal opened the door and let in the impatient customer. "Well," he said to the boys in farewell, "as the Irish say, God love you."

Walking over to City Hall, he thought: I'm lucky at that. She loves me. An American girl loves me and I'm nothing but a Wop. She must have been worried when she knew she was going to have my baby. Sure, I know it's mine. I was the first one. But if she worried, she never let me know. She trusted me. She knew I'd do the right thing. I'll try to be as good to her as I know how so that she'll never be sorry.

Sal, Reenie and Margy walked down one of the corridors of City Hall. It was a payday and nearing closing time. Clerks wandered around carrying their pay envelopes, paying each other back borrowed dimes and quarters. A young girl stood before a counter getting a paper notarized. She was not a worker there, merely a citizen making application for a civil-service job. The clerk had his stamp at hand. He read the paper, the hand holding it seeming to rest by accident against the girl's hand gripping the counter. He read the paper as slowly as he could, making the reading last long because it was pleasant to feel the girl's hand. He looked up from time to time, straight into her eyes, while he asked a question. She answered shyly, with lowered eyes. She didn't like his hand so close to hers but she was afraid to move it; afraid that he'd find something wrong in her application.

A clerk came hurrying through the corridor. "Hey!" called Sal. "You got five minutes?"

"Maybe," hedged the clerk. "Why?"

"Want to be best man?"

"Well . . ."

"Dollar in it for you," said Sal.

"Glad to oblige," said the clerk.

"Sold!"

"And thanks," added Reenie.

They made a little procession walking down the corridor: Sal and Reenie, arm in arm, and Margy and the clerk right behind them, also arm in arm. Three men passed the little group, then stopped to turn around and stare at Reenie's obvious pregnancy. One made a remark to the other two in a whisper and all smiled.

Reenie, hurt and angry, called back over her shoulder, "What's the matter? Haven't you ever seen a doll before?"

"Lay off, Jack," said the best man to the clerk who had done the whispering. The three men were embarrassed. Dropping their eyes, they walked away, hands in pockets.

It was a quick, casual, civil ceremony. They shook hands all around and Sal brought out a dollar for the best man.

"Forget it," said the clerk, pushing the bill back into Sal's hand. "All I want is a kiss from the bride."

Obediently, Reenie offered her cheek. He kissed it gently, then he put an arm around Sal, another arm about Reenie and held them to him.

"Listen," he said. "Don't you take all this too seriously. I'm a married man myself and our kid just got in under the wire. Remember this: It's nobody's business. So long. Take it easy." He was gone.

"He turned out real nice," said Margy.

"For a nickel, I'd bust his face," said Sal. "Nobody asked him to put in his two cents." Sal spoke roughly because he was much moved by the sympathy and understanding of the clerk.

The girl at the counter had had her application witnessed by the notary. She was paying the man the quarter fee. I hope she gets the job, thought Margy, irrelevantly.

As they left the building, Reenie kept looking back. "I don't see my mother," she whispered to Margy. "Wish she would've shown up. It would have meant a lot to me."

"She won't stay mad long," Margy whispered back. "You'll see. Besides, Sal's folks aren't here, either."

"But they don't know and Mama does. I still got Sal's folks to face." Reenie shivered.

They parted from Margy at the bottom of the steps. Margy saw Frankie as they came out but he ducked behind a post where Sal and Reenie couldn't see him.

"I wish you luck," said Margy. "You know that." She put her arms around Reenie' and kissed her.

"Thanks for being such a good friend," whispered Reenie, clinging to her.

"Hey! Break it up," said Sal. "This is no funeral."

"And lots of luck to you, Sal." Margy held out her hand.

"The bridegroom always gets a kiss from the maid of honor," he said. Sociably, Margy kissed his cheek. But he'd have none of that. He grabbed both her arms. "Listen," he said, "let's play like we're both normal and do it right." He put a slow hard kiss on her mouth.

My, thought Margy, it must be very wonderful to have sex in marriage.

The bridal couple rode out to Sal's home in Ozone Park. They walked into the kitchen. Sal told his parents briefly and in Italian, that he was married and had brought his bride home. The father and mother exchanged glances but said nothing. They had never gotten used to their good-looking son's American ways. They dared not protest even though both wished he had married a dark-eyed Italian girl—one who'd understand their ways.

The mother, a thin, sorrowful-looking woman, nodded and told Sal in Italian that they had waited dinner for him. The woman took a big tomato pie out of the oven. The hot olive oil on it bubbled and a wonderful smell of melted cheese, hot peppers, tomatoes, spices and hot bread rose from it. She placed the pie on a wooden board and set it in the center of the uncovered plain wooden table. The old man got out a bottle of thin, sharp, home-made red wine, uncorked it and filled four tumblers. He held up his glass.

"*Salute!*" he said.

After drinking the wine, the mother indicated that they should sit at the table. She declined a seat because she had to stand to' cut the pie. Sal held Reenie's chair out for her the way he always did when they ate at a restaurant. Before Reenie sat down, she looked straight at her mother-in-law and said:

"I want to say that I'll try not to be any trouble to you." She waited. They said nothing. "Did they understand what I said?" she asked Sal.

"Yes," he answered. "They understand English but they don't speak it."

Just then the mother, looking at her son, ripped out a string of tumbling Italian words. She finished her passionate little speech, folded her arms and stared at Reenie.

"Okay, *Mamma mía,*" said Sal with unexpected tenderness in the three words.

"What did she tell you?" asked Reenie. "To get your bride the hell out of the house?"

"My mother said," he explained, "that I should take your shoes off because your ankles are swelling."

He knelt at her feet and pulled off her pumps.

Chapter 27

When Margy got the birth announcement, she was glad that Reenie's baby was a boy. She had been more influenced than she thought by Frankie's talk about the child growing up in disgrace because it had been conceived outside of marriage. If it had been a girl, Margy reasoned, someone would warn her sooner or later not to grow up like her mother. But no one would talk like that to a boy. And even if they did, a boy wouldn't care as much as a girl would.

A note on the reverse side of the card said the boy looked like Sal and would be christened Salvatore but they'd call him Torry so as not to get the names of father and son mixed up. In a P.S., Reenie added that Sal's folks were just crazy about the baby.

Margy went right out to get some wool to crochet a pair of bootees for the baby. The store window was full of made-up samples of afghans, smocked baby dresses, needle-point chair covers and various other knitted, crocheted and embroidered items. Instructions were given free with each purchase of materials. Margy sat on a high stool and let the proprietress show her a new crochet stitch.

The store was a woman haven, filled with the makings for the only creative work that most women did. The owner of the store was sociable and she and Margy got to talking. The woman confided how she had gotten into business for herself.

She had always had a flair for handiwork, she told Margy. In fact, she had once invented four new crochet stitches and she showed Margy a yellowed, ten-year-old clipping from a woman's magazine with her picture in it, announcing that she had won a first prize of one hundred dollars. With that money, she had rented the little store and got stock on credit and before you knew it, she said, she was in business for herself.

Margy thought that was utterly wonderful. She had inherited from her father a belief in The American Dream —not on a grand scale, every poor boy having a chance to be president—but on a more practical scale—that people could own their own homes and could get into business for themselves. As she bent her head over the new stitch, she began to dream of opening a store herself, someday. Oh, not a handicraft store, she wasn't smart enough for that, but maybe a penny-candy store near a grade school, an honest store where only wholesome candy and sturdy cheap toys would be sold.

Margy turned up at Ozone Park one day with the finished bootees. Her visit had been announced by a penny postcard two days before. Reenie took her up to the bedroom she, Sal and the baby shared. The room was rather bare. It had a scrolled iron bed with a thin mattress, a chair and a dresser. The bed had once been white enamel but now was painted a deep pink. Reenie had added her own few possessions. Her lavender sateen bedspread, with gilt braid, covered the bed. A kewpie doll with a feathered skirt—Sal had won it for her at Rockaway Beach a year ago—stood on the dresser. A micaed white cane with a fat silk tassel, souvenir of Sal's skill in knocking down milk bottles at Palisades Park, hung from a tack on the wall. Snapshots of Reenie and Sal in grimly informal poses —legs crooked unnaturally and strained smiles—were stuck in the frame of the greenish-cast mirror over the dresser. The picture of Mt. Vesuvius hung on the wall. Margy noticed a large lithograph of "The Sacred Heart" in an ornate gilt frame hanging over the bed. It was a very red heart crowned by a wreath of thorns. A dagger was thrust through the heart and three fat drops of blood dripped from the dagger. Margy was used to the picture and took it for granted. In fact, as a child, she had worn a replica of the picture, pasted on a thin heart-shaped bit of red flannel, on a string around her neck. But Reenie never quite got over the picture.

"When Sal first took me up to our room," she told Margy, "I wanted him to carry me across the door, you know, the way they do in the pictures? But he said I was too hefty. So the first thing that hit me was that picture. It scared me—that blood. Then Torry jumped up inside me—only I didn't know it was Torry at the time. Well, I'm not superstitious or anything and I didn't believe all that bushwah about babies being marked before birth, still and all, I figured that it didn't cost anything to be careful. You know, sometimes there's a lot of truth in those old sayings. So I never looked at that picture during the last few months I was carrying the baby. Just the same— I know you'll *die* when you hear this—after the baby was born and they brought him in to me, I lifted up his little shirt, and I don't know what got into me, but I really expected to see three red marks under his heart. Of course, there weren't any, but I'm funny that way. It was like a present that the baby was whole and perfect—no harelip or six toes or anything."

"For heaven's sake," said Margy, "why shouldn't a baby be born perfect?"

"I don't know," said Reenie. "Only I wrote and asked my mother to send me my stuff and gave her my address. And she sent it all right. Only I got a letter from her the week before Torry was born and she said I'd be punished because I hadn't been a good girl—you know how I paid board home instead of giving all my pay in? And how I stayed out late nights and worried her and how the baby came before I was married long enough? And so I really thought I'd be punished by having something the matter with the baby."

"I'm really surprised at your mother," said Margy. "She always seemed so swell and all."

"Well, I know how it is," said Reenie. "If I had a girl and she grew up and did what I did, I guess it would just about kill me. Although," she added, "if I knew she was crazy about someone in the first place, I'd try to see it her way and not stand in the way of the marriage no matter what religion or nationality he was."

"Has your mother seen the baby yet?" asked Margy.

"Oh, no. She hasn't been near me—not even while I was in the hospital. Oh, I hear from her from time to time. She's still working in the lunch wagon, only she gave up the flat. Now she lives in a hall bedroom near the lunch wagon."

"You know what I'd do if I were you?" said Margy.

"No. What?"

"Some fine day when you know your mother's not working, I'd just take the baby and go up to see her and hand over the baby and say, 'Here's your first grandson, Mom.'"

"She'd throw me out on my ear!"

"She would not! She'd be so glad to see you! It stands to reason. She's getting old now," said Margy with unconscious cruelty, "and who in the world has she got but you?"

"That's true," admitted Reenie. "Well, I'll bring the baby around to see her someday."

When it was time for Margy to leave, Reenie begged her to stay a few moments longer in order to meet Father Bellini. Reenie was taking instructions preparatory to becoming a Catholic. She spoke very highly of Father Bellini.

"He's not at all what you'd think a priest would be," she said. "He's so human and so up-to-date about everything. He grew up in this neighborhood, you know, and all the people like him. They say he was in love with a girl once and she married someone else. So he decided to be a priest." Margy smiled. "What's so funny?" demanded Reenie.

"Oh, Reenie," said Margy, "they always say that about a priest who's well liked. It's one of those neighborhood stories."

"This one is true," insisted Reenie. "Sal knew the girl. He used to run errands for her when he was a kid."

"Maybe it is true," said Margy. "So what?"

"So it's remarkable that anyone who's a priest could ever have been in love with anyone."

"It's not remarkable. The Church takes only normal men for priests. So they pour all the love they could have for wife and children into the Church and the people of the Church."

When Father Bellini came and was introduced to Margy, Margy had to admit to herself that he *was* different. In the first place, he was bald and all the priests Margy had known had a lot of hair. In the second place, he was Italian and Margy had thought all priests were Irish, merely because all the priests she had known were Irish.

He brought Reenie some reading matter; a book on the life of the Little Flower and a copy of a popular magazine. He called Reenie, Irene, and cautioned her to take it easy and not plunge into household duties too soon after the birth of the baby. He insisted that the baby was highly intelligent considering he was only three weeks old. And he pinned a tiny, shiny medal with a blue bow on the baby's shirt.

As Margy went down the stairs and out of the house, she heard him start examining Reenie on the Catechism. He had a very nice voice.

"Who made the world?" he asked.

"God made the world," answered Reenie.

"Who is God?"

Riding home on the Long Island train, Margy's mind was at peace. She knew that everything was all right with her friend.

Chapter 28

Frankie noticed the two dime-store glass candlesticks with their red burning candles and had a flare of irritation. Whose birthday? What anniversary? Could she by some telepathy have known of his good fortune? As he hung up his hat and coat he said, referring to the candles:

"What's the idea?"

"Let me!" she begged.

As often happened he was touched by something that he understood but was too embarrassed to admit. He was sorry for his sharp remark and realized with an inward sigh that they were getting into the habit of snapping at each other. He tried to make amends. He picked up a holder and held the flame to his cigarette.

"Say these things come in mighty handy after all, don't they?"

It was unfair, he thought, the way her face lit up with pleasure at his amend. Sure, he knew the candles meant something to her; a reaching out for a kind of storied charm in living. He knew that she didn't expect him to understand. All she asked was that he wouldn't make fun of her. He didn't want to be sarcastic, God knows. He remembered how he had felt when Miss Grayce had made fun of him. But he couldn't help being sarcastic at times. She was always getting worked up about things that no one else thought were interesting or exciting.

Women are funny, he decided, the way they pick up the small things of life, things small like beads that could be seen only under a magnifying glass—that they strung together to make into a complicated necklace. And they wouldn't let a man admire the whole necklace. Oh, no!

They expected him to admire each one of the damned beads separately.

Later, as he was finishing his dessert, he said casually, "By the way. I got a two-dollar raise today."

"Frankie!" she screamed in joy. "But why didn't you tell me the minute you got home?"

"What? Oh, I forgot." It was a lame lie. He had put off telling her because he dreaded the way she'd get emotional about it.

She jumped up, ran around the table and sat on his lap. "Now you've just got to put up with it," she insisted, forestalling his familiar protest.

She placed quick happy kisses all over his face. And he suffered her love because he was secretly proud that he could make her so happy just by getting a two-dollar raise. She started babbling about buying a house. He told her to take it easy—that you can't buy a house on a two-dollar raise.

"Yes, you can," she said. "I have it all figured out. The whole secret is in buying in large amounts and saving carrying charges by paying cash for everything and not buying on installments and I'm going to have yellow curtains in the kitchen."

"Is there any more coffee?" he asked.

"Oh, you!" she said, giving him a little shove as she got off his lap. Then she laughed and he smiled and everything seemed all right.

Later in the night, lying next to Frankie in the Murphy bed, she was too elated to sleep. She went over all the events of her childhood and her courtship and marriage and remembered only the happy things. Suddenly she had a feeling that in another moment she would understand everything there was in the world. Drunken people often have that feeling and Margy was drunk on the two-dollar raise. She held her breath and waited for the big understanding. But it didn't come, of course. She felt that she really loved Frankie and wondered how she had ever let the first edge of doubt come into her mind about it. She wanted to make Frankie understand how she felt. It seemed important that he understand.

She slipped an arm around him. He made his body rigid and said, "I've *got* to get some sleep."

"I know."

But she held him tightly, pretending to herself that he really liked it but was sort of shy. She was overwhelmed with tenderness for him. She wanted to make him happy. But she had to acknowledge that the best way to make him happy was to withdraw emotionally from him. Well, she'd take her arm away and let him alone so he could have that happiness or relief. But she had to say something first.

"I'm proud of you, Frankie," she said. "Your bosses must like you an awful lot to give you such a nice raise. I'm glad I married you." He grew a degree more rigid under her arm. "I want you to be so happy," she whispered. "And if it makes you happier not to have me hold you, I'll take my arm away."

But she continued to hold him tightly, hoping against hope that he'd say, I like it. Leave it there. But he said nothing—only stirred impatiently.

"All right," she murmured. "There!" She took her arm away. She was rewarded by his sigh of relief as he relaxed. She turned her back to him and whispered into her pillow. "I would never hurt anybody in the whole world on purpose. Why are you always so afraid that I'd hurt you, Frankie?"

There would have been no answer—even if he had heard what she said.

Frankie invited two of his office friends over to celebrate the raise. Margy prepared the refreshments with excitement. She wanted everything to be perfect. She was so anxious to make a nice impression on Frankie's friends.

The woman, secretary to one of the bosses, wore a severely plain tweed suit, low-heeled brogues and her stiff, straight hair was cut short. She was introduced as Cassandra Wyle, but Frankie and the young man called her Sandy. The young man was called 'Gene. He was good looking, or would be, thought Margy, if he'd get that wavy blond hair of his cut a little shorter. Both were more intelligent and better dressed than the people Frankie and Margy knew. But what was utterly surprising to her was that Frankie got along so well with them. He was free and expansive.

Sandy put a casual arm around his neck and lightly

punched his chin in greeting and referring to the raise said, "Nice going, feller." Margy waited in horror for Frankie to be rude and pull away from her. But he seemed to enjoy the good-natured contact. She noticed that 'Gene extended his left hand in greeting. She thought that was a little more friendly than the right hand and figured that among his class it took the place of the kiss on the cheek among her friends.

It was a pleasant evening. Sandy and 'Gene were amusing and pleasant and easy to get along with and Frankie was transformed. It was as if he were released from a spell. He chattered and laughed and enjoyed himself thoroughly. He was so easy and happy with his friends that Margy began to understand why he was so anxious to get to work in the morning.

As the visitors stood in the doorway saying their goodbys and repeating what a wonderful time they had, Margy, hostess-fashion, put her arm through Frankie's. 'Gene, in the act of raising his hand to adjust his hat brim, suddenly let his wrist go limp and held it that way a second before he let it drop.

"What a touching domestic scene," he said.

"Don't be petty, dear," Sandy warned him.

Rather viciously, Frankie pulled his arm away from Margy. She looked at him and noticed that a hot red color was mounting in his face as though he had been caught doing something nasty. Margy had a feeling of panic threaded through with horror. She had an intuitive feeling of understanding something of which she had absolutely no knowledge.

Later, in bed, Frankie put his arm around her and pulled her to him. Out of a clear sky she remembered something from her childhood—a woman's voice coming through a thin wall partition, the woman next door in bed saying to her husband: "Don't come fooling around me after you've been to a burlesque show." And she had the strangest desire to say the same thing to Frankie.

He said, "You were swell, Margy. They liked you, too. Believe me, I was proud of my home and my wife." He kissed her.

Suddenly she was deliriously happy. She was ashamed of her vaporous fears. The trouble with her, she decided, was that she didn't get out enough; didn't realize that there were different kinds of people in the world.

She returned Frankie's kiss eagerly.

After he went to sleep, she lay awake for a long time, not wanting to lose that happy, relieved feeling. Then she fell asleep. And while she slept, she had the old, recurrent dream. She dreamed that she was a little girl again and that she was lost . . . lost on the streets . . .

Chapter 29

For a while after 'the visit of Frankie's friends the relationship between Margy and her husband seemed to change. He seemed less repressed, more free—as though he had gone to confession and been absolved. It should have pleased Margy but it made her thoughtful and a little uncomfortable. She tried to rationalize the feeling. I'm more used to the way he always was, she thought. I didn't like it—or so I thought. But I'd rather have him the old way. He seems unfamiliar—a stranger, now. I guess I never did know him in the first place.

Much to her horror, she worked up a slight revulsion toward Frankie, physically. Why? she wondered. Why? Oh, I wish those people had never come!

Then something happened that straightened out everything for Margy; made her realize that there was a logical reason for her aversion to Frankie. She found that she was pregnant!

She got up one morning and was taken with nausea. She crawled back under the covers and nudged Frankie. "Frankie, are you awake?"

"What? Well, I am now. Is it time to get up?"

"Not quite. But I want you to do me a favor."

"If it doesn't take too long," he yawned. "I have to be in the office at nine."

"You'll make it," she said—as she said every morning. "Do you know how to make tea?"

"What? Oh, sure."

"Make me a cup, then."

"Why?"

She fought down the next bout of nausea. "Don't ask. Just make it."

"But I don't see . . ."

"Please!"

"Okay!" He got out of bed and went into the kitchen. He came back. "What do you make it in?" he asked. "And where do you keep the tea?"

She gave him simple instructions. He banged things around in the kitchen for a while and finally brought her a cup of hot water beginning to be discolored by a soaked tea bag. Half a lemon was wedged between the cup and saucer.

"See if it's all right," he said.

She squeezed two drops of lemon juice into the cup and took a swallow. "It's just right," she said.

"Are *you* all right?" he asked nervously.

"Yes," she said quietly.

"Is it all right for me to shave then?"

"Of course."

After he had washed and shaved he came back into the living room. He was disappointed at not finding his clothes laid out. He hadn't realized how much he had come to depend on that little service. He took the cup and saucer from her and sat on the edge of the bed.

"Margy, you *are* all right, aren't you?"

"I'm so all right, it's sinful."

"What's the matter then?"

"Nothing. Only . . ." She put her hand on his knee. He twitched it away from under her hand. "Oh, Frankie," she said, "don't pull away from me now. Please don't."

"Listen. I can't sit here all morning playing guessing games. Now I'll have to leave without breakfast or I won't make it."

She had wanted to make a little ceremony of telling him. But seeing his impatience, she told it bluntly.

"We're going to have a baby."

She closed her eyes against the sudden look of revulsion and terror in his face. After what seemed a long time, he asked, "Are you sure?"

"I'm sure."

"It couldn't be that you have a cold—that you're nervous or something?"

"I'm not nervous and I never have a cold."

"There must be something you can do—something you can take."

"But why should I? Besides, it's two months now."

"If you had only told me a month ago."

"But I couldn't be sure a month ago."

He got up and paced the floor holding the cup and saucer very carefully as though safeguarding the crockery would give him a little leeway.

"But I can't understand," he said. "I've been careful."

"I thought you'd be so happy," she said miserably.

"Happy?" he asked incredulously.

"Well, anyhow, it's happened," she said.

"And it's all your fault," he said. "Always putting your arms around me . . . kissing me. . . ."

She swung her feet over the bed and stood up before him in her dollar-ninety-eight pink rayon Lerner night-gown and made the nastiest speech of her life. "What's the matter?" she asked. "Are you afraid of what your friends will say? Are you afraid Sandy will say, 'Tough luck, feller,' or that 'Gene will wave his handkerchief at you and say, 'How perfectly domestic'?"

"What did you say?" he asked. He sounded shocked. Then he became coldly logical. "I am not concerned with what my office friends say or think. Why should I be? They won't know. In the first place I have no intention of spreading the news—no matter how wonderful you think the news is. In the second place it's nobody's business but mine and yours." He narrowed his eyes and asked quietly and almost sweetly, "Just what did you mean by that remark, Margy?"

"Nothing! Nothing!" Suddenly she was terrified by the heretofore formless thing that had acquired shape by her words. "I don't know why I said that. You mustn't mind what I say. A woman in my condition is supposed to say many silly things." She retched painfully.

"Gee, I'm sorry, Margy. I'm such a dope. I don't know anything." The shape dissolved and the thing became formless once more. She retched again. "For God's sake! Lie down," he said.

After the attack passed, they tried to talk about the whole thing sensibly. "Look at it this way," he said. "We're just about getting along. A kid will set us back. Three or four years from now when we're on our feet it would be all right. But now. . . . Oh, Margy! What are we going to do? How are we going to manage?"

"Well, we have fifteen dollars saved. We'll add your two-dollar raise to the fifteen. That will pay for the doctor and the hospital. Easy."

"That's the least of it. I'm thinking of what it will cost after."

"Not much. I can nurse it for six months at least. That will cost nothing. After that, a quart of milk a day—a can of Dextri-Maltose once in a while . . ."

"Suppose it gets sick."

"Why should it? You're healthy—I'm healthy. Why shouldn't our baby be?"

"But . . ."

Once more she stood up. This time there was no nausea. "You'll be late for work," she said firmly.

She made coffee for him. He had to eat toast with it. There had been no time to go to the baker's for buns.

After he left, Margy did some apprehensive thinking. In a way, Frankie's right, she thought. But I want this baby and I'll manage somehow. First we'll need more room— can't put a crib in the kitchen or bathroom. But we can't pay more rent. That means we have to move to a cheaper neighborhood to get more room for the same rent. That will be all right for a couple of years while she's still a toddler. By the time she's old enough for kindergarten we ought to be on our feet enough so's we can move to a nicer neighborhood where she'll have nice children to play with.

I'm really scared, she acknowledged to herself. I heard so much about the pain of giving birth. Mama used to say she'd take poison rather than face childbirth again. Still and all, Reenie had no trouble. Things are different now than when Mama had me. The doctors try harder to save you pain. I should have tried to do better when I was home to make up somehow for the pain I caused her by being born. Still and all, I wouldn't want my baby to make up anything to me. It's not asking to come into the world and I'll never make it pay me back the way Mama tries and Mrs. Malone. I'm the one who must make up to it for the fact that it *was* born.

Frankie finally got up enough nerve to go over and tell his parents. Mr. Malone took it calmly. He grunted and turned the next page of his undertakers' manual. Frankie was relieved. He had expected his father to be hearty and say something like: "Well, well! I didn't know you had it in you."

Mrs. Malone, acknowledging the inevitability of the thing, said she wasn't surprised. She knew her son would be trapped.

"What do you mean trapped?" asked Malone. "Being as they're married almost a year now?"

"I mean, she knows Frankie's too good for her and she was afraid that Frankie would find that out too, after the novelty wore off. She knew he'd wake up someday and leave her sooner or later. So she schemes and schemes to have this baby and hold him."

"It don't take a hell of a lot of scheming," commented Malone over the top of his book.

"Who asked you for your two cents? Just keep on learning how to lay out stiffs," she advised, "and shut up."

"That I will," he said. He looked at her speculatively. "Knowing how to lay out a stiff might come in handy someday."

"Yeah? Never mind. I'll bury youse all, yet."

Malone slammed the book shut and presented it to her. "Learn how first," he said. She threw the book across the room and Malone roared with laughter. Frankie stood there feeling miserable.

She turned to Frankie after the little joke was over with. "With all due respect to your wife, son . . ."

"Naturally!" Frankie jerked his head in a little bow.

". . . She played a dirty lowdown trick on you." In a way, Frankie thought so too, but he resented his mother saying it.

"Mama," he said, "you don't like Margy. Not because she's Margy but because I married her. You would have hated anybody I married."

"How you talk! I want all my children to marry. I wanted you to get married. Only I hoped you'd pick out a better girl—one that came from a better family, anyhow."

"Her family's all right and when all is said and done, she's too good for me."

"*She* told you that, I bet."

"No, she didn't. But never mind. I'm not asking you to like her. All I'm asking is that you treat her decent."

"I'm open and above board. I never put on. I treat people the way they deserve to be treated. If I know somebody what deserves to be treated good, then I treat them good. If they don't deserve it, I just can't be a hypocrite and treat them good even if they did happen to marry my only son. Frankie," she said—and she was sincere—"I only want one thing in the world; to see my children happy. I don't care about myself. I lived my life. When all is said and done, I don't want nothing—although I was a very pretty girl in my time and I always thought I'd marry well . . . not complaining about your father who always worked hard and did the best he could. Well, anyhow, I got nothing against Margy, poor thing. But a mother feels . . . you could never understand, son. Anyhow, you should have done better than Margy."

Frankie looked at his father. Malone's face was twisted in some kind of an emotion. Frankie didn't know whether it was pain at his wife's criticism of him or amusement, or disgust at the sentimental talk. He just didn't know. He had a flash of understanding of his mother. But he was uncomfortable, as always, at emotion. He looked away and said:

"Just the same, you've got to treat her nice, Mama. At least until after the baby comes. After that," he said with a flash of understanding, "I guess she won't need anything from anybody."

"I never allowed my children to tell me what I should do," she said. "And I don't see that I have to be different now."

He tried to be as sincere as he thought his mother was. "She's only a girl, Mama, and maybe she's scared. She'll have to go through a lot of suffering getting this child. She might die, even. You wouldn't want that on your conscience if she died—that you were mean to her."

"Who told you all that nonsense," she asked, "about women being scared and suffering and maybe dying just because they have a baby?"

"You did, Mama," he said quietly. Then he left.

Malone couldn't get interested in his undertakers' manual. He felt sorry for his wife, for Frankie—even for Margy. He looked up at his wife's twisted face and closed his book gently.

"Yes, you did, Nora," he said. "You told him. He was a boy of sixteen at the time and just beginning to turn around and look at the girls on the street. And you was carrying Doreen at the time and you told him how scared you was—how you was going to suffer giving birth and how you might die. I told you at the time not to trouble the boy and you said he's got to learn about life sometime. And then you told him that he mustn't do nothing to cause you grief and you got around to it that every time he looked at a girl, he caused you grief. Oh, you learned him well, Nora, thinking it was for your own benefit. You didn't know you was learning him for some other woman's benefit, too."

She tried to explain. "It's just that Frankie's the best one of all the children I got," she said.

"Yes, he's the best one we got," he said. "He was made out of the love a pretty girl and a decent man had for each other a long time ago. He was carried under a happy heart. He was hoped for and he came into the world . . . wanted." He sighed. "The others came unwanted because we couldn't help ourselves and because there was slip-ups and accidents. But he's the one was wanted."

She opened her mouth to speak. He held up a silencing hand. "Nora, it would be better if you didn't say nothing right now." As gently as he had closed it, he opened his book to the chapter that dealt with the proper and the respectful laying out of the dead.

Margy didn't have to tell her mother. Her mother told her.

"You're going to have a child," she said accusingly one day when Margy was well into her third month of pregnancy.

"Yes, Mama." Margy waited for a lecture. Flo's reaction was unexpected.

"I guess I wasn't a good mother," she said.

"I wouldn't say that," fenced Margy cautiously.

"Of course not. It's not your place to say it. But I say it. I wasn't a good mother."

"Wherever you get your ideas!"

"I know I wasn't a good mother because if a girl has a good mother it's natural to tell her right away when she expects a baby. And you didn't tell me."

"Mama!" she said, trying not to cry.

But Flo went on. "I did my best to be a good mother. But being's I couldn't afford to buy you toys and later, nice clothes, I guess you turned against me."

"No, Mama! No. I knew how it was."

"Well, wait'll you have a child of your own and your heart aches because you can't afford to give it everything its hands reach out for. And when she grows up and grows away from you maybe you'll realize how I feel. . . ."

Flo heard Henny's step on the stairs. Automatically she lit the gas and went about preparing the fried-egg supper. She winced a little when a tear fell into the hot fat and made a drop or two of bubbling grease jump up on her hand.

"I'm going to have a baby, Papa," announced Margy before her mother could break the news.

"I knew it long ago," he said as he hung up his hat and coat.

"You knew it! She knew it! Frankie knew it! Everybody knew it but me," said Flo, wounded. "Nobody tells me nothing."

"Who told you, Papa?" asked Margy.

"Frankie. About a month ago."

"And I only know it now," moaned Flo.

"Well, Papa?" asked Margy.

"Well, what?"

"Aren't you going to wish me luck—or bawl me out? Or something?"

"I think," said Henny, slowly, feeling for the words, "that it will be kind of nice to have a grandchild. We will try to be good to it," he said with a kind of dignity.

"Your father," said Flo, taking the cue of dignity from him, "is right. My grandchild will want for nothing if I can help it." But she had to get in a last gloomy thought. "And if anything happens to you in childbirth, God-forbid-and-knock-wood, I'll take the baby and bring it up like my own flesh and blood, which in a way," she added honestly, "it is."

Well, Flo proffered the usual invitation to stay to supper expecting the usual refusal. I'd-like-to-but-I-got-to-get-home-to-get-Frankie's-supper. Instead, Margy said, "Of course I'll stay."

"What about Frankie?" asked Flo conscientiously.

"He can eat out of the icebox for once," said Margy.

"Or go over to his mother's," said Flo, practical as always.

Margy wanted to hug and kiss her parents. But she knew that Flo would say, Don't be so silly, and she was afraid that Henny would cry. So all she said was, "These are the best fried eggs I ever ate."

But they knew.

Chapter 30

Margy had always meant to go back to the office and visit the girls as she had promised. But for some reason or other, she kept putting off the visit. One day a letter came with the Thomson-Jonson letterhead on the envelope. The name Wayne Prentiss was written over the firm name. The envelope contained a folded copy of the latest issue of the office newspaper. Someone had written an article for it entitled: *I Wonder What's Become of ——.* There was a blank space instead of a name at the end of the title. There followed a parody of the song, "I Wonder What's Become of Sally." Instead of the name Sally, there was a blank space again. After the parody, there was a little doggerel verse about former workers.

> *There was Jean*
> *There was 'Rene,*
> *Their leaving made us blue.*
> *They are wed,*
> *And 'tis said,*
> *They're having babies, too.*
> *But I wonder what's become of ——*

Mr. Prentiss had written the name *Margy* in all the blank spaces of the song and verse. Margy considered that a personal invitation. She was pleased that she was remembered and she made plans to visit the office the next day.

It was a good time to show herself to her old friends. Never had she felt or looked better. She had entered into a time of relaxed waiting. Nature had gone into a conspiracy with her to ease things all the way along the line.

The nausea had stopped long ago and she was pleasantly hungry all the time. The simplest food had a wonderful taste. Her sleep was deep and dreamless. Her pale skin glowed and her hair took on a deeper sheen.

The little hollows under her cheekbones filled out and a fugitive dimple came to her left cheek. Her heretofore adolescent-looking breasts swelled glamorously and she was very proud of them.

The office seemed a little shabbier and a little smaller than she had remembered. She reported first to Mr. Prentiss. He looked more tired than she had remembered. He was not wearing glasses. He rose and smiled as she entered and took her two hands in his.

A shock went from his hands to hers and all the way up her arms. She had never felt such a thrill at Frankie's touch.

"Margy! So you found your way back to us!"

"Yes."

"And how has the world been treating you?"

"Swell."

"Everything coming your way?"

"It seems so."

"And your husband?"

"*He's* fine."

"And yourself?"

"*I'm* fine."

It was not an enriching conversation. Margy had walked into his office poised and full of self-confidence. Now the old inferiority complex came back.

She thought: What am I doing always thinking about him and coming back making believe I want to see the girls when I really want to see him? I'm getting too settled for such a school-girl crush. Besides I'm married now, anyhow. And he wouldn't look at me, really. Way above me. A college graduate and a lawyer. A boss and he owns his own home. And of course, there's his mother. . . . I used to think it was wonderful—the way he had a pat saying for everything. Now it annoys me. Why? Did I get smart all of a sudden in the months I've been married? Still and all it's better to have something to say, I imagine, even if it's in mottoes, than to have nothing to say all the time like Frankie. Listen to me! Frankie's all right. At least we're the same kind of people.

He thought: She's so young and she doesn't know much, yet she leaps into life and grasps it with both hands—not a coward like me. I've had many girls working under me —opportunities—but this one has to stay in my mind. Why? She's not as pretty as some of the others. I've never heard her say anything memorable. Why does she keep coming up in my thoughts? Chemical, maybe. She has the courage I lack. I've had the opportunities which seem important to her. Together we have all the elements of completement. I started thinking of her when she took it upon herself to answer that farmer's letter. It almost cost her her poor little job. She didn't think he was a moron because he wrote to a mail-order house for a wife. Out of a meager little life and an unrealized gift of understanding, she tried to fix things for him. And how I jumped on her for it! Well, there must be discipline or there'd be no work done. No, she is not important in any way except that she seems like life itself to a poor weak thing like me. Mother would say she's not in my class. Mother! And what is class? I've been a dutiful son, Mother. You gave over your life making me one. I can't be a dutiful son any more because now I have no mother. So now I'm nothing.

He sighed and said, "Well, Margy, I suppose you want to visit with the girls?"

"Yes."

"I won't keep you then." He looked at the clock. "It's a quarter to twelve. Suppose you come back here at twelve and we'll have a bite together."

He said it casually but her heart jumped with excitement. She accepted stiffly. "That will be very nice, I'm sure."

She paid her respects to Miss Barnick, who looked the same only more tired. She went in among the girls. They were all there except Reenie, Ruthie and Marie. The girls seemed the same yet were different. Their clothes were different and most had changed their style of hairdo. One looked a little fatter, another much thinner and one or two of the older ones looked, like Miss Barnick, a little more tired. She wondered how it was possible for such changes to take place in less than a year?

They gossiped. They renewed the office gossip of her day, interspersed with new office gossip. They told her there was a new girl in the office just like Reenie—just like Reenie, classy and all. There was a new girl named Ruthie. Only she was different from the other Ruthie. Each one said practically the same thing on greeting her and she made practically the same answers.

"How do you like married life, Margy?"

"Swell!"

"Well, married life certainly agrees with you."

"Thanks."

At five minutes of twelve she went into the washroom to renew her lipstick. The girls began dribbling in to fix up to go out to lunch. For some reason, she found herself in back of a row of girls. Her arms were piled high with purses she had been asked to hold. As the girls primped and talked she looked over their heads at their faces in the mirrors. Why, she thought, I'm one of the old girls now—the ones who stand aside for the younger ones.

"Whatever happened to Marie?" asked Margy.

"Didn't you know?" they chorused.

"She married a rookie cop," said one.

"And he's mean to her," contributed another.

"But she loves it," added a third.

"She's crazy then," said the first.

"Some women are funny that way."

"The way I'm funny for potato salad."

"Oh, you!"

"Any man hit me, I'd kick his teeth out."

"*In*, kid. In. You'd have to get your foot in his mouth to kick 'em out."

"And me wearing a size seven shoe!"

"Anybody ever put their foot in a man's mouth?"

And they screamed and shrieked with laughter.

He was waiting for her at his office door. Although it was a warm June day, he had his topcoat folded cautiously over his arm. The elevator was full of chattering girls. The chatter stopped suddenly when they stepped in. The girls, after a frank, surprised stare, began putting a hand over a mouth to cover a fake cough, a handkerchief to wipe away a nonexistent smudge, a palm over the mouth with the middle finger pushing up the nose tip—all this, Margy knew, to hide the grins on their faces. She knew the girls would talk about it all afternoon: The boss took Margy to lunch!

She matched her step to his, having to make a little hop-skip to get in rhythm. He noticed and tried not to smile. At the first street intersection they came to, he cupped his hand under her elbow and steered her across. Again the shock went up her arm as if her elbow had touched a defective electric toaster. She was sorry there were no more streets to cross to get to the restaurant.

She studied the purple-inked menu with mixed feelings. She had never eaten in a restaurant with any other man but Frankie. She was anxious to do the right thing. The *table d'hôte* lunch was fifty cents. This seemed expensive to her. She thought maybe it wouldn't be considerate to have him pay for a whole lunch for her. The waitress asked her point-blank what she wanted. Margy had read somewhere that you must give your order to your escort and let him give it to the waiter. So she fixed her eyes in a glassy stare on Mr. Prentiss' face and said that all she wanted was a cup of coffee.

"One coffee," said the waitress before he could say anything. "Light or dark?"

"Light, Mr. Prentiss," said Margy wishing him to know that she knew what was what when lunching with a gentleman.

"Oh, no," he said. "Then I'll have to take only coffee too and I'm hungry. Please have the lunch, Margy."

"All right. I'll take what you take."

He studied the menu carefully. Finally he chose chicken croquettes, peas and mashed potatoes. He didn't like it but he thought she did. She did. After the order was given, Margy leaned back in her chair and looked around. Mr. Prentiss looked around too and saw a group of six girls lunching together at a nearby table. The girls stared at him. He took his eyeglass case from his pocket and put on his glasses. Then he took them off and put them back in their case.

"Do you *have* to wear them?" asked Margy.

"Not any more. I had a slight case of astigmatism some years ago. But it's corrected now. I use them out of old habit, I guess."

"Well if you don't have to, I wouldn't if I were you.

You look so much younger without them." Her face reddened painfully at her frank remark. "I mean you look so much better without them."

"If I look younger without them, I'll never wear them again," he said kindly. "And thank you so much for the compliment."

After the food was served, she asked politely, "And how's your mother?"

"My mother," he said, "passed on."

"You mean she died?" she asked, not to correct him but because she was astonished.

"Three months ago."

"I'm sorry." She knew what he was going to say. He said it.

"Well, we all have to go someday."

"That's the truth. But I really am sorry. I wish there was something I could say."

To herself she thought: Good. Now he can live his own life. Then on pretext of brushing crumbs from her chest, she made a furtive sign of the cross, saying to herself, God forgive me for unkind thoughts of the dead.

"You must be lonely," she said.

"Not any more than I used to be."

"Your house. I heard somewhere you had a house in Brooklyn Heights."

"Bay Ridge," he corrected.

"Well, have you given it up?"

"No."

"Isn't it hard for a man to run a house?"

"Not for me. You see, Mother taught me all about housekeeping."

"That's fine," she said lamely. She was remembering a washroom remark of a year ago. A girl had said he'd make some woman a good wife someday.

The waitress brought back the cards so they could choose their dessert.

Without hesitation, Margy looked into his eyes and said, "Huckleberry pie."

Used to his mother taking a long time to choose a dessert, he thought there was something wrong. "Take your time," he said. "Choose something you really like."

Her eye went to the dessert line: Huckleberry pie, rice

pudding, ice cream. "I still like huckleberry pie," she said.

"Two," he ordered. "A la mode."

"Ice cream's ten cents extra," said the waitress.

"I shan't complain," he said, feeling somehow that the waitress had spoiled the occasion.

They walked back to the building. Again the thrill when he took her arm at the crossing. They stood at the entrance of the building preparing their good-bys.

"I enjoyed the lunch," she said politely.

"The pleasure was all mine," he told her. "Well, Margy . . ."

Now the time had come to say good-by. She was reluctant to have it end. She felt that she wanted to give him a little present. So she said:

"I would like to tell you a little secret. No one knows outside of my relations." She paused. "I'm going to have a baby in December."

A flash of disappointment showed in his face. Then he smiled. He took her hand in both his and pressed it. "I'm glad, Margy, very glad."

She didn't hear what he was saying. She was rocked from head to toe again by that electrical shock at the touch of his hands.

"Thank you."

He released her hand slowly. "I always wanted to marry and have a lot of children."

"It's not too late," she said.

"I don't know," he said doubtfully. "I like children," he added. "I don't see any other reason for marrying. I'd have to be sure there'd be children." She felt that he was putting into words some doubt of himself.

"A lot of people marry just for companionship," she said.

"Companionship! I've had enough companionship to last me two lifetimes," he said almost bitterly.

"Yes, well . . ." she said, a little embarrassed at his emphatic tone. "I'm wishing for a girl."

"I'd want all daughters, too," he said. "If I had a son, I'm afraid I'd bring him up to hate his mother."

She didn't ask why. She knew.

Riding home in the trolley she thought: What's the

matter with me getting all thrilled and excited just because a man held my hand a second or two? Why I could easily turn into a loose woman, she assured herself with pleasant fear. The whole trouble, she told herself bluntly, is that I'm a married woman and don't get to sleep enough with my husband.

Chapter 31

Margy was proud of her swelling breasts. She admired herself. But that wasn't enough. She wanted Frankie to look and admire.

She stood before him in her slip. "Look!" she said.

"At what?" he asked.

"My bust."

"What about it?"

"It's filled out."

"So what?"

"So I look better. So I won't have any trouble nursing the baby."

"That's good." He turned away as if to terminate the conversation.

"Feel!" she commanded.

"Don't be silly," he said.

"Don't *you* be silly."

She took his hands and placed them on her breasts. His hands started to curve instinctively over the breasts, then flew open with the fingers rigid. With a sudden laugh she released his hands with a throwing-away motion. He was relieved and angry.

"Say it," he said. "Say what you're thinking."

"What am I thinking?" she asked, puzzled.

"That if I won't, someone else will."

"I thought no such thing," she said indignantly. "Besides, I don't know anybody else." She thought of Mr. Prentiss.

She got into her bathrobe and knotted the cord firmly about her waist. He relaxed, knowing that nothing more was expected of him. But obscurely, he was ashamed of his relief. He tried to make amends.

"I've been noticing," he said, "that your dresses do fit better."

"That's right," she agreed, then with unashamed vanity added, "I can wear the cheapest dress now and it looks as though I'm modeling it."

Her vanity went deeper than that. She felt that she looked very feminine and desirable now and she walked the streets to the stores with her head held proudly.

She was content. She was fed, housed, clothed and fulfilling her destiny as a woman. She felt no woman should want more than that. Of course she wanted more, but it was a dreamy want and nothing that had to be fought for at the moment. She wanted love and companionship. Well, she had Frankie's love such as it was and his companionship, such as *it* was. Maybe, she thought, that's all there is to marriage and I mustn't look for more. Bluntly, she felt the need of a more satisfying mating. She felt the need of security; an owned home so that there'd be no worry about being asked to move, or the rent raised. She wanted to be sure that there would always be food—that she'd never have to say to her child, "Eat that, and be lucky you got it." No, she thought, no child should be commanded to feel lucky just because he had the food and shelter and care that all children born are entitled to.

Her days were filled with household duties and sewing for the baby. She enjoyed making the bed and it became quite a ritual because she had her most satisfying thoughts then. She thought: About two years from now there'll be a little girl following me around when I make the bed. And when I smooth the sheets she'll make the same movements with her little hands and I won't say, go away, you bother me. I'll say, that's a good girl.

She wondered whether anybody had ever written a book about a bed. I would if I was a writer, she thought. People are conceived in bed, born in bed and die in bed—most of them. When we have trouble, we lie on the bed and cry. When we're happy we lie on it smiling, looking at the ceiling with hands clasped under our head. You go to see a girl friend but you don't talk real confidential until you're sitting on the bed together. Your first party dress is laid out on the bed and your wedding dress, too. And the night before a girl marries and lies smiling at the ceiling, her mother comes in and sits on the bed and talks. (Well,

Mama tried to, anyhow.) And the mother seems like a girl again, talking confidentially to another girl.

She wanted to tell somebody her ideas about the bed but there was no one. Frankie would think she was silly and her mother would be embarrassed. She would write Reenie about it but her thoughts never came out well in written words.

Well, when my baby's old enough, she thought, I can talk to her about things like that and she'll understand. She'll understand because she's coming from me—is part of me. She has to be like me. It wouldn't be fair if she was like the Malones, considering that they don't like me and Frankie isn't so happy about her coming.

Always she thought of the child as a girl. She knew that most women wanted sons. She didn't blame them. In some ways girls were a drug on the market and certainly they never got the breaks a boy got. A boy could be president or make a million dollars. What else could a girl do except marry? Well, she could work, of course. In a factory? Never. An office? Maybe. Schoolteaching's about the best work for a woman.

Some teachers, she thought, are nice and some are terrible. Some hate the children they teach because they can't marry and have their own. Some love children. They love 'em—well just because they love 'em or because they wanted their own children but no man ever . . .

I liked my Home Economics teacher. I was in love with my science teacher. I don't remember her name but I remember everything she said. Then there was that English teacher, Miss Griggins. It was hard to learn even how to parse a sentence from her because she was so mean. She's the one who went to the principal and reported that girl, Glad—her name was Gladys something—because she did poor schoolwork. Glad was smart in school but Miss Griggins tormented her because she came to class in spike heels and lipstick—because she had the nerve to do at fourteen what that teacher, with all her money and age and nobody to be accountable to, didn't have the nerve or feeling to do.

Maybe my daughter won't want to be a schoolteacher. Maybe she'll want to go on the stage. Oh, I hope so! I'll buy her ballet slippers and manage to get dancing lessons for her as soon as she's old enough to walk. She might turn out to be another Marilyn Miller.

she hummed happily.

Oh, the baby *must* be a girl! If I have a son I might get to be like Mrs. Malone or Mrs. Prentiss. I can well see how that could happen. Frankie's not affectionate. So I'd look for affection in my son. Without meaning to, I'd bring him up to believe that I was the only perfect woman in the world. I'd be jealous of his girls and I'd think he was too good for his wife. Maybe I'd really believe that he was trapped into marriage. I don't want to be like that. So it's got to be a girl.

Frankie talked the situation over with his best friend and newly made brother-in-law, Marty.

"Look, Marty, we were getting along pretty good and then this had to happen."

"It's a trap of nature," explained Marty, "to keep the world populated."

"Well, what has to be, will be," sighed Frankie.

"Is that bad, after all?" Marty wanted to know. "Ask me now if I want kids and I'll say, hell, no! But if they come along, I'll get used to it, I guess. I figure this way: things is got to be kept going on."

"True enough," agreed Frankie.

"Of course, there are enough other dopes in the world to keep it going," philosophized the friend, "and maybe a couple guys like us should be allowed to step aside."

"Yeah. I'm only one guy. Who'd ever miss my addition to the world?"

"They say," offered Marty consolingly, "that a lot of guys feel that way—don't want a kid at first. But when it comes along, why they're nuts about it."

"There's something in that. Right now I don't want it," admitted Frankie. "But somehow I got the feeling that I'm going to be crazy about the little feller."

"Sure you are," agreed Marty. "That's how nature makes suckers out of all of us."

Frankie did the best he could. Since the pressing need was money, he economized on his only luxury—cigarettes. He took to waiting a half-hour longer when he wanted one. He changed to a brand that cost a penny less a pack.

He controlled the instinctive gesture of pulling the package from his pocket and inviting "Smoke?" when he stood talking to someone for a moment. And when someone offered him a cigarette he said, "You bet! Thanks!" instead of, "I got some of my own here." He saved a few cents a week that way. As he dropped the coins in the dime-store piggy bank on which Margy had painted BABY in red nail polish, he'd say: "He might take a notion to go to Notre Dame someday, you know." Margy'd answer: "I'll see that she gets to college if it's the last thing I do."

All in all, he did the best he could for Margy. Each morning before leaving he said: "Don't do any lifting today, hear? Wait'll I get home." And although she contemplated no heavy lifting during the day, she was touched by his concern and promised to move no furniture during his absence.

Carrying the baby seemed to satisfy all of Margy's emotional and physical needs. She seemed to need nothing from Frankie. He, knowing this, was relieved, and enjoyed her little affectionate overtures, knowing nothing would come of them. They held hands while walking, and he slept with his arm about her. It was an ideal arrangement for him: affection without sex. They lived like two loving and understanding friends.

He wished it could last.

Obeying the doctor's orders to do a lot of walking, Frankie and Margy went for long Sunday hikes in Highland Park. These autumn, Sunday-morning walks were wonderful to Margy. Never had she enjoyed sun and wind and cool air and green grass and trees more. She breathed deeply and felt that the clean earth-scented air was good for the unborn baby.

They had to walk through narrow streets and pass several corners before they could get to the park. As her time came nearer and she began to look unwieldy, he got in the habit of releasing her hand from his, grabbing her elbow and steering her fast past groups of fellows loitering at newsstands in front of candy stores. Unduly sensitive, perhaps, she was quick to notice how the loafers stopped talking as she and Frankie drew near. She noticed the quick sharp look they gave her and the knowing one they gave Frankie; how they looked up at the sky as if unconcerned and whistled a bit of popular song as she and

Frankie went by. At such times Frankie's fingers tightened on her arm and didn't relax until they were well past the newsstand.

Margy didn't care about the loafers. She felt that people were the way they were and there wasn't a thing you could do about it. She knew that Frankie as a young fellow himself used to hang out with a gang in front of a candy store after Sunday Mass and, while maybe he himself hadn't made dirty remarks about pregnant women who passed by, certainly the other fellows had and he had listened. That's what made him ashamed now. He knew what the fellows were thinking and saying.

Margy wished that Frankie was the sort of person who wouldn't be concerned about the remarks. But he *was* concerned and that was that. Her pleasure in the walks wasn't worth the embarrassment she knew he felt. So when she was eight months gone she told him that the walks were getting to be too much for her.

She couldn't help feeling a little hurt when she saw how relieved he was—even though he protested that the walks were good for her and that she really ought to keep them up.

Chapter 32

Margy chose Dr. Paolski because he was the obstétrician recommended by the general practitioner of the neighborhood. She got to know a lot about Dr. Paolski during the six months of her relationship with him. She learned some things from him, others from observation and a lot from talking with other patients during the long hours of waiting in his reception room.

Dr. Paolski's grandfather had been a Polish boy, working—he was a serf almost—as stable boy on a baronial estate in Poland. He fell in love with one of the scullery maids—the one whose job it had been to pluck chickens all day for the baron's lavish household.

The stable boy and the scullery maid had a dream—a dream of starting a new life in America, a land where all men were equal. They married with this dream in mind. Their fellow servants, servants on nearby estates and neighboring serflike peasants, thought enough of this dream to contribute a hoarded coin or two toward it. Enough money was raised to buy a steerage passage to America. The newlywed pair left without the knowledge of, and minus the blessings of, their master.

They found a home in America, half of a four-room cold-water flat on McKibben Street in Williamsburg, Brooklyn. Their first son was born in America. He went to the public school of the neighborhood and grew up to be a smart boy. He started working in a sweatshop when he was sixteen. When he was twenty-two, he banded with four other sons of Polish emigrants and the combine rented a small one-window store on 28th Street in Manhattan and went into the raw fur-pelt business. In time, Stan Paolski accumulated enough money to buy a small detached house in East New York which, in spite of its name, is still in Brooklyn. He took his bride there. In the course of time he had a son whom he named John.

John Paolski, obstetrician, was a Brooklyn boy, born and bred. He studied at a Brooklyn college, interned at a Brooklyn charity hospital. He married a Brooklyn girl, the daughter of one of his father's partners in the fur business, and he set up practice in a semidetached, yellow-brick veneer house on Eastern Parkway, Brooklyn. He purchased the house with his wife's dowry.

His office, delivery room, hospital ward, diet kitchen and living quarters for his wife, himself and two daughters, and for his wife's aunt, were all under the same roof. Unlike most doctor's wives, Mrs. Paolski knew where her husband was at any hour of the day or night.

The entrance hall to the house served as reception room. It always seemed more crowded than it actually was. Five or six pregnant women, some in the last stages, could take up a lot of space. The dining room had been converted into a combined office, consultation and examination room. The kitchen adjoining, stripped of gas range and icebox, served as the delivery room.

There were six beds in the long, narrow, two high-windowed living room. The beds were so close together that there was no room for bed tables. Each bed had a small shelf over the foot of it which held the personal belongings of the patient. Most of these footboard tables held the same articles: a magazine or two of the true-story type, a plant always on the point of withering, cut flowers cramped into vases too small for them, a half-filled candy box and a pile of little envelopes containing whimsical or sentimental rhyming couplets signifying satisfaction on the birth of a baby. A milky glass tumbler, holding a colored-handled toothbrush, stood like a stiff expressionistic flower among the envelopes. Purses, containing makeup, comb and small change were kept under the pillows of the owners.

There was a little sun parlor, glass enclosed on three sides, attached to the dining room. The babies were kept there and visitors who wanted to gape fondly at the little bundles had to go out into the yard and look in from the garage driveway which separated the Paolski house from the house next door.

A kitchen had been set up in a corner of the basement.

The babies' formulas (that is, those babies who were not breast fed), and the mothers' meals were prepared there. Another corner of the basement contained washing machine, tubs and ironing board.

Mrs. Paolski's spinster Aunt Tessie did the cooking and laundry work. It was considered a fine arrangement. Aunt Tessie had no man, no home of her own. It was lucky for her that she had relations to look after her. Aunt Tessie slept on a cot near the washing machine. Once, Mrs. Paolski's mother, who was Aunt Tessie's sister, asked was it right that Tessie lived and slept in the cellar? It was not a cellar, Mrs. Paolski told her mother indignantly. It was basement living quarters and quite ideal, too—warm in winter from the furnace and cool in summer from being underground—or did Mama want to take Aunt Tessie to live with her and Papa? Mama agreed that it was a very fine basement—not damp like some.

A little beaverboard closet held Aunt Tessie's sparse wardrobe consisting of reluctant discards from her relatives' outfits. Since Aunt Tessie was supplied with room, board and clothes, and never went anywhere, she had no need of money. Naturally. Nevertheless, the good doctor often slipped her a five-dollar bill now and again—on Tessie's birthday and at Christmas. Sarah always said that Doctor would wind up in the poorhouse—the way he was generous. But since Aunt Tessie saved the five-dollar bills and since her meager will left her estate to the Paolski children, Sarah didn't worry too much about her husband's big heart.

Sometimes Aunt Tessie had a very disloyal thought. She thought that maybe her working for food, shelter, old clothes and ten dollars a year to keep in trust for the Paolski girls was kind of a break for Sarah and Doctor. But she never said anything about it because it was quite true that she had nowhere else to go.

The Paolski family lived on the second floor. The bathroom at the head of the stairs served family and nurse. (Aunt Tessie had her own private toilet in the basement.) The bathroom also served as a repository for the patients' bedpans. The "den" upstairs had been made over into a kitchenette and the master bedroom into a living room. The two daughters shared the other bedroom. Doctor and his wife slept in the attic. It was "finished off" and had one window. It had no heat in winter but Doctor and wife agreed it was healthful to sleep cold. It was inclined to be stifling in summer but Doctor explained that it was good to perspire; some body wastes were eliminated that way.

Sometimes Doctor decided to spend the night downstairs on the assumption that Mrs. So-and-so might decide to hemorrhage and he'd feel better if he were on the spot. On such occasions he stretched out on the black leather couch in his consulting room and Mrs. Paolski, who didn't like to sleep alone in the attic because she was afraid of mice, rested on the living-room divan. Of course these emergencies didn't come often; only on a sweltering night in August, for instance, or a bitterly cold night in January.

The house was home and hospital. It had provisions for everything except a corridor for husbands to pace off the agony of becoming fathers. They had to do their pacing on the street in front of the house. The neighbors were used to the sight of some man always pacing the sidewalk with slow measured steps. The neighbors liked it. Day and night there was a pacer. It was like having a perpetual watchman in the neighborhood. It gave householders a sense of security. There were never any burglaries on the block. Sometimes two men awaited birth; either they struck up a friendship and paced side by side or else passed each other every half-minute at a given point. At such times they looked like men picketing to protest the unfairness of life.

Dr. Paolski provided fair facilities for mothers who couldn't afford regular hospital fees and who were too proud to lie in at a charity hospital and too literate to call in a midwife. His fees were reasonable: twenty-five dollars for the delivery which included pre- and post-natal care. (Five dollars extra if it were a boy and circumcision was desired.) He asked three dollars a day for bed, food, nursing and care of the newborn. If a woman needed or wanted an anesthetic, that was three dollars extra.

All in all, Dr. Paolski provided a needed service at a low cost. He couldn't be blamed for cutting corners.

Chapter 33

Margy worked out her budget. Delivery and anesthetic—she'd have to have one, she was not brave enough—hospitalization—that came to seventy-two dollars. Cab each way, two dollars. She'd have to tip the day and night nurse a dollar each. Seventy-four. Make it seventy-five. She'd like to have a dollar extra in case she wanted to send out for a newspaper or something. Yes, seventy-five dollars would do it. It seemed very expensive to Margy.

Two weeks before the baby was due she had a conference with Frankie on finances. "We need seventy-five dollars," she said. "At the least, seventy-four. I've saved and I've saved but I only have fifty-six dollars."

"You said you'd manage," said Frankie.

"I meant it. And I tried. I saved your two-dollar raise. I tried to economize. But somehow the food bills got higher. I seem to be so hungry all the time."

"Well, don't worry, Margy. It's too bad that you have to go through the pain and trouble of childbirth and worry on the side about paying for it."

"Oh, the worry's good. It takes my mind off my own scaredness at least."

"Well, it'll work out all right. I'll cut out smoking altogether."

"Oh, no, Frankie! Your one comfort; your only extravagance. Besides, you don't smoke much."

"I'll lay off for two weeks then—the two weeks you're in the hospital. It won't be hard. Every time I feel like a cigarette, I'll think of you in the hospital. Doing without a smoke won't seem like anything at all, considering."

"We'll save two weeks on the gas, electric and ice bills while I'm in the hospital," she suggested hopefully.

"And food," added Frankie. "I'll stay at my mother's house and eat breakfast and supper there. That will save a lot."

He didn't feel too happy about the idea of eating at his mother's house. If he ate too eagerly of anything she'd say: "That's right, Frankie. Eat more! You don't get good cooking like this in your house."

"We ought to take out hospital insurance," he said. "I've been reading the ads. 'You never know when illness will strike,'" he quoted somberly.

"No, Frankie." She was firm about it. "I've never been sick, neither have you. We can't afford to pay out premiums year after year on such a gamble. We have life insurance. That's enough."

"But you never can tell," he persisted. "Like they say, illness strikes suddenly."

"People like us can't afford to be sick. We've got to keep well. If we lose our health . . ." she knocked on wood, he followed suit, "we're sunk."

"Everything's all right now, maybe. But what about when we get old?" he asked, feeling the full weight of his twenty-two years.

"It will be forever before we get old. And by that time we'll be on Easy Street. We'll have our own home, you'll have your own business and our children will be all through college."

"*Children?*" he groaned. "Gee, Margy, we can't have any more. Honest! A guy's got children, he gives hostages to fortune. I read that somewhere when I was in high school."

"What do you mean—hostages?"

"I mean when you have children you're in hock for the rest of your life."

"But if you bring up one you might as well bring up two or three; two close together and when they're ten and twelve, one more. So that when the two oldest leave home, there's still a child left in the house."

"No, Margy. One's enough. And I'll see to it personally," he said evenly, "that there'll be no more."

"But what good is a normal woman without children?" she cried out. "I've got to have children, Frankie."

"Why? Why? Give me one good reason why." He

thought of his mother's reason. "Aside from the fact that you want to tie me down."

Then she said something she hadn't known was in her mind. "We've got to have children because you and I have nothing between us."

There was a sudden intense quiet like the throbbing stillness after the cutting off of a high note in music that has been held too long. Her hand went to her mouth as if she would put back the words. She fought frantically for something else to say—something that would nullify her words to him. But she couldn't think of any magic phrases. Bless me, Father, for I have sinned, she whispered to an invisible confessor. She wanted to kneel before Frankie and ask him to forgive her for hurting him so. She moved forward in her chair but just then the baby stirred within her and she had a foolish notion that the baby would be harmed somehow if she knelt to ask forgiveness of its father.

His eyes were drawn to the little sudden movement under her taut skirt as the child within her stirred. And he winced with pity. She's the one who'll have all the pain and risk, he thought. Why does she fight so for it, he wondered, as if it were some great privilege? He got his hat and coat out of the closet. He spoke to her quietly.

"So you finally said it, Margy."

Familiar from childhood with the dread ritual of quarreling, she made no answer, knowing that like steps, one angry word made a path for another angry word to follow. He put his hat on carefully; he buttoned his coat slowly.

"Where are you going?" she asked as she had heard her mother ask her father many a night.

"Out," he said.

And his inflection was the same as her father's.

Of course they made up later that night. He explained his attitude quietly and logically and he begged her to understand. She assured him she did. And she really did understand. Unfortunately, understanding doesn't always connote sanction, conversion or forgiveness. She had an idea that whoever wrote something about to understand all is to forgive all, just didn't know what he was talking about. She apologized tearfully for what she had said.

She assured him that they had everything in the world between them.

They made up and were close for an hour. But there was a tear in the fabric of their marriage, and in spite of meticulous mending with words of forgiveness and understanding, there was a ridge that showed where the rent had been made.

It turned out, however, that their hurting quarrel had been for nothing. Frankie was never called upon to assume the responsibilities of parenthood.

The baby, a girl after all, was born dead.

Chapter 34

She happened to get the best bed in the room—the one next to the window. Visitors had room to stand at the side of this bed. Visitors to the other beds had to stand at the foot. Frankie took off from work and came over to see her as soon as they phoned him the news. Lines of grief took away the last vestige of boyishness left in his face. Embarrassed by the stares of the other five women, all newly-made mothers who were pityingly curious as to how he'd take it, he bent down to speak into Margy's ear. His back bumped the window ledge so he knelt down and rested his chin on the pillow.

"I'm sorry, Margy. Awfully sorry."

"I know, Frankie. I know."

"I can't tell you how terrible I feel."

"Poor Frankie!"

"Don't hold things against me, Margy."

"Why should I?"

"I acted like a heel saying I didn't want the baby and all. But *you* know."

"I know."

"I sounded off a lot but it was just talk. I would have been crazy about her."

"Would you, Frankie?"

"Don't you believe me?"

"Of course I believe you."

She knew he was sincere in what he was saying. He had been sincere, too, when he gave all his reasons why he didn't want children. Well, he was right, she was right. Or maybe they were both wrong. She didn't know. She didn't feel like talking about it. She wanted to go to sleep and forget for a while.

"Talk to me, Margy."

"About what?"

"Anything. Get it off your chest——the way you feel and all."

"Why?"

"What? Oh, because you were always such a one to talk things out. You'd talk a streak about the way wax looked dripping off a lighted candle. And now you have nothing to say about this. It doesn't seem natural."

"But there's nothing to say, Frankie. I was in labor for a day. You know about that. Then I heard the doctor say, 'Breech presentation.' Then the nurse said, 'Which forceps?' Then they gave me ether or something. When I woke up they told me the baby had been born dead. That's all."

"Didn't you cry when they told you?"

"I don't remember. I was too busy turning another corner at the time."

"What? Where? What corner?" She turned her head away. "Margy?" he whispered. She closed her eyes. "Margy!" he called in a little panic. Her breath went in deep and she held it shudderingly.

He got to his feet, mechanically brushing off his knees, a habit that was automatic with much kneeling in confessional and pew and at the altar. On his way out of the hospital he spoke to the nurse.

"I wish you'd have the doctor take a look at my wife," he said.

"What seems to be the trouble?" asked the nurse with bright routine interest.

"She talks a little like she was out of her mind—about turning around corners—things like that."

"She's still feeling the effects of the anesthetic, probably. But I'll have Doctor take a look at her."

"What seems to be the trouble, Mrs. Malone?" asked Dr. Paolski.

"Nothing. Only where I carried the baby, it's empty. But the emptiness hurts like it was a live thing. It seems to be eating me away inside."

"Oh, you're merely feeling afterbirth pains. They'll pass after a while. In the meantime, I'll have Nurse give you something."

It was a small funeral. No need for hearse, flowers or outside mourners. Frankie, his father and mother and Margy's parents rode out to the cemetery in the undertaker's limousine. Henny Shannon, holding the small white casket on his knees, sat next to the driver. Frankie, having had to take another day off from work, sat between his mother and mother-in-law. Malone sat on the drop seat facing them. The driver pointed out things of interest along the route. The passengers looked obediently and murmured conventional replies.

They should have felt tender and understanding, one toward the other, because they should have been drawn together in what people call the common bond of sorrow. But the bond between them was horror and hate and it pulled them away from each other. There was horror of being in that small closed space with something dead among them. Malone, for all his study of the dead, felt the same horror as the others. And there was hatred. Flo sat there hating the Malones. She'd always hated them anyhow—all except Frankie. And she only liked him because he was her son-in-law. Henny hated Frankie because through him grief had come to Margy. The Malones hated the Shannons because their daughter had brought this hardship on their only son.

Frankie was the only one not hating anybody. He was too busy worrying about his job and about money. He'd be docked two days' pay this week and there hadn't been enough money in the first place for the doctor and hospital. And now this! Forty dollars for the burial—very reasonable, the undertaker had assured him. Frankie knew it was reasonable but he worried all the same. He'd have to ask Margy could he pawn her wristwatch and her silver. Birth and death were two expensive items.

It was Margy's first Sunday afternoon in the little hospital. The narrow room was crowded with visitors. Frankie, his parents and Margy's parents stood in an ungraceful line on the window side of Margy's bed. The stares from the five pairs of eyes beat down on her face like a hot noon sun.

Mrs. Malone wished she had been nicer to Margy. At the moment she thought of her more as a suffering woman than a girl thief who had stolen her son. She meant to be comforting and understanding.

"Well, Marge," she said, "it's God's will."

"Yes, Mrs. Malone," said Margy obediently.

Mrs. Malone twisted her corseted hulk and looked behind her. "Lose something?" asked her husband.

"No, I'm trying to see where the stranger is," she said.

"What stranger?"

"A stranger to Marge who goes by the name of Mrs. Malone." Mr. Malone got the joke and guffawed. Everyone in the room stopped talking to stare at him, and Frankie was embarrassed.

"There's no Mrs. Malone here as far as you're concerned, Marge," she said. "Call me Mother."

"Yes, Mother." But the word stuck in Margy's throat and had to be washed down with another word. "Yes, Mother Malone."

Mr. Malone, bright as a new nail, came in with, "Mother Macree. Shure I love the dear silver . . ."

"Shut up," she said. He shut up. "Yes, you figure it all out," she said to Margy, "and you'll see it's God's will."

Margy tried to figure it out. If there's a God, she thought, and her fingers twitched with the instinct to make the sign of the cross to exorcise her blasphemous *if*, I can't believe He'd give a woman this great longing to give birth only to take the baby back. No! God must have more to do with His eternal time than to punish birth-torn mothers that way. Something went wrong and no use putting it off on God.

"If you can only make yourself believe it's all for the best," continued Mrs. Malone.

How can it be for the best? thought Margy. What best? What is gained by the way you suffer if no living child comes as a reward? All you get out of it is knowing you can suffer an awful lot without dying. And of what use is information like that to a person like me?

Mrs. Malone wanted to give Margy some kind of a gratuity. "Maybe I didn't always treat you right," she began. (No. That was giving too much away.) She made a fresh start. "Maybe you *think* I didn't treat you right. But it wasn't because it was you. I would have acted the same about any girl Frankie married. Suppose your baby was a boy and lived and you brought him up and sacrificed for him and just when he got old enough to be a comfort to you, he meets a strange girl and marries her and . . ." Flo interrupted because she couldn't keep still a moment longer.

"And how do you think I felt, Mrs. Malone, when a strange boy came along and took away the only child we had? But I try to be nice to Frankie just the same."

"And why not?" bridled Mrs. Malone. "You got a good son-in-law, Mrs. Shannon, believe you me."

"And if you ask me, you people got a damned fine daughter-in-law," said Henny.

Margy tossed restlessly. Frankie worried. "You're all bothering Margy," he said.

"Oh, it doesn't matter, Frankie," she said wearily. "I'm not listening anyhow."

"I guess we wore out our welcome," said Mrs. Malone.

Flo tried to fix things up. "If you didn't mean nothing out of the way, Mrs. Malone, neither did I," she said.

The apology was accepted. They dropped the argument and began to talk brightly of casual things. Flo saw a tear slide out from under Margy's half-closed lids. She took a try at comforting her.

"No use feeling bad, Margy," she said. "What's done is done and crying won't help. We must think of the living," she concluded vaguely.

Margy sat up in bed. "You mean well, Mama. You all mean well. But nothing you say seems to mean anything to me." She tried to explain.

"I don't miss the baby. How could I miss something I've never seen? I miss waiting for it to come. I miss planning for it." She started to talk fast and feverishly. She didn't mean to say all she did but once started, much of the accumulated heart hurt of her short life tumbled out in fast-spoken phrases.

"You see, I wanted this baby so bad. I needed it to prove something; to prove that this could be a good world. I was going to get all the things I never had for this baby to prove that there are more than dreams in a person's life. First, I was going to give it love.

"Ever since I was a child no one ever held me and said, 'I love you, Margy.' Oh, I know you loved me, Mama and Papa. You, too, Frankie—in your way. But no one of you would come right out and say it. I can excuse Mama and Papa—they never had the way. They had the way of the older generation. But you, Frankie . . ."

"Margy, Margy," he said. She waited. Maybe he'd say it and maybe everything could be saved. He thought of saying he loved her, but he couldn't. He couldn't alone with her and he could even less with his parents there.

Her father and mother said nothing. She hadn't expected them to say anything.

She said, "I always wanted a doll—a sentimental thing to want, I guess. But I never had one. I almost believed that there were no dolls left in the stores. I would have gotten a doll for my baby. Yes, I would! Even if we had to eat bread and salt washed down with water for a month to pay for it. A child forgets a time of hunger but never forgets the aching want of other things.

"And if she ever got lost, I wouldn't've hit her when I found her. I would've been so happy to get her back again. I'd . . ." She stopped talking. Her throat was tightening up and she didn't want to cry in front of them.

Flo's thoughts ran under her daughter's words. She never understood me. She doesn't remember how hard I tried. All she remembers is the quick slap; the times I didn't get her a doll or a new winter coat. She couldn't know that I loved her because I never could say it in so many words and I had no way of proving it. She never knew that the slap, the scolding was a way of taking it out on her because she made me feel bad because I couldn't do for her all that should have been done. Oh, I wish her child had lived! She would have gone through what I went through, then. She would have learned then why I couldn't do better. She would have come to understand that I was a good mother in my way.

Mr. Malone remembered the time Frankie had wanted a pair of skates and how he couldn't afford to buy them for the child. The boy had bought one rusty skate from the junk dealer for a nickel. The memory came sharply into focus: the child hopping up and down on one foot propelling the skate which was on the other foot. It had bothered Malone. He had instructed the boy to alternate the one skate so he wouldn't grow up lopsided.

Frankie was always a one, thought Mrs. Malone, to

want to go to a boys' camp in the summer. But there were the other children and not enough of money or anything else to go around. Maybe she should have tried harder to get the money to send him. But no, she decided, she had done the right thing. If she had indulged Frankie, the other children would have begged and teased for things. I couldn't give to him and deprive the others. But if I had a chance to do it over again . . . she sighed.

Henny Shannon had his thoughts: A doll for a girl, tin soldiers for a boy. A girl practices being a mother, and a boy a general. They should have things like that—things all children want. If they don't get nothing along that line they grow up figuring they're not entitled to much. They grow up learning to be glad just to have a roof over their head and something to eat. They figure they get a break when they get a job—any old job just so it pays a few dollars. Because they didn't have a doll or tin soldiers or skates when they were kids they grow up figuring they got no right to expect anything at all but the chance to work so that they might live and to live so that they might work. And people ought to be allowed to expect a little more out of life than that.

I told her I didn't want children, thought Frankie. She'll never forget that. But if this child had lived I would have tried to see to it that it got better breaks than we got. But what's the use of telling her that now? No use telling anybody anything if you can't prove it.

As if she could know all their thoughts and was now taking it upon herself to correlate them into a whole, Mrs. Malone spoke for the group.

"Marge," she said, "there's things you'll never understand until you bring up a houseful of children. Parents don't mean to deprive their children. But the way things is, they got to deprive them sometimes. A good child understands how that is. A bad child grows up brooding on it. Now I don't blame you for feeling mean. You lost your baby. That's a terrible thing. But you'll get over it, believe it or not. We all feel bad. What happened to you happened to us in a kind of way. After all, it was my first grandchild. And that has a meaning to me. I get all choked up when I think of the other day when we rode out to the cemetery. A person wouldn't be human if things like that didn't make them feel just terrible. But like your mother said, it's all over. Like she said, we got to think of the living. I guess you understand now, Marge."

But Margy was tired of understanding; of trying to know how it was with others. She leaned forward on her elbow and looked straight into Mrs. Malone's eyes. "Mother Malone," she began.

In an instant, the way a dream covers years in a split second, Mrs. Malone had a vision as soon as Margy spoke her name. The vision was that Margy knew her, Mrs. Malone's, worth at last. Margy would now be to her what her own daughters had never been—friend and confidante. From now on Margy would say to Frankie: "Go see your mother, Frankie. I'll stay home." "Frankie, your mother's a wonderful woman. You owe everything in the world to her." "Spend more time with her. Go see her every night. I'll step aside because I know she has more right to you than I have." "Don't buy me any presents for my birthday or Christmas. Put the money toward a present for your mother." "Ah, you can't do enough for your mother, Frankie. She's a wonderful woman."

All this passed through Mrs. Malone's mind before Margy repeated more insistently. "Mother Malone, I want to tell you something."

"What, Marge?"

"Mother Malone," said Margy, "I hate you!"

"What did you say?" croaked Mother Malone, her face flooding slowly with a turgid red color.

"I *said* . . ." Margy spoke quietly, not opening her teeth to let the words out. "I said, I hate you!"

The last thing Margy saw, before she turned away from them all and closed her eyes, was the red color receding from her mother-in-law's face, leaving in its wake sloppy red splotches.

They say, thought Margy, that when a person suffers grief or pain, it makes them nobler in character. That's not true. Not in my case, anyhow. When things were right with me it was easy to pretend people always meant well and easy to overlook mean things said and done. But after you go through something bad you realize that all the rosy ideas you had about things and people were childish make-believe. Or it could be that after suffering something you don't have enough feeling left to pretend to yourself that it's a right world. Or could it be that suffering wipes all foolishness out of you and brings you up to the truth and the truth is that a lot of people are small and cruel?

Take Frankie's mother. Did the suffering of giving birth make a big person out of her? No! She went through what I went through but it didn't make her ache for me when she knew what might be ahead of me. And take me: I went through once what she went through four times. But it doesn't make me feel sorry for her in any way. It makes me hate her.

I don't feel holy and broad-minded just because I had pain and have grief. I feel cheated all the way along the line. I feel hate, too. I hate Frankie's folks. I mustn't hate Frankie because I'm married to him and I have to live with him. It wouldn't be right to hate Mama and Papa, because my flesh and blood and bones come from them and it would be hating myself.

I hope I get over this feeling of hating everybody and thinking that nothing at all in the world is any good. I *must* get over it. Because how can I—how can anyone live in this world unless they have regard for other people and a lot of hope for a decent future?

If I ever got to really believing that things would never be any better than they are right now, I guess I'd just as soon lie down and die.

Chapter 35

But Margy was young and resilient.

Against her will, almost, she found herself interested in the concentrated life of the home-hospital. She found herself speculating on the family life of the Paolskis. She wondered how it would affect the two daughters—growing up with babies being born daily or nightly in the converted kitchen beneath their bedroom. Did they think that the whole of life was the routine of birth? Did the screams of the women wake them at night or were they so used to them that they slept through them? Would they feel lost if they went to live somewhere else and, passing through a hall on entering or leaving a house, not see a row of beds and patients out of the corner of their eye?

She enjoyed chatting with Aunt Tessie when Aunt Tessie brought up her tray. She became friends with her fellow-patients. She began to enjoy the evening visiting hours which were for husbands only. Toward the end of her stay there, an evening seemed like a bit of a party.

The five mothers and Margy had enjoyed the supper Aunt Tessie had prepared for them. They commented on the luxury of having a tray in bed; admitted, as they did every night, that the dainty salads were a treat because they had no time at home to fix a salad and even if they did, *he* wouldn't touch it. All *he* wanted was meat and potatoes and a piece of coffee cake from the bakery.

The husbands seemed to arrive at the hospital all at the same time as if they had waited on the corner for each other. Each night it was a different husband's turn to treat the girls to ice cream. Each night one of the men walked in carrying a carton of a quart and a half of strawberry ice cream. No one knew why it had to be strawberry but Brooklyn men seem to prefer that flavor above all others—even though they don't eat it, they like to buy strawberry ice cream.

Each night Nurse made the same remark before she turned the carton over to Aunt Tessie for serving. "You really shouldn't've brought cream. They'll all get too fat." But after the mothers had been served and each mother had contributed a generous spoonful of her cream to make up a dishful for Aunt Tessie, Nurse sat on the radiator shelf swinging her heavy legs, taking part in the good-natured banter while she spooned out the ice cream that clung to the sides and bottom of the carton, and ate it.

The mothers, freshly made up, with hair neatly brushed, lay back on their plumped-up pillows. Those who were mothers for the first time usually wore be-ribboned rayon bedjackets over flimsy nightgowns—the last item of sexy finery most of them were ever to own. Repeaters—mothers for the second, third or more times—usually wore long-sleeved, buttoned-to-the-neck flannel gowns. They preferred warmth to beauty.

Each husband leaned over a bed shelf and conversed privately with his wife until after the ice cream had been eaten. With the clearing away of the plates and spoons, the talk became general. Men exchanged remarks with each other and with wives other than their own. The women traded understanding smiles and looks with each other as they recounted trifling incidents and funny happenings of the hospital day. All, save Margy, were glowingly serene as they sat back against their pillows with their proudly swelling breasts straining at jacket and gown.

"Nurse tells me that my son, Mike . . ."

"Michael," corrected his wife.

". . . is making passes at the girls out in the nursery," said Mr. Jones.

"He takes after his old man," said Mr. Brown.

Laughter.

"Nurse is a riot," confided Mrs. Williams with an arch smile at Nurse, who swung her legs more energetically. "Know what she did today?"

Several husbands assured her that they didn't but they sure could guess. Then they leered good-naturedly at Nurse.

"Well," continued Mrs. Williams, "she brought my Shirley in for her . . ." Mrs. Williams paused coyly.

"For her two-o'clock nursing," prompted Mrs. Brown shamelessly.

"Well, anyhow, you know how my Shirley only has three hairs on the top of her head?" She waited. The other women assured her that they knew how Shirley only had three hairs. "Well, what does Nurse go and do but tie a big pink bow around those three hairs. I thought I'd *die!*"

"She's a little vamp, that one," was Nurse's evaluation of the three-haired Shirley. Mr. and Mrs. Williams tried not to look too proud.

A thought occurred to an older, more thoughtful woman. She felt that maybe the talk was hurting Margy because Margy had no baby to brag about. She changed the conversation suddenly.

"Do you think the snow will stick?" she asked.

All of them got it. The smiles died from their faces and they carefully avoided looking at Margy as their eyes went to the windows and they gave opinions concerning the lasting qualities of the newly falling snow.

Margy wished they wouldn't. It made her feel ill at ease; isolated from normal life. She spoke for the first time that evening, wishing to bring things back to normal.

"Mrs. Brown, you tell them what happened when Nurse brought in Carol . . ." Margy timed the pause, timed her smile, ". . . for *her* two-o'clock nursing." They laughed. Margy's weak gag had gone over or so they pretended.

"Oh, it was nothing," deprecated Mrs. Brown.

"It was so!" insisted Mrs. Williams indignantly. "Tell it."

"Let Margy tell it. She can do it better than me," conceded Mrs. Brown.

"Tell it, Margy. Tell it," chorused the women. So Margy told it.

"Well, it seems that when Nurse brought Carol in . . ."

"For her two o'clock . . ." prompted Mr. Jones.

"Aren't men *terrible?*" squealed Mrs. Jones.

"Like I was saying," continued Margy, "Nurse brought Carol in. She lifted her little head . . ."

"And she's only five days old, too," interpolated Mrs. Brown proudly.

"Who's telling this?" demanded Margy, pretending anger.

"You are," conceded Mrs. Brown meekly.

"Let me, then. Anyhow," continued Margy, "she lifted her little head and looked straight at each one of us in turn. Then she yawned—like she was bored, closed her eyes and let her head fall down on Nurse's shoulder."

Everyone laughed. They laughed too loud; too thoroughly. It's not that good a story, thought Margy bitterly. It's just that they're sorry for me.

Eventually the nurse brought the evening to a close by consulting her wristwatch, bouncing off the radiator shelf and announcing:

"Nine o'clock. Beddy-bye time. We must have our beauty sleep."

Obediently and with some relief, six husbands craned over six beds and kissed six wives good-night. The husbands left in a body after Mr. Williams cautioned Nurse not to take any wooden nickels and Mr. Brown admonished her not to do anything he wouldn't do.

Five fathers and Frankie walked around the house and stood in the driveway under the falling snow. Nurse came to the sun parlor and snapped on the light. They stared through the glass at the fruit of their loins lying pink and crumpled in containers resembling packing boxes.

"Look at that loafer over there," said Mr. Jones, pointing proudly at an unpressed infant. "Yes, sir, if my old lady didn't go and get me a son."

"Who do you suspect?" asked Mr. Brown, jealous because his wife had got him only a girl.

"Nobody. I'm wise, see? I got me a Frigidaire, home."

Like a disapproving gesture, the light in the nursery snapped out. The men walked away as one of them told the hoary old iceman joke. They laughed heartily. As they reached the street someone said:

"How about a beer before . . ." he let his voice go falsetto ". . . before beddy-bye time?"

The men laughed again. Louder this time.

Frankie was the first one to say, "Sure."

The women, bedding down for the night, heard the man laughter through the closed windows. They smiled at each other.

"The men! They sure have the life," philosophized Mrs. Brown contentedly.

"You said it!" agreed Mrs. Williams.

"They have all the fun and we have all the trouble," said Mrs. Jones.

"Ain't that the truth, Margy?" asked Mrs. Williams. No answer came from Margy's bed.

"What do you know! She's asleep already," said the woman in the bed next to Margy's.

"If I could sleep like that. . . ." said Mrs. Brown who had a passion for unfinished sentences.

"If you could sleep like that, what?" asked Mrs. Thompson, a woman who abhorred the vacuum made by unfinished sentences.

"Why I wouldn't be in the situation I'm in tonight," said Mrs. Brown with coy lewdness.

Nurse's voice cut into the laughter. "That's about all, girls. Sleep tight, now, and don't ask for the bedpan during the night unless you really have to go."

The lights clicked off. Margy turned her face to the window. She was wide awake. From within the dark room, she watched the rhythm of the falling snow outside the window.

Chapter 36

Margy was supposed to stay in bed ten days. But on the seventh day she was up and around helping the day nurse carry in the babies for feeding and giving bottles to the two babies who were on formulae. On the eighth day she told Dr. Paolski that she wanted to go home. He demurred, saying she had had a harder time than most women and there was the shock of losing her baby. He agreed, however, that she would be happier at home when she pointed out that her bed was needed. A woman had come in the day before and was occupying the couch, with a screen around it, in the doctor's office. (And it was damned cold sleeping in that attic, too.) When she paid him, she was pleasantly surprised when he refunded six dollars, charging her only for the eight days instead of the full time the way he had a right to do. She considered the six dollars a windfall until she remembered that it would just make up the pay for the two days Frankie had lost from work.

The little imitation leather week-end bag she had carried to the hospital had never been fully unpacked. She went through the bag before she packed her nightgowns and toilet articles. The dozen Birdseye diapers and three Vanta shirts that out of loyalty or sentiment she had bought by mail from Thomson-Jonson were still sealed in their tissue envelopes. These could be returned and something else bought for the credit check. There were also three flannelette nightgowns that she had made by hand. She stared at the featherstitching—pink for a girl. She didn't want to take them home. They'd be reminders. . . .

She turned them over to the day nurse with instructions to give them to some mother who might run short or come ill prepared.

"I'll do that," promised the nurse. "I'll say they're a present from a woman who walked out of here with empty arms." Margy winced at the sugary sentimentality of the little speech.

Although ready to leave, she hung around until two so that once more she could help with the babies at their feeding time. She said good-by to the six mothers—the one on the couch now had Margy's bed. She exchanged addresses with them and promised to visit each one. They knew and she knew that the promises would never be kept because seeing their babies would remind her that her own would have been that big if it had lived.

She gave the day nurse a dollar tip and left a dollar in Mrs. Brown's care to give to the heavy-legged night nurse. She shook hands with Dr. Paolski who said he was sorry —sorry as hell. She said he shouldn't worry. It was one of those things. He said he'd be seeing her again in a year's time, he hoped.

She went down to the basement to say good-by to Aunt Tessie. Aunt Tessie was sitting on her cot reading a day-before-yesterday issue of the New York *Graphic*. Frantically she crammed it under her pillow when she heard the step on the stairs. Apprehension left her when she saw it was only Margy. She stood up and her face looked withered and lined under the hard unshaded light of the one-hundred-watt bulb overhead which was needed day and night in that dark corner. They murmured conventional good-bys as they shook hands. As Margy turned to go, Aunt Tessie said:

"Look! I'd like to tell you something. I know you feel bad. But it's better to lose something than never in your life have anything *to* lose."

"I don't know," said Margy. "I don't know."

Chapter 37

Margy stared hungrily out of the trolley window. Familiar scenes had a clear unfamiliar look like scenes in a foreign country, read about, but seen for the first time. Details stood out sharper, colors seemed more vivid and the street sounds had fresh meaning.

She was disappointed when she didn't have that same fresh sense of sharp discovery when she walked into her home. It was like something she had left behind a long time ago. It seemed small and shabby and dusty. The seam in the tapestry that she had hardly noticed before now stood out like an ineptly healed scar. There were pockets of dust within the petals of the artificial red roses in the black bowl. The few slender shabby books made the heavy bookends seem silly. And there was too much blue everywhere. She found she didn't like blue any more.

She went to the hope chest where she had stored the little dresses and slips she had made for the baby. Might as well get that first stab over with, she thought. To her relief, the tiny garments were gone. She surmised that her mother had taken them away.

She took down the blue tapestry, shook the dust out of it and put it and the bookends in the hope chest. She threw the artificial roses in the trash bag.

The icebox smelled musty. The few odds and ends of food she had left there were moldy. She threw everything into the garbage can except the bottle of ketchup and two eggs which she hoped might still be good. She opened the windows and the icy wind that came in and filled the folds of the curtains and made them stand out like pennants felt good to her. She swept, dusted and washed until her little home was fresh and clean again.

In cleaning the bathroom she saw a pile of Frankie's

soiled linen lying in the tub. Suddenly she felt very tired. She wanted to lie down but the bed was up in the wall. She felt it might be too heavy to lift down so soon after coming from the hospital. She felt cold. She found she was trembling. She closed the windows and got a blanket from the closet. I did too much, she thought, the first day home. She opened the oven of the gas range and lit it. She sat before the warming oven wrapped in the blanket.

As the warmth entered her body, she relaxed and felt again the pains of emptiness—the ones the doctor called afterbirth pains. She wanted to cry but she had the same feeling she had had when her mother kept slapping her the time she was lost; that she mustn't give in and cry. Her eyes grew hot and her face settled into ugly sullen lines as she fought down the desire to cry her eyes out.

She looked into the warm black cavern of the oven and thought: Many women sat this way before a gas oven after they had turned it on and not lighted it. I wonder what their thoughts were.

She leaned forward and saw the gas flame flickering through the round holes of the bottom of the stove. As she looked, the flame sucked inward and disappeared. She jumped up in a panic and turned off the gas. She looked fearfully around the little kitchen as if she feared some malignant presence was there fixing things so she'd die.

And she didn't want to die! No, not ever. She wanted to live—to keep on living, no matter what happened.

She noticed that she hadn't closed the kitchen window all the way. She felt relieved, knowing that the wind coming in had sucked out the gas flame—that no invisible evil being was responsible.

After a while she put fresh makeup on, brushed her hair and went out to the stores. She remembered there had been mail in their box when she came home. But she hadn't had the key. She took it from its place under the alarm clock.

There was a letter from the furniture company, the gas company and the insurance company. Of course, Frankie hadn't been home to pay the collectors when they called. She stuffed them unopened into her purse. There was a letter from Reenie and one with the Thomson-Jonson letterhead.

She read the letters as she walked along. Reenie wrote

that she just didn't know what to say. She was so sorry and she hadn't come to the hospital because it would have made her feel too bad. But she'd come to see Margy as soon as she could at home. There was enclosed a card with Father Bellini's name engraved on it. The card had a message. It said: "Do not lose your faith, my child." Clipped to the card was a smaller card with a Sacred Heart medal attached to it.

The other letter was from Mr. Prentiss. He had heard of her loss, he wrote. No words that he could say . . . but he knew she'd take hold somehow. . . . He had so much confidence in her strength. Into each life some rain must fall, he wrote. However, each cloud had a silver lining.

The words of a popular song came to Margy's mind. "Look for the silver lining. . . ."

Sunny. Marilyn Miller's show. I was going to buy my girl ballet slippers, she thought. I was going to call her Marilyn.

She walked down three steps to a basement store. As usual, the door on which was chalked TONY. ICE. was locked. Summer and winter it was always closed and locked. Yet she had expected it to be open this time. Why, she didn't know, except the world seemed to have changed so much she thought this, too, must be changed. There was a grubby pad on a hook and a stub of a pencil on a string. She wrote instructions for resumption of ice delivery. Ice wasn't needed in winter if people had a box attached outside the window. But the landlord didn't like boxes on the sills. Just the same, resolved Margy, I'm going to put up a box. I can save sixty cents a week that way. And if the landlord doesn't like it, he can get another tenant. I'm tired of always considering other people and being afraid to do this or that.

The bakery man seemed pleased to see her again. He knew she had given birth to a baby and that it had died. Frankie had told all the tradespeople when they inquired. The bakery man said nothing. But after he had wrapped her coffee ring, he slipped a sugar cookie under the string, the way he did sometimes when shy little children came in to make purchases.

The delicatessen woman was less tactful. "I hear you lost your little one," she said.

"Yes," said Margy.

"It's tough. Sure is tough."

"Yes," said Margy.

"How did it happen?"

But Margy didn't want to talk about it. "I'm in a little hurry," she said. "I'll take a stick of butter and a pint of milk."

"I can see you didn't change any," said the woman, huffed because Margy had changed the subject so abruptly. "You forgot your empty again."

"If my head wasn't tied on . . ." Margy began her familiar apology.

"I got to charge you a deposit."

"That's all right. I'll bring in two bottles tomorrow."

"Make sure they're from this store."

"Listen," said Margy. "We all have our faults. One of mine is that I forget to bring back bottles. That doesn't mean I'm a crook and would put over a different bottle on you—not that you'd let me—for the sake of two cents."

"No? Well, you wouldn't be the first that tried to put a ringer over on me."

"I've been dealing in this store a year now and I've never done that. Furthermore, this isn't the only store in the neighborhood. You can keep your butter and your milk."

"Don't be like that just because I want my own bottles back."

"I'll be any way I please."

She walked out of the store trembling. It was the first time she could remember quarreling with anyone over a little thing. She bought butter and milk at another store.

She had the potatoes peeled for supper before she remembered that Frankie didn't know she was home and that he'd go to his mother's for supper.

He got home at nine. After a lingering supper at his mother's home he had gone out to the hospital. He had had a pinch of fear when he saw another woman in Margy's bed. The nurse had explained. It had been Frankie's turn to bring ice cream that night. He brought it home because he had been too surprised to leave it at the hospital. There was a lot of it. It was runny on the outside but still firm in the middle. They ate it.

Afterward they sat at the kitchen table and went over the little pile of accumulated bills. There was a gas bill, an electric bill, a polite but subtly threatening note from the furniture company saying they'd like to believe that the Malones had overlooked two weekly installments on their furniture bill by accident and trusting that it wouldn't happen again. A printed slip from the insurance collector stated correctly enough that he had found no one home when he came for the weekly premium and trusting that someone would be home the next time as it was a serious thing to let a policy lapse, he was very truly yours.

Frankie produced the undertaker's bill last. She read: *Item: To Burial, Malone Infant.* There was the imprint of an oblong rubber stamp .that said *Paid* with the date written in in ink and someone's initials. He put two pawn tickets on top of the paid bill.

"It took everything I could scrape together to pay that one bill," he said. "It made me feel bad to have to pawn your wristwatch and the silverware but there was no other way out."

She shoved the bills, notes and pawn tickets away from her and stood up.

"Going to bed?" he asked.

"I'd like to write to my old boss, first."

"But why?"

"Maybe I can get my old job back."

Very carefully he arranged the papers in a neat pile and put them in the kitchen-table drawer. Without comment he walked into the living room, got the bed down and brought out the bedding from the closet. She followed him into the living room.

"It would help out," she said. "We'd get out of debt. We have to get out of it or we'll be sunk the rest of our lives."

He said nothing. He went into the bathroom, leaving the door open. He turned on the water. When she went to him, he was washing his hands. He turned one hand over the other in rhythmic, anguished movements—the way she used to do when her father and mother quarreled. She knew how he felt. She put her arms around his waist from the back and looked at him through the mirror of the medicine chest.

"Why do you object so, Frankie? Other men's wives

241

work. Times've changed. No one looks down on a man any more because his wife works—especially if they have no children."

He shrugged her lightly holding arms away as he turned off the water with one forceful twist of his wrist. He reached for a towel and dried his hands thoroughly before he answered.

"What are you trying to do," he cried, "put a finish to our marriage?" He threw the towel at the bar. It missed and fell to the floor. He walked out of the room.

She thought: My going to work won't finish it. It started to end the first time you pulled away from me when I put my arms around you.

It took her a long time to pick up the towel and an even longer time to smooth it out and hang it up. When she went out into the living room, she saw him standing at the window, expectant, as though he were waiting for her.

"Margy, what are you trying to do to me?"

Suddenly she became alert—wary. So many unformed thoughts—nebulous questions in her mind. And now the answer was coming.

"I always wanted to support my wife like a normal man. And I could have done it, too, if it hadn't been for the baby. Now don't get me wrong. If that child had lived, I would have wanted to support it the way I want to support you. I would have done the very best I could for it."

But you wouldn't have been able to love it, she thought, no more than you are able to love me.

"But I was right in the first place. People like us just can't afford to have children. If I had a better job, more pay, it would be different. You can't see it my way, I know. But I'm right. And a lot of other people would say so, too."

Yes, he was right, thought Margy. There was a class of comfortably fixed, educated, altruistic people who made a profession or a hobby out of uplifting the masses. They would claim that Frankie was right—that there should be no children unless economic conditions were favorable.

But she was right, too, in wanting children. Her want went beyond the logic of economics; it was rooted in nature—the survival of man. She knew women who said: "Of course I want a child. But not until we can afford to give it *everything*." She considered that these women were cowards—using a modern economic cliché to hide their cowardice.

She didn't argue the point with him as to who was right; who was wrong. Bad quarrels come when two people are wrong. Worse quarrels come when two people are right. Anyhow, it was over now, and there was no use arguing.

"You said something," she said. "What did you mean? When you asked me what was I trying to do to you?"

"Skip it."

"No, Frankie. It's time you told me. It wasn't fair that you didn't tell me from the beginning. I knew there was something wrong with our marriage but I didn't know what."

She sat next to him on the bed and waited. After a while, not looking at her, he began to talk.

"People are born a little a certain way," he began. "Then as they grow up things seem to happen that make them more that way." He thought over what he had said and wasn't satisfied with the way it had come out. He tried a different approach.

"My father was always rough and ready. My mother got to be that way, too, in competition with him. But underneath she was different. I was the first child. She kept me pretty close to her. She was always talking to me, trying to make me different from my father. He got on to it and did the opposite. He tried to toughen me; made me go out and fight with the boys; went out of his way to talk dirty in front of me. I didn't want to be the way she was making me—a sissy. And I didn't want to be his way—loudmouthed, dirty jokes all the time. So . . ."

"But don't get me wrong," he burst out. "I don't want to go around sleeping with fellers. I . . . I don't want to sleep with anybody. That's about the way it is," he said.

"I like girls—always did. But after I'd take a girl to a dance and we'd stand in the vestibule and she'd want to . . . it used to disgust me. But I felt different about you. You seemed sensible—your feet on the ground—no baby talk; no lovey-dovey stuff."

"I'm sorry," she murmured, "that I fooled you. I didn't mean to."

"The whole thing's not your fault," he said. "Not mine.

It's just one of those things. But I did want to marry, have a home of my own and support my wife in it. Just to prove that I was like any other man."

Why didn't he want a child, then, to prove it? thought Margy. Ah, well, she concluded, when someone is mixed up about certain things, it's hard to figure out what makes him want one thing and not another.

"But in the long run, I shouldn't've got married," he concluded. "I had no right . . ."

"Of course you had . . . have a right," she said. "Only it should have been a different type of girl. Someone who fitted in with you better—who didn't brood or expect a husband to be a sweetheart all the time. Yes, someone like Sandy, the girl in your office, who calls you feller. Only someone not all the way like Sandy."

"I guess I don't look so good to you any more."

"Don't belittle yourself, Frankie. No. Please don't. You're so decent and hardworking and honest. You always try to do the right thing. You turned out fine, considering what your mother and father did to you."

"Margy!" he called out. There was pleading in his voice and a little fright, too.

For once her woman's instinct failed her. Her first impulse was to take him into her arms and say, There, dear. But she hesitated because he had repulsed her too many times. Yet maybe this was the time to take hold again; to put her arms around him. Maybe he needed her now—wouldn't push her away.

But she wasn't sure any more. She did nothing.

"Margy," he said, "don't write that letter to your old boss."

She waited a long time before she answered. Then she said, "We're both very tired."

He waited a long time before he replied. He said, "It's been a day."

She turned out the light.

She lay beside Frankie in the dark. And she felt lost and unhappy. She missed the child she had carried within her during the summer, fall and early winter. With sudden aching desperation, she put her arms around Frankie and held him tightly. She waited, holding her breath. If he relaxed in her arms, she knew she'd weep scalding, cleansing tears. They would be one together in common trouble and common understanding. She would try to fall in love with him.

But almost frantically, he struggled out of her arms, saying in something like horror: "Margy! It's less than ten days since . . . you can't be thinking of . . ."

She let her breath out in a shuddering sigh.

The end!

"No, dear," she said gently. "That will be the last thing in my mind for a long time. It's just that I feel so alone and I want to be close to somebody and I thought maybe you felt alone, too, and I thought it wouldn't hurt if we held each other a while. Nothing more than that."

He took her in his arms, then, and they lay talking in the dark. They talked about little inconsequential things; the gossip of the neighborhood; news of Cathleen and Marty, her husband; about how Mr. Malone was talking of giving up trying to learn the undertaking business and how Mrs. Malone was screaming about all the money wasted on lessons.

"And that reminds me," he said. "I'm in a sort of a fix. I didn't think you'd be home for two more days and . . . well . . . my mother expects me for supper tomorrow night."

She thought: Let him have his mother. Let her have him. It will be good for him to have someone when I let go. She said: "That's all right, Frankie. I'll go over and eat with Mama and Papa. Your mother will be happy and my folks will be happy. It works out fine."

"You won't have to bother cooking," he said.

"That's right," she agreed.

That's the way it's going to happen, both thought in their different ways. First there'll be the eating apart for a while. Then we'll decide it's foolish to pay rent on the apartment when we're never there. We'll live apart pretending it's just for a little while. We'll see each other every night for a few hours. Then things will come up—excuses—a night when it's raining too hard or one of us is too tired. Meetings will be skipped. We'll go back to having dates once in a while. And in time the whole thing will be over and we'll pretend that we don't know how it ever happened. And people will say: "But they always seemed to get along so well!"

His thoughts left hers and went off on a personal tangent. Maybe I should go West, he thought, and start my life over. But what do I know about the West? Nothing, except I always read in books and in history that a person always went West for a fresh start or to find a fortune. I might get out there and find it's no better than here and I might have trouble getting the kind of work I'm used to. No, I'll have to stick it out here. I'll work harder and try to save more. Only I don't want to live with my mother any more. I'll stay there a while to please her and then I'll get a room nearer my work. Save time—maybe carfare that way.

Thus he made plans to reconstruct his life.

People say, thought Margy, that a sharp clean break is the sensible and kind thing. I don't believe that. Marriage is too important to be ended by a sudden announcement. He'll stay at his folks and I'll stay at mine. As time goes on, we'll see each other less often—have even less to say to each other than we have now. And there'll come a time when the marriage isn't there any longer.

She thought of Mr. Prentiss. I mustn't make a mistake the next time, she thought. Maybe he lived with his mother too long. Maybe . . . still, he likes children; he'd be a good father. I always think of him. She sighed deeply and decided she'd cross the bridge that was Mr. Prentiss when she came to it.

Frankie heard her sigh and his arms tightened about her. She felt him draw closer to her. Her desire to love him was gone. It would never come back. But the need to comfort him was still there.

"Go to sleep, dear," she whispered, "and forget everything. Don't worry and never be afraid. Let me hold you the way I'd hold my child. And you can make believe you're a little boy again, safe with your mother. Just for tonight."

He was the first to fall asleep.

The dream started before she was fully asleep. She moaned, trying to cut off sleep and avoid the sad dreaming. But she was so tired—so tired. Her day had started in the hospital and ended at home. She had done so much —thought so much. The dream formed relentlessly and went forward inexorably.

She felt the hot summer wind on her legs and looked down at her new brown sandals. Again she was a child lost on the streets of Brooklyn. Then she came to the gates and as she reached out her hands to touch them, a change came and she was no longer a child. She was a woman. She pushed the gates open and walked through. The way ahead was known to her. She would never be lost again.

She awoke suddenly as if a spring had been released inside her. Frankie was lying on the edge of his side of the bed and she on the edge of hers. There was almost a whole bed space separating them. She listened to his even breathing for a moment. He was sound asleep.

She got out of bed quietly and felt her way into the kitchen. She switched on the light after she had closed the door. She felt the radiator. Some heat was still coming up. She got her box of stationery and a bottle of ink and a pen from the cupboard. She started to write a letter.

Dear . . . she began. But the *D* was too thick and there was a scratch on the paper where the *e* should be. She held the pen under the hot-water faucet and watched the crusted ink wash off and briefly discolor the porcelain of the sink before it ran down the drain.

The pen point looked shiny and new. She took a new piece of paper and dipped the pen in the ink bottle.

Dear Mr. Prentiss, she wrote. *I am writing you this letter . . .*

Best-selling fiction in Tandem editions

Edith Pargeter's memorable trilogy
of medieval England and Wales

The Green Branch 55p

The Scarlet Seed 55p

The Heaven Tree 60p

Romance and history combine in a swift-moving story of border warfare, power politics and private feuds on the Welsh border in the reign of King John.

'A highly dramatic and intense story, beautifully written.'
Glasgow Evening Times

Barbara Michaels

Sons of the Wolf 50p

The Master of Blacktower 50p

Ammie, Come Home 50p

'Miss Michaels has a fine sense of atmosphere, of period, of humour and of storytelling.' *New York Times*

Catherine Cookson

Slinky Jane 45p

Hannah Massey 45p

The Garment 45p

Compelling and moving novels, set in the North Country which Catherine Cookson has made famous.

'In an age when so much rubbish is published and writers are two a penny, Mrs Cookson comes as a boon and a blessing. She tells a good story. Her characters live.' *Yorkshire Post*

My Only Love, My Only Hate

Marguerite Neilson

The two families had been at each other's throats for generations. How it had begun – ancient political rivalry, a quarrel over land or inheritance, or a point of honour – few of them knew or cared. While their elders bickered and threatened, paying only lip-service to the Prince's edicts, the young men blooded their swords and their servants brawled in the streets. In such an atmosphere of bitterness and scarcely veiled hatred, it would have taken a miracle to bring peace to Verona.

A miracle – or a chance meeting. But whether the young man, eager for excitement, who made his way, masked into the Capulet mansion; the girl who dreamed of an enduring love, an immortal romance; were the instruments or the playthings of fate, would be resolved in a few days of sultry heat and deadly passion.   35p

Serpent In Eden

Juliet Dymoke

The love between the general – the most famous face in Venice – and the shy, lovely girl he wooed and won from her father's house, was instantaneous. Their life on the sun-drenched island of Cyprus could have been a passionate idyll, but for a threat nearer at hand than any of the Turkish battle squadrons which constantly menaced Venice's outpost.

One of the general's closest companions saw that he could manipulate the girl's innocence and her husband's growing possessiveness to his own twisted purposes. In his privileged position it was easy to spread the innuendoes, and play off his pawns, one against the other, so that the very intensity of the general's adoration only fed his suspicion of his wife's loyalty. And the man who brought the crisis to a head was the one, of them all, who had the least desire or need to.   35p

Jill Tattersall

A Summer's Cloud   25p
The Midnight Oak   30p

England is at war with Revolutionary France, and in their different ways both Henrietta Clyde and her cousin Sophia find their desire for romance and excitement more than compensated for by rumours of smuggling, revolutionary plots, and sinister strangers.

Lady Ingram's Retreat   30p

There was more to Ingledale, the great house on the Yorkshire moors, more to Sir Luke's intimidating manner and his young daughter's childish fears than Arabel Murray could possibly fathom.

Lyonesse Abbey   30p

Tessa knew that she must solve the mystery that haunted the Abbey, or she could never truly be Damon's wife. And she wanted that more than anything in the world.

Midsummer Masque   35p

A menacing tension brooded below the surface of the Clune household, and a situation in which murder was to be the least of the threats Rowena Manville had to face before the secret of Gryphons was revealed.

Thomas Costain's best-selling historical novel

The Black Rose   50p

Walter of Gurnie, bastard son of the Earl of Lessford, fled from England to escape the enmity of his family and the bitterness of his love for the Lady Engaine. Wealth and fame and a chance to claim the woman he loved were to be found only in the fabulous realms of the East, if he could win through the savage hordes of Kublai Khan's Mongol warriors to the Celestial City of the Manji Emperor.

Two brilliant reconstructions of Scotland's dramatic story, by the distinguished Scottish author, Jane Oliver

The Lion is Come   40p

The epic story of a warrior king, Robert the Bruce, King of Scots.

Sing, Morning Star   40p

The love story of Malcolm, King of Scotia, and Margaret his Queen.

Edith Pargeter's memorable trilogy
of medieval England and Wales

The Green Branch   55p
The Scarlet Seed   55p
The Heaven Tree   60p

Romance and history combine in a swift-moving story of border warfare, power politics and private feuds on the Welsh border in the reign of King John.

'A highly dramatic and intense story, beautifully written.'
Glasgow Evening Times

The Pageant of England

Thomas Costain

In four colourful volumes, the author of *The Black Rose* brings to life the story of England's most dramatic and exciting era – the troubled period between the Norman Conquest and the emergence of the Tudors, when the foundations of monarchy were being hammered out between monarchs and people. He blends a novelist's story-telling skill with a historian's accuracy to tell of the private lives of kings and queens, of plot and counter-plot, civil wars and foreign conquest, of nobles and peasants, merchants and priests, and all the vast and brilliant panorama of the age.

'Crowded with epochal events and grandly heroic personalities . . . much bloodshed, and battle and violence and suffering . . . lively, fascinating.'
New York Times

'What he cares about is the colour and pageantry . . . the personalities, triumphs and disasters . . . Above all, he has the unique and surpassing ability to write a good story.'
San Francisco Chronicle

The Conquering Family 80p
The Magnificent Century 80p
The Three Edwards 95p
The Last Plantagenets 95p

Edgar Rice Burroughs

Three series by the Master of Imagination and Adventure

The exploits of David Innes in the perilous lands of the earth's core

Adventure in uncharted Caprona, a land of Dawn Age men and monsters

Universal warfare between moon-dwellers and the Earth of the far future

Name..

Address..

Titles required...

....

....

....

....

....

....

The publishers hope that you enjoyed this book and invite you to write for the full list of our titles.

If you find any difficulty in obtaining these books from your usual retailer we shall be pleased to supply the titles of your choice upon receipt of your remittance.

Packing and postage charges are as follows:
U.K. One book 18p plus 8p per copy for each additional book ordered to a maximum charge of 66p.
B.F.P.O. and Eire 18p for the first book plus 8p per copy for the next 6 books, thereafter 3p per book.

WRITE NOW TO:
          Tandem Publishing Ltd.,
          123 King Street,
          London W6 9JG

          A Howard & Wyndham Company